RH1NO

AN EPIDEMIC THAT TAKES OVER THE CITY

D. C. OUTSKIRTS

iUniverse, Inc.
New York   Bloomington

RH1NO
An epidemic that takes over the city

iUniverse books may be ordered through booksellers or by contacting:

iUniverse
1663 Liberty Drive
Bloomington, IN 47403
www.iuniverse.com
1-800-Authors (1-800-288-4677)

Because of the dynamic nature of the Internet, any Web addresses or links contained in this book may have changed since publication and may no longer be valid. The views expressed in this work are solely those of the author and do not necessarily reflect the views of the publisher, and the publisher hereby disclaims any responsibility for them.

ISBN: 978-1-4502-4579-1 (sc)
ISBN: 978-1-4502-4614-9 (ebk)

Printed in the United States of America

iUniverse rev. date: 10/29/2010

CHAPTER 1

A steady drizzle of rain covered the streets of a quiet residential area in Philadelphia. Hunt Rhinehart discreetly stood in the doorway of a two-story townhouse, attentively watching a house across the street. It was quarter to eight in the evening. He'd been standing there for fifteen minutes. Fortunately, the rain kept the block fairly empty. Otherwise, neighbors and pedestrians would've certainly taken special notice of Hunt's six-foot-two muscular frame and his long trench coat. Hunt stood there, patiently waiting and watching.

A couple walked out of the house next door, drawing Hunt's attention. Eying the couple, Hunt instinctively slipped his hand inside of his trench coat and pulled out a semi-automatic handgun as the man glanced at him. The man nervously turned away, pretending as if he didn't see Hunt or the gun.

"Can we please get out of the rain?" the woman asked the man without noticing Hunt.

"Yeah sure," the man quickly replied before grabbing the woman's hand and running down the block with her.

Hunt turned his attention back to the house across the street just in time to see the door slowly opening. He tapped a tiny transmitter in his ear and in a low tone he said, "Nobody move."

Hunt's heart raced as he watched two men walk out of the door. He mentally confirmed the identity of his target. "Yes," Hunt thought, tightening his grip around the handgun. The shorter of the two men, standing at five-two and about one hundred and fifty pounds, was in fact the suspected Middle Eastern terrorist known as Impregnable Ali.

Hunt tapped his earpiece again and said, "Target is confirmed, everyone stand by." Hunt surveyed the second man and immediately recognized him as Ali's long-time bodyguard, Saheed - a muscular big barrel of a man standing at six-three, two hundred and fifty pounds. Hunt watched as Ali and Saheed gingerly walked up the block, and then patiently followed them from a distance. He wasn't worried about losing them; he knew they were heading to a local mosque three blocks away. Still, he wanted Ali captured and taken alive before he reached the mosque.

Things appeared to be going as Hunt planned, until he spotted a woman approaching up ahead in front of Ali and Saheed. Hunt quickened his pace trying to get closer to Ali, thinking the woman might get in the way.

Then the drizzling suddenly morphed into a downpour, giving Hunt the cover he needed to quickly close the space between him and his target. The only problem was the downpour caused the woman to quicken her pace as well. The woman noticed Hunt raising his gun as he approached and abruptly stopped in her tracks and covered her mouth. The woman's wide-eyed expression alerted Ali and Saheed that something was going on behind them, and Hunt sensed it.

"Don't move!" Hunt shouted. But it was too late. Saheed had already pulled out a small caliber handgun, spun around and rapidly pulled the trigger. The first shot startled Hunt, but he swiftly dropped down and returned fire. Hunt didn't want to use deadly force, but Saheed left him no choice. Saheed let off three shots before Hunt fired a single shot into his face, knocking him a few feet back. The woman screamed and Ali didn't bother looking back; he just knocked the women out of his way and took off running. Saheed was hit, but still on his feet. Hunt fired two rounds into his chest, dropping him like a ton of bricks. Then, like the sweep of a magic wand, a few dozen FBI agents and police officers blanketed the block.

"Don't shoot the target!" Hunt yelled, jumping up and chasing Ali, who was a half block away. "Give it up Ali!" Hunt shouted, closing the distance between him and Ali.

While running, Hunt slipped his gun into his coat pocket and pulled out a retractable baton. He then waited until he got within a few feet of Ali, stopped and threw the baton at him. The baton hit Ali in the back of his leg causing him to stumble, but not fall down which did not matter much because his momentary pause was all that his pursuers needed to capture him.

An agent appeared on Ali's right side and fired a compressed-gas powered talon, which released a huge net that engulfed Ali and sent him falling to the ground.

Ali struggled to free himself, but the sixteen foot nylon net was indestructible. The chase was over. Hunt slowly walked up.

"Good work," Hunt told the agent before pointing towards Saheed's body. "Now go clean up that mess."

Hunt stood over Ali, who was still struggling, and told him. "You can knock it off. Spiderman couldn't get away at this point."

CHAPTER 2

One week later… In Atlanta, Georgia another surveillance detail was taking place. This time the target was not considered to be hostile.

*   *   *   *   *

"One hundred and twenty-eight pounds mommy…" Kimberly stated. "That's more than what you weigh, right?"

"It's close," replied Faith.

"And it's just a baby," stated Kimberly.

"Who would think a baby could be born and weigh that much," stated Melvin.

Faith smiled as her two children looked at the baby rhinoceros. She was the world's first rhino conceived by artificial insemination. Arriving into the world at 128 pounds, which was 2 pounds lighter than Faith. Her seven year old daughter, Kimberly, had been close when she compared the weight differences.

Faith could tell that Kimberly was amazed at the animal from the way she stared. It was brought to Atlanta only a few days ago from the Budapest Zoo and was ready to embark on a world tour just like any other superstar, Faith thought. As she held onto Kimberly's little delicate hand, Melvin who was nine, stood nearby. He didn't like his mother to hold his hand out in public. He felt it took away from him being a big boy. Faith gave him his freedom, but she watched him very closely being that the exhibition was crowded.

* * * * *

"She seems to be a good mother," stated one of the FBI agents that had been assigned to monitor Faith.

"Yeah," agreed the other agent. They sat just outside of the park in an unmarked car peering at Faith and her kids through high powered binoculars.

"What are her vitals?" The first agent who had commented on her maternal traits asked.

"She is thirty-two years old, five-foot-six, shapely, single mom, extremely intelligent and a workaholic. She is the lead analyst at the Center for Disease Control and Prevention," concluded the agent.

"You left out the part about her driving a big truck," joked his partner.

"I left out everything," countered the agent who was looking over the dossier that held all of Faith Millicent's information. As he looked at the photo of Faith standing next to her Hummer truck with her healthy, caramel colored skin and close cropped auburn hair, he thought that her eyes, which were the prettiest green that he had ever seen, conveyed her compassion.

Her children were adopted; both had been born independently to drug addicted mothers. The boy, Melvin, was handsome with brown skin, brown eyes and a short afro. Kimberly was adorable, thought the agent, with her dark chocolate skin and shiny little braces on her teeth. She looked like a little girl should, in his opinion, with pig tails in her hair and a curious look on her face.

Faith has a sister, the agent mentally noted picking up the photo of Yvonne Kincaid. "Here's the sister," he told his partner. "She's a looker as well."

The second agent took the photo and compared the stark differences between the sisters. Yvonne was two years younger than Faith with tawny brown skin, five-foot-four and one hundred and five pounds. Her eyes were hazel and told a different story.

"What does she do?" asked the second agent.

"She's a hair and makeup artist," answered his partner. "She's also married. Married four years, to this light skinned fellow, six-foot-two, thirty-one years of age, one hundred ninety-five pounds with green eyes and his name is Jeff Kincaid."

"What does he do?" The first agent asked.

"Look pretty," he replied sarcastically. "He's a model, go figure."

"Is he cheating on her?" asked the first agent.

"Not that we have uncovered," he answered.

"This is the mother," stated the first agent moving along. "Name is Fanny, widowed, sixty-five years old, favors the younger daughter; complexion wise anyway. She lives up in Water Edge. That's an upscale subdivision in Stone Mountain just outside of Atlanta."

"Hey, they're on the move," stated the second agent; taking the dossier from his partner so that he could drive.

While driving, his partner asked, "Who's this?" Holding up a photo of a light skinned, black man with light brown eyes, who looked very intelligent and dressed like a professor.

"Oh yeah, that's a fellow named John Lovejoy, he just transferred to the CDC. He's supposed to be a big shot expert in flu pandemics. They say he was the architect who helped pen the new Pandemic Severity Index."

"Wow, twenty-nine years old," noted the second agent. "I see that Lovejoy and Faith Millicent are the only African-Americans in their department down there."

"Correct," affirmed his partner.

"Any romance between the two?" asked the second agent.

"Who knows," his partner responded with a shrug.

They were now driving down Peachtree Road and it was late in the afternoon. The agents figured that Faith would be heading home now. She lived in the Dunwoody area of Atlanta, Georgia in a condo.

Her three bedrooms, two-thousand square foot condominium was in a skyscraper building called the 'Manhattan.'

"Oh look," stated the first agent. They're stopping for ice cream," he teased; adding that he could use some ice cream too. They watched Faith and Kimberly walk into the ice cream parlor and several seconds after Melvin had run in.

"Have they gone over to her apartment yet?" asked the second agent.

"Yes, but couldn't get in" his partner stated. "Seems the little lady, has an elaborate security system. Her door doesn't take a key; there is a biometric identification panel instead. Only approved visitors can get in by placing their thumb and forefinger over the panel to unlock the door. So, that's the closest we got. I hear she has a penchant for stainless steel and silver. Her entire kitchen is done up in that stuff."

"How do you know?" asked his partner.

"The condominium complex has all custom work on file and we received a copy of it," answered the first agent.

"Who are these two?" asked the second agent; holding up a photo of Buddy and Edna Defoe.

"They are Ms. Millicent's colleagues at the CDC and married as well," answered his partner as the second agent scanned the information that accompanied the photo.

"I see Edna Defoe is forty-one years old, an ex-professor from Brown Medical School in Rhode Island. She is petite and weighs one hundred and ten pounds. She has olive skin, friendly brown eyes and long blond hair." Her husband on the other hand looked like a baker, the agent thought. Buddy Defoe forty-four years old, five-foot-five and one hundred and sixty pounds.

In the photo he wore a three day shadow on his face. His eyes were blue and he sported a cleft in his chin. Quickly the agent thought of the men that played in westerns. He and his wife Edna were the same height which made them look compatible. Buddy's information also noted that he was extremely competitive.

As Faith exited the ice cream parlor with her children, everyone was enjoying an ice cream cone. The agent with the dossier in front of him picked up another photo. It was a man named Jules Marceau who is the director of the National Vaccine Assistance Program within Faith's Millicent's department.

"That's the last subject," noted the first agent.

"French National and an American citizen; we need to find out which nation he is truly allegiant to."

The second agent nodded as he sized Jules up. Sixty-six years old, pot-bellied, mustached and balding with an abrasive disposition the report alleged. He's five-foot-eight, two hundred and forty pounds with harrowing sharp blue eyes.

Faith and her kids were back in route to their home. The agent that was navigating the unmarked car several vehicles behind them didn't think that Faith had done a suspicious thing since they had begun trailing her. He told himself that would be put in his report.

CHAPTER 3

"Excuse me," stated Faith bumping into a man as she rushed into the CDC. What was supposed to be an uneventful day had not turned out that way.

First her sister had awakened her at five-thirty in the morning to say that she and Jeff were off to a photo shoot in Houston for Vanity Fair. Then an urgent message had come through from the CDC telling Faith that she needed to report back to the center immediately. Faith had been on a two week sabbatical which was abruptly cut short. She didn't know why, all they told her was to pack a bag.

So, Faith did as she was told. She packed bags for her children as well and Kimberly grabbed a teddy bear that Yvonne had brought her, which she could not bear to be without. Faith dropped the kids off at her mother's home before she made her way into work.

Faith's department was located on the fifth floor. Getting off the elevator, she walked briskly into her office saying a few hellos and good mornings on the way.

"Nice to have you back," Buddy said while she was walking towards the door.

Faith said, "Yeah, thanks," as she entered the office her and Edna shared.

"Hey," Edna stated as she immediately stood up to go pour Faith a cup of coffee.

"What's going on?" asked Faith while walking over to her desk and looking at the small mountain of paperwork that had accumulated in her absence.

"I'll let Jules tell you," answered Edna. Calling their supervisor by his first name was not unusual, they all did.

"He told me to send you over as soon as you showed up, so here," concluded Edna as she handed Faith her cup of joe and a note pad. Faith liked to take notes during meetings so Edna was thinking ahead.

Faith took the coffee and pad after placing her handbag on her desk. "I guess I'll drink on the way," commented Faith; messing with Edna whom she often called pushy.

"That was the idea," countered Edna as Faith walked out the door.

As Faith walked across and a little to the left, she saw that his door was open. But he was talking on the phone. So she didn't enter, she stood to the side of the door until he finished his call. Actually she didn't have to wait long - he hung up a couple of seconds later.

Faith knocked on the door lightly even though he had already seen her. "Good morning, are you ready for me now, sir?"

"Yes, yes replied the director, come in Ms. Millicent and please have a seat." Faith sat down in a very comfortable chair directly across from his desk. Jules never fawned over his subordinates when he wanted their expert opinion on something. He just stared them down as he was doing to Faith now.

"What is it Jules?"

"How was your vacation?"

"Lovely, now, what is it?"

"We have a situation in Houston that involves a possible terrorist attack. The Department of Homeland Security called me early this morning and asked me if I had anyone that I could send down to take a look."

"I didn't see anything in the news."

"Yes, I know," answered the director. "They're keeping this one close to the chest. One is because it did not cause considerable harm and two, because they don't want the public to panic. But there is a concern that either a chemical or biological weapon was used down there. Obviously, something went wrong but that does not negate the fact that poison was used."

Faith thought about her sister and Jeff heading to Houston. Faith liked the field work more than the in-house research. "Okay, I'll go down and have a look sir."

"Oh yeah, you'll be taking Lovejoy with you, just in case it was a biological weapon. You can't use the centers airplanes because this exploration is hush, hush, so be discreet. I've already briefed Lovejoy and he has booked your flight as well. Please keep me informed," concluded Jules.

"Yes Sir," replied Faith while standing up.

Each week Faith would look over the Centers morbidity and mortality report. There had been a rash of food-borne illnesses reported since she'd taken leave along with several reports of sexually transmitted diseases becoming antibiotic resistant. Faith was curious about this, so on her way out of the office she inquired.

"Sir, I saw a report while I was out; about that dreaded Yersinia being back. Could you have someone send me the morbidity and mortality report along with some data from the Gonococcal Isolate Surveillance Project so I can stay abreast?"

"Okay, but this Houston situation is priority," he reminded her.

"No problem, boss!" Faith stated while walking out the door.

* * * * *

The meeting had been quick. Faith didn't get a chance to take notes or even enjoy her coffee. When she got back to her office John and Edna were waiting for her.

"I've booked our flight; we leave out of Jackson airport at noon."

"Okay," replied Faith putting her coffee and note pad down on her desk.

"I'll have to meet you there," stated John. "I didn't pack a bag. Oh yeah, bring a lot of vouchers," John added while smiling at Faith. Edna had a sly smile on her face that Faith caught.

"What?" Faith asked.

"He loves to take road trips with you and he's fond of your children," Edna mentioned.

"Everyone is fond of the children and we haven't taken that many road trips together, so knock it off." Since John was going to run home and pack a bag, Faith decided to make a run home as well. Edna was still watching her, like she wanted to say something else. "What now... you know Jules could have sent you, smiley face."

"He could have, but he didn't because you're top notch around here in the sleuth department," acknowledged Edna as the words followed Faith as she left the room.

CHAPTER 4

When Faith arrived at the airport, it was packed. The taxi pulled up right out front of the main entrance. She didn't see John standing off on the side, but he saw her. "Faith!" he called out, approaching the cab. "Let me get your bags."

Faith did a double-take. Usually, she saw John strictly in suits and very nice ones. Now, he stood before her in track sneakers and a warm-up suit. It gave him a very different look, she thought. He looked like a collegiate athlete.

John grabbed her bag in his hand after the cab driver opened the trunk. "This is it?"

"Yeah, that's it," replied Faith shaking off her surprise. "How long have you been here?"

"For about thirty minutes. I checked the terminal for our gate, and confirmed the departure time. We still have a few long minutes. So your entrance, I don't know if it was choreographed, but it's perfect."

Faith smiled, and paid the cab driver. "I do my best," she told John, as they walked into the terminal. They stopped off at a little first, so that Faith could get her cup of joe and then board the plane.

"You fuel up with this stuff?"

"Yes, I do," confessed Faith, taking the window seat. "It's my only vice."

"That's too bad," noted John.

Faith got comfortable. "Why is that too bad?"

"Because if you're going to have a vice, I feel that it should be something exciting, pleasurable and steamy. But if you get caught doing it, then it's evil, maybe degrading or even sexually immoral. Being addicted to coffee doesn't cut it for me."

"Okay, then." He'd just told her too much, Faith thought. They felt a little something, then the plane was in the sky, and Faith looked at the ground as it ran away from her.

"You don't agree?" John asked, bringing her back to the subject.

"About vices?"

"Yeah."

"No, I don't. What you're talking about is more than a vice. It sounds criminal."

John laughed. "Truth be told Faith, most vices are criminal. But I do hear people speak about having the vice of laziness or untidiness. And that upsets me." He was still laughing. "I mean, don't waste a vice on triviality."

Faith stared at him for a minute. "You're different outside the center. It must be the attire."

"It's the mischievous boy inside me."

"The urchin outside of work," Faith smiled.

"Yeah, he agreed. "I saw how you looked at me, when you arrived at the airport."

"Well, I'm used to seeing you in your corduroy trousers," she told him. "So forgive me. You just looked a bit Corinthian."

"Given to luxury?"

"No, more man about town," she told him.

"Okay, I'll take that too."

The in-flight movie, a love story, came on. John liked that.

"Have you seen this before?" He asked her.

"No, have you?"

"No, but I hear it's quite good."

"You're into love stories?" Faith was ready to appreciate his sensitive side, if he chose to show it.

"Yes," he answered. "That and dopey love songs."

"Why?"

"Because it's fun," John said honestly. "Our job is serious enough, so I think we're entitled to have and even seek out fun wherever and whenever we can." He paused for a moment. "That's why I find myself asking you out occasionally. I'm hoping to have some fun with you, a little comradeship."

"Is that so?" asked Faith, looking sexy as hell to John with her green eyes sparkling, and her short hairdo drawing him in.

"Yes, it is." He was hoping his honesty would make her drop her guard a little.

"Honestly, John, your last name scares me."

"You don't have to take it if you don't want to," he joked. "You can remain a Millicent."

"What?" Faith blurted out, causing several passengers who were seated nearby to look over at them. "So, you want to marry me also?"

"Well, of course, but we would need to fall in love first," he told her.

Faith laughed, giving him a view of her pearly white teeth.

"Slow down, I haven't even consented to take your home number."

"You have my cell phone number and I do take that phone home with me."

"Oh please," ready to back the conversation up. "Your name… that's where it started, Lovejoy. It sounds like the name of a Casanova."

"Not hardly. I haven't been on a date in a year, and all I see is dead people, like the little boy in that movie. What kind of Casanova is that?"

"I don't know." Faith was honestly amused by his candor. She forgot about the movie momentarily, more interested in what made John Lovejoy tick. "Where are you originally from John?"

"North Carolina born; Compton, California raised, and now residing in Atlanta," he told her. He was cultured she learned, and well traveled. Once Faith began to share, she took over the floor for the remainder of the flight. Their seats reclined like the chaise lounge their director, Jules, had in his office. The only difference was that Jules allowed a person more room to stretch their legs. But still and all, Faith found the seat and the conversation extremely comfortable.

Once they arrived in Houston, John quickly retrieved their luggage as Faith rented them a Hyundai Santa Fe, since they were probably going to have to lug equipment around. It was getting late, so they headed straight to the hotel.

Since they'd arrived at George Bush Intercontinental Airport, Faith booked them at the Holiday Inn Intercontinental. She almost got them a double occupancy room, as she did when she and Edna traveled. But she didn't when they checked in, and they were given two room keys. She saw a hint of disappointment cross John's face.

"We're right across from one another," she told him, handing him a key.

"Okay," he said cheerfully, masking his expectation. "That's good, because when I'm thinking about the fundament, I may need you." Faith, at her door, looked back at him. He smiled, and stuck his key in the door. "What?" he asked, opening his door and tossing his luggage right in.

"You're not talking about my behind, are you?" she asked; the word 'fundament' stood for 'buttocks', but not exclusively.

John blinked at her. Then what she was asking him registered.

"No, no, I'm talking about the other meaning," he told her. "The underlying theoretical basis of principle."

"Okay, just checking."

CHAPTER 5

'*Knock. Knock. Knock.*'

Faith, in the shower, heard the knocking at the door. She got out and wrapped a huge towel around her body. Trekking to the door, she looked out the peephole and saw John standing there, smiling. He raised his hand and flashed a Starbucks bag at her. Faith looked at the clock on the wall. It was seven-thirty in the morning. She unlocked the door and let him in. "I thought I had at least another hour," she told him.

"Sorry," he replied, admiring her wet look. "I thought we'd get an early jump on things. I got you a crepe suzette. Jules has me hooked on them, and there's some java in there for you."

He raised the bag up and Faith snatched it. "Thank you," she said, walking back towards the bathroom.

"You're welcome," replied John, looking at her shapely figure. This time, he was thinking about her behind.

Faith managed to dry off and get dressed in ten minutes, while periodically taking small bites of the thin dessert pancakes John had brought her. They had a sweet tangerine sauce inside of them that wasn't offset by the coffee.

"I spoke with a guy from the Federal Bureau of Investigation," John informed her from the hotel room's common area. "They have some evidence for us to go over, down at their command. I told them I'd have to speak with you first, to see if you wanted to go by there, or go to the crime scene first."

"Crime scene," yelled out Faith, with her mouth full. "I like to get a feel for things first.

"Cool, me too," he hollered back.

Faith took five more minutes, and then she emerged from the room. She had on a crinkled top and a matching skirt. Her toes were out in a pair of trendy sandals. John stared at her feet.

"What?" she asked him.

"What if we have to run?"

"Then they called the wrong people for this job," she told him, and they headed out the door.

The crime scene was in the downtown area, in the vicinity of the Crowne Plaza Hotel and club quarters, at a small cafeteria called Linden Plaza. When they got there, Faith immediately understood why the authorities would believe that the place was prime for a terrorist attack. Because it centered on the same reason the owners of the Linden Plaza most likely opened their business here, she thought: Location, location, and location. It was like a public square she thought, or basically a plaza. It was broad and paved off, with plenty of room for couples strolling by to have a look or in the case at hand, become exposed.

The Feds were waiting for them when they arrived; the entire block was on lock down. Faith and John needed an escort to get on it.

"Mr. Lovejoy?" stated a big Caucasian man while approaching the police rope.

"Yes," confirmed John, shaking the man's hand. "This is my colleague, Ms. Faith Millicent."

"I like the sound of that, ma'am. That's the premise under which I work: *Faith*. Let them through," he instructed. Two men in suits, who were standing on the right and left sides of him, promptly held up the rope so Faith and John could walk under it.

"My name is Buzz Shaw," stated the gentleman, smiling broadly and shaking Faith's hand this time. He was very powerful. Faith could tell because, even though he shook her hand gingerly, it felt crushing. His blue eyes were piercing; he was clean-shaven with blond spiky hair, at least six-feet tall, and two hundred pounds, she estimated.

"I'm forty-eight," he told Faith, as he led them over to the café.

"Why are you telling me that?" Faith asked.

"Because I see you taking a pedigree of me," he told her. "Don't worry; people do it all the time and when you've been in law enforcement as long as me, you notice everything. I see you guys had breakfast already."

"You can tell that also?" Faith asked. "What… do I look fat?"

"Not at all, ma'am," he told her. I can tell because it's early and both of you look very alert and I figured you to be approximately one hundred and thirty pounds, ma'am." He told Faith lowering his voice so John couldn't hear the number. When Faith smiled, he knew that he had been accurate.

"Now," he continued, "Don't worry about breathing anything harmful. You got here late. All of the really bad vapors are gone. We had the Environmental Protection Agency down here yesterday. They gave the place the thumbs up and Mr. Lovejoy, that's a mighty fine name you have there. I can imagine what your lady friends tell their friends. If it's nothing good, at least it's a good ice breaker," he noted. "Kind of like my name, although Buzz is my nickname. My original name is Cain. Like the eldest son of Adam and Eve. I suppose my mother was thinking of that when she named me. But I changed it, or actually I really don't use it. A guy killed his brother out of jealousy in the bible, you know. And it means to create a great disturbance. Doesn't sound right telling people when I investigate great big disturbances," he chuckled.

Faith wanted to say, 'can we get to it,' but couldn't get a word in edgewise until he shut up; probably to take in more oxygen, she suspected.

"Is this it?" asked John, trying to bail them out.

Mr. Shaw was very sharp. He caught on right away.

"Yeah, that's it," he replied. "I won't hold you up any longer. Do what you do, and I'll be right over there," he told them, pointing to several other men who stood nearby conversing. They all wore large gold badges on the lapels of their jackets. The badges held the F.B.I. insignia, which made Faith wonder: where was Mr. Shaw's?

"Did he say that he was with the F.B.I., or with the Houston Police Department?" she asked John.

"I'm not sure," replied John looking at a chalk outline that sat prominently on the floor. He walked around the place and counted four outlines. Faith saw them as well, but neither one of them commented.

There was a waiter in the place, speaking with a police officer. When the officer saw Faith and John looking, he waved them over.

"You're with the CDC?" he asked.

"Yes," replied Faith.

"He's all yours." The police officer closed his memo pad and walked away.

"Hello." Faith pulled out a small pad. "My name is Faith Millicent, and this is John Lovejoy. Could we ask you a few questions? What is your name, first of all?"

"Jesus," stated the man. He was Hispanic, so Faith wrote that down. His name was Latin, but it was spelled like that of Christ.

"You work here... tell me what you saw?"

"I was waiting on tables, the place was pretty crowded, but nothing unusual for this place," stated the man.

Faith listened closely, trying not to miss a word; he had a thick accent, and spoke very fast.

"The people all fell down on the floor at the same time," he continued to say. "They were all bleeding from their mouths. Then we tried to help them, but they died."

Faith wrote down everything that he said. Then she looked at the floor where the people died again, before looking at John.

"Is that it?" asked John.

"Yes," stated the man. "There is no more."

John looked around briefly. "They all collapsed at the same time, not one behind the other?"

"Yes, at the same time," confirmed the man.

"Did anyone complain of chest pain, shortness of breath, or did they have a fever, while you were helping them?"

"Yes, they say that it hurts their chest. And the gentleman that I help was burning up."

"Thank you." John walked away, leaving Faith standing there.

"If I need to speak with you again," asked Faith, "where can I contact you?"

"Here, Senorita."

"You don't have a home phone number?" Faith asked.

"No phone," he told her. "Here, I'll be here."

"Okay," said Faith. "Thank you." He walked off when the big man approached.

"Well, Ms. Millicent. Have you solved my case yet?" He asked her.

"I'm working on it," said Faith sweetly.

"I need results," stated Mr. Shaw. "I have five people dead, and no suspect."

"Five?" stated John walking back over.

"Yeah," stated Shaw. "One of the victims was a woman. She was seven months pregnant, so that one is a double.

"Do you have an autopsy report?" asked Faith. "If not, we're going to have to take a look at the bodies."

"Got it right here," stated Mr. Shaw, pulling several loose sheets of paper from his back pocket. He gave some to Faith and a few to John. Then he left them alone for a minute.

Faith and John looked over the reports each of them held. Then they switched documents.

"I was just talking about something like this with Jules," stated Faith, "which reminds me; he never got that paperwork to me."

"You were talking about a biological attack?" asked John.

"No. There's an E. coli problem with the nation's vegetables. And we discussed Yersinia and undercooked pork," she explained.

"Anyway, Yersinia was found in their systems. So that's what killed them."

"Looks that way," stated John.

"What's the matter?"

"They all collapsed at the same time," he said. "What are the chances of that happening?"

"One in a million," answered Faith.

"Try, one in a billion," corrected John. "And did you notice one person had no food in their system, and the pregnant women only had salad? Something's wrong."

"Did you check out the kitchen for rodent droppings?" asked Faith.

"Yeah, I looked by the trash cans, and in the storage bins. I didn't see any."

"So what's up?" asked Mr. Shaw coming back over.

"Yersinia Pestis killed those people," Faith told him. "It's a bacteria."

"I know. It's deadly."

John looked at Mr. Shaw, and got the impression he was a military man, not a bureaucrat.

"It's a weapon, isn't it?" asked John bluntly.

"Why do you say that?" asked Mr. Shaw.

"Because all those people died at the same time," stated John. "It couldn't be the eatery's food - not everyone had eaten yet. Rodents and fleas carry the bacteria, but those two entities are not present in this particular establishment. Are they, Mr. Shaw? If that is even your name."

"Very good, Mr. Lovejoy," stated the man. "I asked them to send me the best. I guess that's the two of you. You're right. It was a weapon. A biological one, we believe."

"Who's we?" asked Faith. "I didn't catch the agency that you work for."

"I didn't say," he responded. "I need to know how you knew that it was Yersinia Pests," he asked. "Because you knew before I gave you the autopsy reports."

"The symptoms that they all suffered from," answered Faith. "The fever, chest pains, and the blood in their mouths; that would be the bloody sputum or expectorated saliva that came up from the victim's respiratory tract."

"Exactly," stated Mr. Shaw. "So now, you do know what my problem is?"

"What?" John wasn't really aware. Faith didn't speak; she knew, and Mr. Shaw sensed this.

"Tell him for me Ms. Millicent, will you please?"

"Mr. Shaw needs to know how is it that these people died so quickly, when the symptoms take days to appear."

"Bingo!" he said. "It's a plague, but not any old plague."

"Pneumonic," interjected John speaking about pneumonia, which was an acute, or chronic disease marked by inflammation of the lungs, and caused by viruses, bacteria, and physical and chemical agents.

"You are correct, Mr. Lovejoy," agreed Mr. Shaw. "But I was gonna say manmade."

Everyone was quiet for a moment, just taking everything in.

Then Mr. Shaw said, "I'd like for the two of you to have dinner with me tonight at Sasha's. At eight o'clock. That's down on Hardy Toll Road."

"We didn't agree yet," said Faith.

"It wasn't a request," stated Mr. Shaw, and left.

*   *   *   *   *

After checking out a little bit of Houston, Faith and John headed back to their hotel. Once there, Faith retrieved several faxes from their director. Jules had sent her the documentation she'd requested.

There was nothing really in the material, except for a notation that spoke about the last antibiotic treatment for gonorrhea that was dropped, being penicillin in the 1980's. Faith already knew this.

She made a note to fax back to Jules for the Center to push the pharmaceutical companies to develop new antibiotics. In Faith's opinion, they had dropped the ball in the report concerning the E.

coli problem. All Faith saw there was a request for more funds by the organizations that monitor the nation's food supply. *Give it to them*, Faith wrote across the top of the report. Then she went to go get ready for their dinner engagement.

John came over to collect her at seven o'clock. On their way downstairs, he informed her of a telephone call he'd made.

"I spoke to a friend of mine, down at the Federation of American Scientists. He's in the Biology Policy Group, over there," said John. "He states that not many people would have the know-how to weaponize pneumonic plague, and even if they did, why use that as a biological weapon? Why not something much more deadly, like Anthrax, or weaponized Botulism?"

"I thought about the same thing," Faith replied. "Why not use mustard gas? There's no antidote for that or phosgene? A gas like that is much easier to make and much more deadly."

"You want me to drive?" he asked her when they got to the vehicle.

"Yeah, go ahead," stated Faith. "I want to call my sister anyway. Her flight gets in tonight."

They got in the vehicle and John took control.

"You think that the weapon was released in the air? Like the Aum Shinrikyo cult releasing that Sarin in the Tokyo subway system, back in 1995?"

"Twelve people died in that attack," noted Faith. "That would be a possibility, but I doubt it - everyone in the place should have been affected."

"I know." John hit his GPS so he would know where the restaurant was. "I'm just throwing theories out there."

Faith called Yvonne first, but there was no answer. She called her mother's home next.

"Hello?"

"Hi Mom, where are the kids?"

"They're getting ready for bed; you want to speak to them?"

"Yes, please Mom," Faith thought about the pregnant women who'd been killed, and felt lucky.

"Mommy!" Kimberly got on the phone. She sounded upset. "Mel won't talk to Teddy, Mommy."

"Don't worry about that, baby. Mel just won't have a friend like Teddy then. It's his loss," Faith said, trying to smooth things over.

"Yeah, it's his loss," agreed Kimberly. "Are you having fun Mommy?"

"No," said Faith. "I'm working."

"Oh," replied Kimberly. "When are you coming home?"

"In a few days, baby. You be good for me, and let me talk to Mel."

"Okay, bye Mommy." said Kimberly. Her brother got right on the line.

"Mom, what's up?" he asked.

"You," said Faith. "Would it hurt you to play with your sister by talking to her bear?"

"Teddy bears don't talk," stated Mel. "That's stupid!"

"Mel." Faith got stern with him. "Your sister and I talk to her teddy bear. Are you saying that I'm stupid?"

"No, Mommy."

"Well, then don't ever say that again. I left you in charge of your sister's well-being. That means you must play with her, and not upset her. If she likes talking to her bear, play along with her, Mel. Do it for me, okay?"

"Okay, Mommy. I'll do it for you - but don't tell my friends."

"Thank you baby," Faith felt like laughing. "And I won't tell. I love you."

"I love you too, Mommy," he said. "Goodnight."

"Goodnight," replied Faith, and hung up.

"I'd talk to a teddy bear for you too," said John.

Faith looked at him and smiled. "I'm going to hold you to that," she told him.

The restaurant was right up ahead. John pulled into the adjacent parking lot.

"How do you want to play this?" John asked.

"Play it?" repeated Faith. "I'm not quite following."

"This guy doesn't want to have dinner with us because he likes our company," suggested John. "He's looking for something. It's only fair that we get something in return."

"A quid pro quo." Faith understood. "Information for information."

"Sure," confirmed John. "I like to be in the know."

"Got you," stated Faith. "I agree."

The restaurant was a cozy looking place. As soon as they walked in, a man wearing a black suit and dark shades pointed them in the direction of Buzz Shaw. Shaw was seated discreetly in the back, conversing with a buxom woman who Faith took to be a waitress.

"Here's my party now," stated Mr. Shaw as Faith and John arrived at the table.

"Hello," stated the vivacious young woman. "I'm Tasha. If you need anything, just holler for me," she told them, smiling as she dragged her healthy plump self away.

"Evening," stated Faith, taking a seat. John didn't speak. Instead, he nodded an acknowledgement.

"I had a little something to eat," stated Mr. Shaw. "Would you like to order anything?"

Faith looked at the plate in front of him. There appeared to be remnants of several Buffalo wings on it. "Not right now," she said. "Maybe later."

John just shook his head, and indicated no.

"Okay, Tasha will be back," Mr. Shaw said. "She's a lovely girl, isn't she? I love black women," he confessed, looking at Faith. It sounded like a confession to her, anyway.

She wanted to ask him if that was a vice, just to mess with John, but she didn't. Instead, she smiled and took it as a compliment.

Mr. Shaw took another bite of his wings and chewed for a moment. He and John stared at one another, but not hostilely.

"You know," stated Mr. Shaw. "I always think of chicken when I eat buffalo wings. And chicken makes me thing of roup."

Faith squeezed up her face at the word 'roup.' She was considering having the wings herself, but couldn't now. Roup was an infectious disease of poultry and pigeons characterized by inflammation and discharge from the mouth and the eyes.

"How do you eat, and speak about stuff like that?" She asked him.

"Easy," he replied. "I don't worry about it. We all have to go sometime. When it's my turn, there'll be nothing I can do about it."

"Mr. Shaw--" said John about to ask a question before he was cut off.

"We're all on the same team," interjected Mr. Shaw. "So call me Buzz and hopefully, I can call both of you by your first names."

Faith and John didn't protest, but John did continue. "That's just it Buzz," he said "We don't know that you are or what team you're actually on."

"The United States Government," he told them. "Your director, Jules Marceau, knows me. That's why I called him. He'll vouch for me. But right now, I need some information from the two of you. So what's it gonna be?"

"We'll cooperate as much as we can," replied Faith. "We just don't want to be left in the dark."

"I'll tell you as much as I can, fair enough?"

"I guess so," replied John. "What else can we use as a bargaining chip?"

"Your expertise," Buzz answered. "You know how they say knowledge is power?"

"They also say, 'he who knows the most wields all the power and influence' so where does that leave us?" countered Faith.

Buzz gave them a brutal grin. "Are you familiar with Aristotelian logic?"

"Aristotle, the Greek philosopher?" asked John. "Or his school of thought, such as a person who tends to be empirical, relying on observation or experiment; or scientific in his methods or thought?"

"Both," stated Buzz.

"Buzz is speaking about syllogisms, John," stated Faith, "which is Aristotle's deductive method of logic, conclusively his theory of the syllogism, the formal logic based on Aristotle, and dealing with the relations between propositions in terms of their form, instead of their content."

"You're losing me," stated John honestly. "Buzz, you said all of this to say what?"

"I wish to touch on the syllogism, like Faith has said," confessed Buzz; "that being a form of deductive reasoning consisting of a major premise, a minor premise and conclusion. For example: All mankind must die one day. That is the major premise. I am a part of a mankind: That is a minor premise. Therefore, I will certainly die one day. That is the conclusion."

"I'm still not following you," said John.

"I am," replied Faith. "Buzz is trying to tell us that there is a threat to mankind that he wants to discuss with us, like he's James Bond. And this is a motion picture, am I correct?"

"You were until you began to get condescending," he told her, suddenly upset. "I realize that I'm speaking to you in a way that sounds conjectural, but I have no choice. This is a matter of national security, and I have to be absolutely sure."

"I'm sorry if I offended you," Faith told him. "That wasn't my intention."

"Apology accepted."

"But what is it that you have to be sure of?" asked Faith.

"Whether to bring you and Mr. Lovejoy in on this conundrum."

"I thought we had agreed you would call me John."

Buzz paused and looked around the restaurant inquisitively. Then his eyes fell on John and Faith.

"What I am about to tell you both," he stated in a low voice, "doesn't leave this table. And if you don't come aboard with me on this assignment, you are to forget this and never speak about it again. Exactly fourteen days ago, the Department of Homeland Security received correspondence from an unknown source. It threatened the citizenry of this country with death by plague, pestilence, affliction, or calamity whatever you want to call it. But it is serious and it's not a threat anymore. The incident that we called the CDC in on is the fifth one, totaling thirty-one deaths in five different states."

"Oh my God," uttered Faith.

"My point exactly," replied Buzz. "We need God's help on this one also."

"How do you know that the attacks are all related?" John asked.

"Because the notes that we have received are all signed by the same person. They also always give up the location of the attacks, not the general area, but the exact location. The only problem is the notes are received at the same times as the attacks are taking place. So there has been no room for response except to clean up the mess made."

No one spoke for a good minute. Faith and John were evaluating the information that they had just received.

Then Faith said, "You say that the person signs the notes. Could we see one of them?"

Buzz produced the last note sent. It looked like it had been written by a child.

"They're writing with their other hand, not the primary one," Buzz informed them. "So no fingerprint analysis can be done."

"Cimmerian," stated John, reading the signature at the bottom of the note.

"Yes," confirmed Buzz. "You know who that was?"

"Yes," said Faith. "That was one of the mythical people described by Homer as inhabiting a land of perpetual darkness."

"In other words," explained Buzz, "if we don't pay the requested amount, they will turn the United States into a very dark and gloomy place."

"How much is the request for?" John asked.

"One billion dollars," said Buzz.

"Are you considering paying it?" Faith asked, afraid. But she didn't know why. She just suddenly had a premonition that things would get worse.

"I wish I could write a check myself," stated Buzz. "But the President refuses. The United States Government's official stance on this is that we don't negotiate with terrorists. So it's now basically a race against the clock. We have thirty days before Cimmerian is threatening to release the mother of all plagues right here in the United States."

"Whoa," said John. "Why don't you pay the amount and try to catch them when they try to collect the money?"

"I don't have the authorization to stage such a sting."

"So who does?" Faith asked.

"The person that explicitly stated to me that I am not to negotiate under any circumstances."

Faith shook her head, with the feelings of dread growing stronger inside of her.

"So at this point," she asked, "the situation is what?"

"Combustible," replied Buzz. "Like I said, we have thirty days."

"To do what?" asked Faith.

"To figure out who is posing this threat, neutralize it, and keep the task a private affair," suggested Buzz.

"I don't see how we can possibly do all of that in thirty days," said John. "That's impossible, don't you think?"

Buzz didn't answer that question. He had learned a long time ago that negative talk was worst than negative thought. It not only crippled you, but it jinxed you as well.

"I know we can't do it," admitted Faith. "But even if you could, I don't know how you can possibly keep thirty-one murders quiet. And I don't know how we can help you. We study infectious diseases. John knows about biological agents."

"And chemical agents," interjected John.

Faith glanced at him and saw that he was excited, not afraid like her. It was a guy thing, she figured.

"All you have to do is look over the crime scenes for me. Identify the method of murder. This last one was a disease that's right up your alley. If you can tell me how they're affecting the attacks, beautiful. If you can't, so be it. Just help me out, and as far as keeping thirty-one murders under wraps, let me handle that."

"But I don't see how--" Faith said about to continue her protest until Buzz cut back in.

"Did you hear anything about any unusual murders before we called you in?"

"No," Faith slowly admitted.

"How about you, John?"

"I can't say that I did."

"Exactly," replied Buzz, tossing a copy of the Houston Chronicle on the table.

Faith picked it up, and read a report about a gas leak at the Linden Plaza Eatery, which the article stated sickened five people. According to the paper, the sickened parties had been treated and released.

"Is this legal?" she asked.

"Legality isn't my department," stated Buzz.

"What is?" asked Faith.

Buzz didn't smile anymore. In fact, his face didn't possess a smidgen of humor.

"Let's hope you never have to find out," he told her.

Faith let it go after that; his words chilled her to the bone.

"Who else is in the know on this thing?" John asked. He knew Homeland Security had called the CDC. That's what Jules told him, and he had spoken to and seen F.B.I. agents, so that made two law enforcement agencies.

"Everyone," stated Buzz. "The F.B.I., Homeland Security, NSA, C.I.A., INTERPOL, you name it. Not everyone knows the specifics. The commanders do, and that's all that counts. So, you will have unlimited resources at your disposal. So what do you say? Are you in or not?"

*　　*　　*　　*　　*

Neither Faith nor John, were very patriotic, not in the sense that they would die defending their country, but they did value the American way of life and believed in the Hippocratic Oath. So they agreed, and were on board the mission.

"I appreciate your assistance," stated Buzz raising his arm and calling another man over.

"This is Hunt Rhinehart," stated Buzz. "He's with the World Health Organization."

"Sir." Hunt shook John's hand.

"John," introducing himself returning the shake.

"Hunt," stated the man, turning to Faith. "Ma'am," he said, shaking her hand also.

Hunt Rhinehart, thought Faith. What kind of name was that? Hunt was Caucasian, six-feet with sleepy looking dark eyes. They looked black, but Faith settled on brown. He looked like he was in excellent shape. She could see the muscles through his turtleneck sweater. He was about one hundred and ninety pounds, thought Faith; and no doctor or health worker. Hunt was a military man if Colin Powell was ever a leader, she thought.

"Hunt is a part of the team," stated Buzz. "If I don't contact you, he will."

The man had on combat boots, observed Faith. Now, what health worker wore them?

Hunt noticed her gaze and abruptly asked her, "What's wrong?"

"Nothing," replied Faith earnestly.

"Don't mind her, Hunt," stated Buzz, "She's just sizing you up. Tell her your age."

"I'm thirty-seven."

After Hunt was seated, their waitress Tasha came back over.

"Is anyone ready to order yet?" she asked cheerfully, looking at Faith.

"Can I have some water?" asked Faith.

"One water," repeated Tasha, writing the order down on a small pad.

"I'll take an order of shrimps," stated John, looking at the next table where the party was having shrimps.

"And I'll have some more wings," said Buzz.

"Okay," said Tasha, writing everything down. "Will that be all?" she asked, looking directly at Hunt, who hadn't ordered anything.

He nodded at her, and she took that as a yes and moved away.

"I take it that you have already filled them in on the preliminaries?" Hunt sounded like a very educated man. Now, Faith was puzzled about his military affiliation.

"Yeah, they're all prepped."

"Okay," said Hunt. "Pardon me if I rush right into this, but I don't have much time. I fly into New York later on tonight to speak with the Secretary of State. But I wanted to sit down and speak with the two of you first. Buzz says that both of you are very bright."

Hunt paused after saying this, thinking that someone might wish to respond. When no one did, he continued to speak.

"There have been five attacks," he began. "We have a representative from the B.T.W.C. That's the Biological and Toxin Weapons Convention. This person states that the weapons and biological agents that have been used have the markings of those secretly cultivated by the North Korean Regime. There is an installation in the rural town of Chongju that has been long suspected of developing biological and chemical weapons. If the weapons used here originated in North Korea, we'll have to take that as an act of war, even if they sold the weapons to a terrorist organization and are not directly involved with the material anymore. This is why we need for you to identify the agents and specify their place of origin. We don't want an international incident, if one can be avoided."

Faith knew for sure now that he wasn't with the World Health Organization. They could identify the agents themselves. And she knew also because he spoke too much about avoiding an international incident. That was soldier talk.

"If the weapons didn't come from North Korea, but Iran or Syria, we need to know that as well. Did you tell them the agent that was used in the first attack?" Hunt was staring at Buzz.

"No, I didn't get around to it," he replied. "Why don't you do the honors?"

"Anthrax," stated Hunt. "Six people were killed, and two were critically injured. It was Inhalation Anthrax that we believe was ground down into a fine microscopic powder. It was sprayed in the air like a mist, we believe."

He had the floor and no one interrupted him. The only time he stopped speaking was when Tasha brought the food and water. She sensed they were in the middle of a private discussion, quickly put everything down in front of the person it belonged to, and sashayed away.

Faith sipped her water, mesmerized by the details that Hunt was laying out. John ate his shrimp, but listened intently as well.

Buzz knew the information already Faith suspected, because he appeared more engrossed with his second helping than the threat.

"The second attack," continued Hunt, "consisted of a mustard gas attack. The stuff is so potent; it alters and damages the DNA of those that come into contact with it. The mustard gas attack was surprising. The Anthrax routinely pops up here and there, but not since World War I have we seen an attack of mustard gas. Germ warfare was employed in the next three, like this latest. It reminds us of the Soviet Union and the program that they had under the Civilian Research Group, called Biopreparat. They developed biological weapons in the form of Anthrax and pneumonic plague like we have just seen here. If there is another attack using biological or chemical weapons, the Nuclear Threat Initiative is threatening to put the public on notice. I don't think that they will, but it has been my experience," stated Hunt Rhinehart, "to take threats seriously."

CHAPTER 6

"I need another drink." Faith walked over to the hotel's mini bar.

"Pour me one too." asked John. "Please?"

They were back at the Holiday Inn, where they had been for hours, mulling over the information that Buzz and Hunt had given them: Folders and dossiers of paperwork, pictures, data and conclusions. The pictures were very upsetting, but not as upsetting as the projections.

The powers-that-be, meaning the United States Government, expected to lose tens of thousands of people during the fight to bring whoever was responsible to justice.

Tens of thousands, thought Faith, over and over. They expected, she told herself.

"Here," she told John, after pouring him a glass of red Bicyclette Rose wine. That was all the hotel had.

"Thank you." He set the glass down next to a pile of paperwork.

"It doesn't make sense," mumbled Faith, in between drinks.

"What's that?"

"Tens of thousands. How could they be comfortable with so many people dying?"

"That's just an estimation," said John, trying to comfort her. She was obviously very distressed over that number. So he gave her another.

"Only thirty-one have been killed Faith. Not even a thousand."

"Only thirty-one, you say," repeated Faith. She was looking at a photo of a child from the first attack. Who kills innocent children? She thought. "It's not an estimation, it's an epiphany of things to come. A comprehensive and perceptive conclusion of reality, by means of a sudden intuitive realization."

John put his papers down, and came over to sit next to her on the couch.

"Don't beat yourself up. We didn't cause this condition or circumstance." Gently, he picked up her hand and cradled it in his. "You won't be any good to yourself or this cause if you let yourself go," he told her.

Faith knew he was right. She looked in his eyes and saw a relative calm.

"How can you be so calm?" she asked him.

"Because although this is a horrible occurrence on a massive scale," he informed her, "this kind of stuff is what I came into the profession to study and prevent. We both did. So I know that we have a job to do and in order to do it," he told her softly, "we have to remain calm, and rationalize the situation. I concede that this is an epiphenomenon only in the sense that it is an additional condition in the course of a disease, not necessarily connected with the disease."

He was speaking her language now and it soothed her.

"The primary infection." said Faith. "The disease itself is greed, money. They're doing all of this for money."

"Exactly," agreed John. Faith moved into his arms and rested her head against his chest. She cried silently, wetting the front of his shirt, but he didn't seem to mind.

John gave her a moment as he held her loosely. When she settled down and came up, Faith kissed him softly on the lips.

John didn't kiss her back initially. But then he did, only because he felt that she needed to be kissed, and he wanted desperately to be the one kissing her. What almost made him stop was the sweet taste of the French wine on her lips and tongue. He didn't want to take advantage of her, or the situation.

It appeared opportune to him. But Faith assured him that it wasn't. When she mumbled, "It's alright, we can have one night."

One night in paradise was his, thought John as he kissed her back and gently lifted her up from the couch and walked into the room. Faith's clothing fell from her body like leaves in the Fall. John's clothing followed and in a minute they stood before one another, nude, necking and native. In the sense that they felt as though they existed, naturally in nature and belonging to only this moment in time. Laying her down on the bed gently, he moved down in between her limbs.

Faith wrapped her legs around his back, but then released him. "We need to use protection," she told him.

"Oh yeah," he mumbled, getting back up and running to retrieve a condom from his trouser pocket. She wasn't intoxicated, he told himself, smiling all the way back to her.

She rested with her head up on a fluffy white pillow, her legs up, and a beautiful smile on her face when he returned.

John tore open the condom and dressed his manhood. Then he took up his prior position. This time, Faith guided him into her and pulled him close, so that their bodies nestled against one another. John kissed her passionately and she reciprocated his advance.

Although she felt very good, the real feast for him was done with his eyes, just looking into her face as they pleasured one another.

Faith had a spot on her upper chest, just above her right breast, that John noticed and began to kiss before he moved on to her breasts. It was considerably lighter than the rest of her body. It was her nerves, or birthmark as ordinary people called it, he figured.

He took his time with each lovely mound. They were like peaches, he thought. Soft, juicy with red tinted skin.

For two hours, John loved and made love to Faith, concluding with the notion that he had been right about her all along. She was special inside and out, he thought.

*   *   *   *   *

Faith had dozed off while John lay awake, thinking not about death and disease, but life and love, hoping that the one night Faith spoke about would go on forever.

At eight o'clock in the morning, Faith abruptly sat up in bed. She looked over at John and his eyes opened.

"I gotta pee," she wiped the sleep from her eyes as she climbed out of bed. She was still nude, so John enjoyed the show as she made her way from the room.

A minute later, John heard the water in the shower running and got up himself. He walked down to the bathroom and could see a silhouette of Faith's body through the glass doors to the shower. The glass was cloudy but anyone who was half way observant could appreciate the feminine figure in the profile.

"Do you want some company?"

"No!" She replied quickly, a little too quickly for John's taste.

The Faith from Atlanta had returned -- the absolute professional.

"Could you send for some coffee for me, John?" She asked sweetly.

"Yeah," he said. Walking out of the bathroom, he realized the moment they had shared had passed.

When Faith emerged from the shower fifteen minutes later, John was in the common area of a suite which served as the living room, sitting on the couch. He had his pants and socks on now, his underwear also, Faith supposed, but no shirt.

She wore a big fluffy white robe that the hotel supplied and a towel wrapped around her head. Faith walked all the way in the living room and began straightening up. She quietly picked up the open bottles of wine and placed them in a waste paper basket. Then she put the used glasses in the sink. She saw her coffee sitting nearby and sampled it. John was about to address her, but she took out her cell phone and began to make a call.

"Why don't you use the room phone?" he asked her just to make conversation.

"Habit," she replied matter-of-factly. "Hello? Yvonne, where are you?"

John watched her as she listened to the other person on the line speak. Then when it was her turn to respond, she walked out of the room. He figured that she was probably talking about him at that point and hoped that she was saying something nice. She didn't stay gone for long, so his mind didn't get an excessive amount of time to wonder.

"Why do you think the person that is killing these people" asked Faith, "is taking work from the poet Homer?"

"I don't know, Faith," replied John hesitantly. "The police are probably trying to solve that part of the conundrum. We should probably tackle the scientific part."

"You're right," agreed Faith, and headed back to retrieve her phone from the other room. "But first I want to talk to Jules."

She came back with it and asked John, "You want some breakfast? I'm gonna order room service for some hominy grits."

"Yeah," John nodded. "I'll take some of them also."

"Okay." She called the front desk and ordered them both breakfast. This took two minutes and then she called Jules.

"Hello," she said, once the director answered his private line.

"Faith?" Jules asked, like he was unsure of her voice.

"Yes Sir. I'm here with John. We have some questions we'd like to ask you."

John liked how she had conveniently put him in the equation. He didn't have a problem with it, but he did acknowledge that she felt she needed an ally.

"Sir, we met your friend, Mister Shaw, and another man named Rhinehart. They briefed us on the matter at hand. Are you aware of all the details?"

"I was made aware this morning," stated Jules "by the State Department. And I must say Ms. Millicent, I had no idea. What are you and Mr. Lovejoy's position on this?"

"We're aboard, Sir," replied Faith. "We just have some concerns, like who are these two men. Mr. Shaw won't tell us what agency he works for. Mr. Rhinehart stated that he's with the World Health Organization, but I seriously doubt that. I'm concerned about why the need for secrecy, if their lies can even be called that."

"Well, Ms. Millicent," replied her director, "First of all, Mr. Shaw isn't a friend of mine. It is true that I have met and worked with him in the past. But we are nothing more than acquaintances. I don't know this other gentleman. The fellow Shaw has always represented himself to me as Buzz Shaw. I don't know what agency within our government he works for, either. But I assure you that he has the nation's top hierarchy support."

"But why the misinformation?" Faith asked. "I need more to go on."

"Ms. Millicent," stated the director, "I really should not be saying this, but I will say it anyway off the record because I respect you and your work. Mr. Shaw, from what I know and believe, doesn't exist in any agency database. I looked, many years ago. Most people in key positions will disavow any knowledge of the man."

"Why is that?" asked Faith, cutting the director off.

"It is my belief that Mr. Shaw doesn't arrest people."

Jules paused at this point, and Faith wondered why. Then it dawned on her: Buzz Shaw was a law enforcement officer who didn't arrest people. If he didn't do that, she asked herself, what was it that he did?

The conversation that she and John had with him the previous night came back. He wasn't concerned with the legality of the situation, he had said. He'd also suggested that Faith and John should not want to find out what it was that he really did. The only thing that Faith could think of was the same thing that they were investigating: murder.

"You're not suggesting sir..." stated Faith, as the revelation hit her.

"You don't have to say it," retorted the director. "I just wanted to make sure you understood the entire situation. Things are not always done how the framers of this country intended. Sometimes desperate measures must be taken, and when those times arrive, men like Buzz Shaw are called in to conduct clandestine operations. This, I'm afraid; Ms. Millicent is one of those times. It isn't my place to say what or who is either right or wrong - I have no opinion one way or the other. I am here to only do my job."

Faith was numb. She was surrounded by people who were all playing God, she thought, each for their own personal reasons.

"Ms. Millicent?" Jules stated when Faith got very quiet. "Are you still there?"

"Yes sir. I'm still here."

"What is it that you and Mr. Lovejoy have left to do?"

"We have to speak with the coroner just to see if there may be something he left out of the report. Then we'll be heading back. It shouldn't take more than a day or two more, sir."

"Very well," replied the director. "I'll see you when you return. God speed to you."

Faith hung up, tossed the phone down on the couch, and plopped her body down right next to it. Then she pulled the towel from her head. Her hair wasn't yet fully dry, but it couldn't be considered totally wet either. John waited a minute before he engaged her in conversation. He was now wearing an undershirt with a button down shirt over it. Faith couldn't remember seeing him put the articles of clothing on, although she had been standing right in front of him the entire time she'd been on the phone. She took a moment to regroup.

Knock. Knock. There was a knock at the door and Faith began to get up.

"I got it," said John, beating her to the punch. He answered the door and was greeted by room service. Their breakfast was sent into the room on a small metal cart; John tipped the man who had brought it up, and thanked him."

"The food's here," he announced, trying to pull Faith out of her stupor. She stared at him, and then shook her head indicating a yes.

"What did Jules say about our fake James Bond?" John asked, in an attempt to be humorous.

Faith didn't laugh. She looked at John and said, "He has a license to kill."

*   *   *   *   *

It took Faith all of five minutes to explain to John every sentiment that Jules had expressed to her, after which they were on the same page.

"Come on, Faith." He waved her over to the breakfast. "Eat. You need the sustenance."

They ate in silence for a few minutes. Then John asked, "Are we going to speak with the coroner for real?"

"Yeah," replied Faith, "and I have to go meet up with my sister. The coroner is important because he listed everyone as dying from the same thing: Pneumonic Plague. He also attributed this to the victim's food intake, but one victim didn't eat. So, we need to know what the port of entry was for that victim."

John nodded. She was right, he thought.

"I'm going to get dressed." Faith stood up. "I'll be ready to go in ten minutes."

"Cool," said John. "I have to make a quick stop at my room. I'll be right back."

*   *   *   *   *

An hour later, they were standing inside of the coroner's office waiting for an audience with a man named Hatcher, who didn't keep them waiting very long.

"Good afternoon," he greeted them. Mr. Hatcher was a very tall African American with huge hands, noted Faith. "What can I do for you?"

"Hello, Sir," began Faith. "We spoke on the phone. I'm Faith Millicent and this is my colleague, John Lovejoy."

"Yes," the coroner nodded. "Please have a seat."

"Sir," continued Faith, "you handled the inquest for the people killed at the Linden Plaza Eatery"

"Yes," repeated the coroner.

"And you listed the prescribed cause of death, but I was wondering about one of the victims. The bacterium that you have listed as being the primary cause of death is a food-borne pathogen, but the victim didn't have any food in their system. So what did you determine to be the exact port of entry?"

The coroner took a moment to consult some documentation. He frowned as he looked over the material, and Faith and John frowned as well, as they watched him.

"I never determined that," he finally conceded. "As odd as this may sound, I believe this particular bacterium entered these victims' systems as something else, and changed rapidly. For those with food in their alimentary canal, I don't believe the food aided this pathogen. That wasn't its mode of transportation. It used another vehicle to get in and around, one I couldn't locate. Once it made it to the stomach of some of the victims, it used this cisterna as a reservoir in its manifestation."

Faith stared at the man. "So, you're saying that once the microorganism gained entry into one of the susceptible hosts, it mutated?"

"Exactly" said the coroner, "without any telltale signs of infection."

"Sudden death," John used the medical term.

"A death that isn't preceded by any condition that would appear fatal," stated the coroner. "They all just dropped dead."

Faith was still for a moment. Then she asked, "Did you identify the original microorganism?"

"Not yet," replied the coroner. "But trust me, I am aware of the time frame of this situation, and understand that there is no time for dalliance. I have a clinic working right now to determine what the initial infection was. When this coroner's jury has done that, I will notify Mr. Shaw."

"Could you also contact me at the CDC?" Faith handed the man her card.

"Yes, of course. If that will be all, I would like to get back to work."

"Thank you for your time." Faith stood, shaking the man's huge hand. John followed suit.

"You know," stated the man, "I was a knickerbocker, before relocating to Houston. I could have been Diedrich Knickerbocker," he added humorously. "I know the entire history of New York."

Faith smiled politely. She was used to out-of-towners referring to her as if she was one of the descendents of the Dutch settlers of New York just because she had lived there prior to relocating to Atlanta. She'd made the mistake of telling Mr. Hatcher that on the phone. She did, however, admire the twist he had put on his comment, by speaking about, and using the name of, the fictitious author in the book by Washington Irving.

"Atlanta is my home now," she informed the man.

"Hotlanta," he commented, walking them out of the place. "That's a beautiful haven, also. I don't know what's going on down there with the home ownership, but Houston doesn't really have that problem. Our cost of living index is slightly below the national average."

He was speaking about Atlanta's high foreclosure rate, thought Faith, and comparing it to Houston's thriving housing market. It was true that Houston had very low cost of living compared to the national average, she thought, as they approached the facilities exit area. But now, its quality of life ranking was damaged in her opinion, in light of the information she was now privy to.

"Thanks again," stated Faith. "I'll look forward to your call."

Outside of the building, she caught John smiling at her. "What?"

"You know... he was feeling you," said John.

"Go ahead," she replied. "He asked me where I was originally from. How should I know he was a history buff?"

"Where to now?"

Faith took out her cell phone. "I want to connect with my sister," she told him. "I don't feel comfortable leaving her in Texas right about now."

The maternal instinct that Faith possessed as a juvenile for her sister was coming back now that she felt a threat was around.

"Hello Yvonne," she said. "Where are you?"

They were finished with their business in Houston and were lounging around at their hotel, and really didn't want to be disturbed, but Faith insisted.

"Where too?" asked John as they got into their vehicle.

"The Hotel Derek," replied Faith. "It's over the Galleria, so take the Northwest Freeway. That will put us in the area."

As John drove, Faith took a moment to think about what the coroner had told them. A mutating microorganism, she thought. That sounded familiar, like the virus that caused AIDS. God forbid, she told herself. We don't need another calamity like that.

When they got to her sister's hotel, Yvonne and Jeff were waiting for them outside.

"What's up?" asked Yvonne.

"John, you know my sister. This is her husband, Jeff Kincaid."

"Hi John," Yvonne caught herself, acknowledging her rudeness. John was shaking Jeff's hand. "We need to make a run," said Yvonne. "So can we talk while we drive?"

"Yeah, sure," replied Faith. "I'll ride with my sister. Jeff, could you ride with John?"

"Sure," replied Jeff, not sure why he couldn't ride with them in his rental.

"Thank you," said Faith, nodding at John walking toward the car with Yvonne.

"What's this about?" asked Yvonne climbing into the driver's seat of a Toyota Highlander she and Jeff had rented. Faith got into the passenger's seat.

"Did you take care of all your business yet?" asked Faith, "regarding Jeff's photo shoot?"

"Yeah, that was yesterday. We're trying to see about another gig while we're down here. What's up with you and Loverboy?" she asked.

"It's Lovejoy," corrected Faith. "But please just call him John."

"I'll call him whatever I want to," countered Yvonne. "What do you care? You're not an item."

"Just…"

"You are!" shouted Yvonne, cutting her sister off. "You're together aren't you?"

"No, we're not."

"You're lying," countered Yvonne. "I can see it in your face. You Hottie!" she shouted.

"Nothing happened," Faith lied, but not too convincingly. Faith and her sister had a special bond. They could communicate with each other on different sides of a crowded room without exchanging a word, just through a look, not even a gesture. When Yvonne said she knew something had happened between Faith and John 'Lover boy' Lovejoy, as she thought of him, she was one hundred percent sure.

"Faith, don't even try it!" She shouted, stopping at a traffic light. "You had sex. Was it good? Jeff and I had sex at Hartsfield-Jackson, in the restroom, while we were waiting for our flight to leave."

Faith jerked her head to the side ready to reprimand her sister, but Yvonne continued talking over her.

"We're not going to do that anymore," she said. "Because you have to damn near take a number to have sex in there. That's how many people were waiting to do it," she said, laughing. "But we continued with our tryst on the plane. I'm already a member of the mile high club, me and Jeff. So, for us, it was like returning to the scene of a crime. You should do it there with John. So when the two of you are back at work you can take bathroom breaks together."

Faith knew that her sister suspected something had happened. So she needed to throw her a bone and give her sister something to nibble on, or she would never stop sniffing around.

"We didn't have sex!" shouted Faith, breaking into the conversation with a lie. "All we did was kiss. That's all!"

Yvonne stared at her, and then smiled. "That's a start," she told Faith. "But you're an adult, you could have done more."

"I'm not ready for more and I don't think that we are going to take it further."

"Why not? He's cool and you're not attached to anyone else."

"Let me just do me please and I didn't come to talk to you about that."

"Okay, okay," said Yvonne. "But I know something happened. The eyes, Sis, they never lie. What do you want to talk about?"

"We all need to leave Houston as soon as possible," stated Faith. "There's a possible terrorist threat going on in the city."

"How do you know? I didn't see anything on the news about any threat."

"They're keeping it under wraps, but five people are dead. That's why they sent me down here to investigate."

"Damn Faith!" You could have told me this on the phone and we could have been out of here by now."

"That's what I've been trying to tell you, but you won't shut up about Loverboy and making love."

"Interrupt me next time. You have the green light to do that any time there's something that I really need to know."

Faith shook her head as Yvonne pulled over, 'If it was only that easy,' she thought.

"I'll be right back." Yvonne climbed out. "You can call and make us a reservation to leave. Jeff and I came in through Hobby Airport - it's quicker over there. So, you might want to try them."

Faith took out her cell phone as she watched Jeff and Yvonne make their way into a Houston television station. Then John came over. He stood outside of the vehicle waiting for Faith to finish on the phone. It took Faith five minutes to set them up with a one-way ticket back. Then she hung up the phone.

"So, we're finished here?" John said.

"Yeah," confirmed Faith. "Unless there's something else that you think we should look into?"

"Not that I can think of," replied John. "That guy Hatcher gave us a lot. Let's see if Jules can get him to send us some tissue samples that we can test ourselves."

"That sounds like a good idea." Faith, looking at him, thought about what Yvonne had said. *He's cool.* Yeah, she thought.

"Jeff's down to earth," continued John. "He told me that I should pursue you because the Millicent women are some wild girls." He smiled broadly, making Faith smile as well.

"Did he?" She shook her head, thinking about how it seemed everyone was trying to push the two of them together. Faith wanted so badly to tell them: Been there. Done that! And she suspected that John did also by the kool-aid smile that he wore.

Yvonne and Jeff emerged kind of quickly, thought Faith, as she saw them coming back out of the building giggling. When they got to the vehicle, Faith asked them, "You're finished already?"

"Yeah, we just had to make a first impression with some studio heads for some possible work in the Spring. It was just an introduction," stated Yvonne. "So, did you make the flight reservations?"

"Yes, we're good to go," said Faith getting out of the vehicle. "John and I have to take our rental back, and then pack. We'll meet you at the Hobby Airport. Even though we have more to do, I bet we'll still beat you there."

"Don't count on it," said Jeff, as Faith and John began to walk to their ride. "Yvonne told me what time it might be, so we'll see you there. Star track style," he joked. "At warp speed."

*   *   *   *   *

"When are you going to get by to see mom?" Faith asked.

"I saw her last month," replied Yvonne. "Why, did she say something to you?"

"No, she just asked how you were and she mentioned that she hadn't seen you in awhile."

"It hasn't been that long," disputed Yvonne. They were aboard a flight headed back to Atlanta. "She's probably experiencing delirium tremens."

"What?" Faith, remembering the telltale signs of alcohol consumption she'd seen at her mother's home before she left for Houston, became agitated. "That's not funny!"

Delirium tremens was an acute delirium caused by alcohol poisoning, something that Faith didn't want to associate with her mother. Yvonne felt her sister's unease with her comment, so she attempted to clean it up.

"Relax," she told her. "First, I wasn't even talking about that. I meant to say tremor."

"What's the difference?"

"One is an uncertain, insecure feeling. The other, the one I meant to say first, is trembling."

"Don't play with me, Yvonne. If you know something, tell me!"

"Ain't nothing to tell," said Yvonne smiling and looking past Faith over at Jeff, who sat about five feet away from her. She got out of her seat. "I'll be back."

Yvonne played around too much, thought Faith. The girl knew that her sister was a slight worrywart, but she still didn't tame her tongue.

"Hey," said John coming over and taking Yvonne's now unoccupied seat.

"Hey," Faith replied back.

"I was thinking," stated John. "I have a friend up in New York who's a specialist in Schizomycosis. He can tell you from the final stages of a disease what bacteria, fungus or pathogen caused it. He may be able to identify the bacterium that the coroner couldn't."

John was excited, but Faith seemed far away. She stared at him and nodded occasionally as he spoke. But he could still see that he didn't have her full attention.

"I'm trying to schmoose with you," John told her. "Are you okay?"

"Yeah," wondering where Yvonne was. She wanted to ask her another question about their mother. "I just have something on my mind," she told him. "Something Yvonne and I were discussing a minute ago. Excuse me." Faith got up and brushed past him. She made her way down the aisle to the women's bathroom.

"The lavatory is in use," stated a tall Chinese woman who was by the bathroom when Faith got there. She walked away smiling, as if she knew a secret.

Faith stood outside of the bathroom wondering if Yvonne had gone in there. She stood there for a full minute before she noticed heavy panting.

She looked down the aisle to see if anyone was looking or coming. The coast was clear. So she put her ear on the door.

"Okay. Okay. Okay," she heard a woman's voice saying. It sounded like Yvonne's. But she wasn't sure until Yvonne purred in her distinctive dialect, "Ooh, that's my spot!"

Faith moved back and hit the door hard with her fist. "Get a room!" she lightly yelled, and walked away.

Inside the bathroom, Jeff stopped what he was doing to his wife and Yvonne covered her mouth with a broad smile on her face.

"Should we stop?" asked Jeff. He was holding her legs up in the air, standing comfortably between them, with his pants down around his ankles.

"Hell no!" Yvonne took her hand away from her mouth. "That was only Faith frustrated and pent up," she told him, pulling him back in closer to her body.

Jeff continued his erotic assault while kissing Yvonne all over her neck. Yvonne placed her hands back on his broad shoulder and pulled him into her, loving her man in so many ways at the moment. She kissed him on the lips and stared into his eyes. She was still smiling about the interruption. The possibility of getting caught while doing something risqué to her made the entire experience that much more gratifying.

"Why should we get a room," she said to her husband, "when the sky's the limit?"

CHAPTER 7

Stepping up to the door, Faith heard the familiar sound of the French rock and roll music that Jules was very fond of. It was called Ye' Ye' and Faith didn't care for it very much. She knocked on the door with a little force.

"Come in!" called Jules, turning the music down. Faith let herself in.

"Oh, Ms. Millicent," stated Jules. "You're back. Where's Mr. Lovejoy?"

"He went to his office to check his messages," replied Faith. "I came right over."

"As you should have." The Director picked up the phone and called John Lovejoy's office.

Faith and John had gotten back late last night. Faith picked her children up and took them home where they all slept in the same bed. The photos she'd seen, of the children that had been killed, had her missing her babies. So she slept with them and held them tight.

Mel had resisted, wanting to sleep alone. He thought it wasn't cool, or grown up, to sleep with his mother, but Faith won in the end.

Jules didn't start questioning Faith until John came over. "Would you like some coffee?" he offered Faith as they waited for John.

"Yes please," replied Faith.

"You're not taking yours au lait?" asked Jules.

"No, black please," replied Faith.

Jules never stopped trying to get her to take her coffee with milk. Faith had come to believe that he only asked her now to test her will, wondering when she would get tired of saying no, acquiesce to his preference, and call it a day.

"Here you go." Jules handed her a hot cup of coffee, and sat, as John knocked at the door and was invited in.

"Sorry," offered John, taking a seat and realizing that he had held them up.

"So brief me," ordered Jules.

Faith went first, explaining the crime scene to him and the dinner engagement that she and John attended with Buzz Shaw and, later, with Hunt Rhinehart.

After she finished with that, John broke down what they knew about the chemical and biological weapons that had been used.

"The historical scourge," remarked Jules baffled by the bacteria, Yesinia Pestis, involvement in the Houston deaths. This was a pestilence that hadn't been seen causing widespread death in a good while.

"And you say that death was instantaneous?"

"They all collapsed at the same time," answered Faith. "So, you could say that. But I'm a bit apprehensive about drawing that conclusion because we don't know what took place inside of their bodies prior to their systems breaking down. The Houston coroner's opinion is that the pathogen entered the victims' system as something else. Then it mutated and became a pneumonic plague."

"So, the question is," stated Jules, "what was it before?"

"Exactly," concluded Faith. "You know, it disturbs me that the two law enforcement officers we met don't have any qualms about tens of thousands of people dying because the government has a policy not to negotiate with terrorist entities. I'm not saying that's right or wrong," added Faith, "That's the Commander-and-Chief's call. I understand that; but I mean, damn, you can have an opinion on it."

"Don't lose focus, Ms. Millicent," warned the director. "Our job is to identify the dreaded affliction and take it out. The other judgments are someone else's job. I understand the principle because I have been in this position before. It is a painful place to be, but what can you really do about it? Some people must die in situations like this for the greater cause."

"I understand that," said Faith, "but tens of thousands?"

"Ms. Millicent, tens of thousands sounds like a very big number, but it's nothing compared with three hundred million or more if the pestilence escapes from our borders."

He was speaking about the estimated population of three hundred million people living in the United States. So when you did the math, thought Faith, preserving the entire nation did make sense. Still, standing around and watching thousands of people die didn't make sense to Faith, either.

"Like I told you on the phone," said Jules, "I know Mr. Shaw's history a little bit, but not the other fellow. Shaw's been *hors de combat* for some time."

The phrase meant out of action and disabled, thought Faith. The latter, Shaw hadn't appeared to her, so she scratched that definition.

"Those in the military community call him A Stormy Petrel," continued Jules, "You know what that means?"

"Yes," said John. "That's a person who appears at the onset of trouble. They used to refer to rebels this way."

"Yes," agreed Jules. "Buzz Shaw is a sobriquet. I know he states that Shaw is his last name, but I believe it is an assumed name just like the name Cimmerian that the killer uses. There is a rumor that our Mr. Shaw popped up in Germany in 2006 after six German citizens were hospitalized with lung problems. The official inquiry stated that an aerosol sealant called Magic Nano was to blame.

Shortly thereafter, he disappeared again. He dropped off the grid and resurfaced in Apex, North Carolina. Do you know why?"

"There was a chemical explosion there in October of 2006," frowned John.

"Yes," continued Jules. "A hazardous waste facility went up in smoke."

"I remember that," Faith spoke up. "They were so afraid that they just let the fires burn themselves out."

"A chemical cloud developed," said Jules, "engulfed by torrent winds. This chemical cloud spread throughout a nearby valley. Over seven thousand people had to be evacuated. Explosions went on inside the facility for four hours. Many people believe that the explosions were a cover for some other sort of military operation that was taking place in the Raleigh, North Carolina area, which required Mr. Shaw's presence. But I don't know. By the morning, they had to expand their evacuation efforts to include ten thousand more residents nearby. God must have been watching the scene because it began to rain. That extinguished the fire and provided relief to the area. The fascinating thing about the entire incident, in my opinion, was the fact that no one could identify the chemicals involved."

"Wait a minute," replied Faith. "I need to just clarify what Mr. Shaw's involvement in both of the incidents was."

"I don't know," said Jules. "I am merely informing you that he was there. In Germany, they didn't want to tell us what had caused the people to get sick."

"I heard that it was the nanoparticles," said John, "that the product contained."

"They use nanoparticles in hundreds of consumer products out there on the market. Why no other instances of sickness occurring?" asked Jules. "In North Carolina, there were a lot of unanswered questions; the facility was fined thirty-two thousand by the Environmental and National Resources Department of North Carolina. Whip-tee-do," concluded Jules. "That still didn't answer the question of Mr. Shaw's presence and involvement. I'm telling you all this because your guess is as good as mine."

Both Faith and John nodded their heads. Jules was obviously stumped, thought Faith. And now, so were they.

"We'd like you to have the officials in Houston send us sample tissue from the victims down there," stated Faith. "We'd also like any other tissue samples preserved from the previous four attacks, so we can run tests."

"Done," answered Jules. "This one is of the greatest priority and you will have every office in the center at your disposal."

"I keep hearing that."

"You keep hearing what?"

"That everyone will be at our disposal. Buzz Shaw and Hunt Rhinehart said that to us, concerning every law enforcement agency in the nation."

"Is that not a good thing?"

"No, too many chefs spoil the meal. John and I will handle the preliminary investigation and I'd like Edna and Buddy to do all the follow up work. That will be all the hands-on help we'll need." Faith looked at John to see if her suggestion met his approval. John nodded; they were still on the same page.

"You want the Defoes?" said Jules. "Very well, whatever they're working on can wait. What else?"

Faith shook her head, unable to think of anything else besides some badly-needed rest.

"We'll keep you updated," John looking at Faith. "We're not sure at the moment what else we'll need. Our needs may change as rapidly as this bug. So we'll see."

"You two have changed since your trip." Jules was staring at the both of them. "You interact differently."

Faith was nervous, picturing her and John's lovemaking. Could Jules see it?

"It's like you two have some sort of telepathy thing going on," added Jules. "I like that."

Faith stood up and smoothed out the lavender summer dress that she wore. John sensed her nervousness and stood up himself.

"If that's it, sir," he said, "we'll go get right on things."

"Yes," replied Jules. Do that. Get right on it."

They turned and headed for Faith's office. Faith was breathing a little easier.

There were two male co-workers standing in the entrance to Faith's office, conversing loudly with Edna and Buddy about baseball.

"Excuse me gentleman," said Faith, edging around them. John headed to his office. Faith was alone.

Buddy was standing over his wife's desk, talking excitedly as usual. "Let's ask Faith," he said. "She's an avid baseball fan."

"Yeah." Faith ran her fingers across her computer panel to turn it on. "So?"

"You know what 'wins above replacement player is,' right?" Buddy asked her.

"Yes." replied Faith looking up. "That's a measure of a player's ability to help his team win games. The acronym is called W.A.S.P."

"That's right," replied Buddy, clapping his hands together excitedly. "This is the argument - they're saying that Derek Jeter is overpaid in relation to his WASP stats."

"Who says that?" asked Faith.

Buddy pointed to their two co-workers and his wife.

"He should get paid more than Alex Rodriguez," stated Edna defiantly.

"She's biased," Faith smiled. "Edna just likes the way Jeter looks."

"You're damn right!" admitted Edna, not afraid that her Buddy would get upset. They were cool like that, thought Faith.

"I've heard people say that about Alex Rodriguez, being over-paid," admitted Faith. "Just like they say that about J.D. Drew, but I don't think that's correct in either instance. What makes Jeter's marquee value, as they call it, so high, are his good looks, skills, and persona. People, the fans, love him. So they watch the Yankees, go to their games, and purchase all of their memorabilia. So, surely he is bringing the franchise in big money. That's why I don't believe that he's really overpaid. But that's just my opinion."

"We'll talk later," stated Buddy seeing Jules coming toward the office. His co-workers took off and Buddy headed toward the door where Jules promptly intercepted him.

"You're working with Millicent and Lovejoy on the 'Cimmerian' thing." He was standing in the doorway. "They will fill you in on the particulars; you also, Mrs. Defoe."

Jules walked away, leaving Edna and Buddy there to wonder.

"What's up?" asked Buddy turning back to Faith.

"Why don't you let John fill you in? I'll bring Edna up to speed. But first, I have to use the ladies room."

*   *   *   *   *

When Faith returned, Edna was alone in their office fielding questions over the phone; concerning the number of available doses of flu vaccine for the impending flu season. Faith took a seat and waited for her to pause momentarily.

"What's up?" Faith asked between calls.

"They've got me helping out the Immunization Services Division," said Edna. "So hold up a minute before you brief me," she told Faith. "Better yet, call these two numbers for me, and ask them how many doses of flu vaccine we can expect from them."

Edna gave Faith the two numbers. They were for Novelties vaccines and Galax-Smith-Klein, longtime suppliers of flu vaccine within the United States.

"We need two hundred and eighteen million doses available," stated Edna. "According to the new federal guidelines, we have roughly one hundred and thirty million doses. So I'm trying to work with a company that may become our fifth supplier. They have a pretty good track record – they've been in the business of vaccine production since 1968. They currently supply sixteen other countries in Asia, Europe, and South America."

"Okay," replied Faith picking up the phone. "So let's knock this out, and I'll brief you on the 'Cimmerian' situation afterwards."

As Faith dialed the first number, she thought about the annual fatalities suffered in the United States at the hands of influenza.

It was estimated to be around thirty-six thousand hospitalizations thought Faith, which was nothing compared to what they were facing now.

CHAPTER 8

"One billion dollars," repeated Jules to himself, alone in his office. That was a lot of money, he told himself. All the things he could do with that amount, life could and would be so much different.

Jules opened up the bottom half of his desk drawer and took out an old picture that was brown around the edges. The photo was of his parents. He liked to look at this photo and imagine what their life was like. His mother, although smiling in the photo, lived a hard life at the time. Jules knew this. She was twenty-one and his father only twenty-four.

His mother was French and his father as well. They met in America and, being fellow countryman so to speak, connected and began a friendship. His father worked on the docks and his mother was an *au pair* girl; that was a foreign girl who worked for a family in exchange for room and board and, occasionally instruction in the family's native language, English in this instance.

Jules set his parents' photo aside and looked over the faxes he'd received. Then he viewed the photographs of the victims from each attack. Horrible business was that of terrorism, he thought, just horrible.

He picked up the phone and called his friend in New York. They weren't really good friends, more like business partners. He was the head of a large pharmaceutical company and Jules fed him information from time to time. The phone was ringing. It was late, but Jules knew his friend wouldn't mind, not after he received the information that Jules had for him.

In Jules' opinion, the man was a hoity-toity kind of person, very self-important, and pompous. But when a person was a billionaire, thought Jules, that attribute comes with the money.

"Hello," stated a very baritone voice.

"Yes, hello," replied Jules.

"Jules, is that you?"

*   *   *   *   *

"You know, dear," stated Buddy, "had the first and second attack not occurred, the rest could possibly have been mistaken for natural occurrences."

"That's probably why Homer sent the note," theorized Edna.

"It's Cimmerian," corrected Buddy.

"Same thing." argued Edna. "Eggs for breakfast?"

"Yes, please." He was looking at the morning paper and, also at the medical records of people who had been killed by a microbial threat and not a conventional biological or chemical weapon.

Buddy and Edna had a simple routine. They went to sleep every night at nine. Sometimes they had sex, but most of the time they didn't because they had work on their minds. They rose at five-thirty every morning, showered, used the bathroom and in Buddy's case, shaved. Then they ate breakfast together and headed for work.

They had to be at the Center by nine in the morning. They were never late, usually early, being that they were both workaholics.

"I know what they didn't look at," stated Buddy, "when they looked for the chain of infection in the deceased."

"What's that?" Edna cracked two eggs into a little ramekin.

"The genetic make-up of the victims," answered Buddy, "in relation to their ethnicity and place of origin. That may have played a part in the pathogen's mutation."

That kind of brainstorming was the couple's preferred way of solving problems and medical conundrums. They did that all the time, bouncing ideas, thoughts and complex opinions off one another.

Edna added a dash of pepper to the eggs, as well as a little bit of vinegar to assist the proteins' coagulation. "Why don't you think they looked at that?" Edna asked.

"Because it's not noted; every other possible theory that they considered is spoken about either in the text or a footnote, but not that."

"Okay. They didn't look there," agreed Edna, "Why should they?" She poured the eggs into a saucepan with a bit of water. She stirred the water prior to pouring the eggs in so that the water formed a whirlpool. This caused the eggs to take on a funny shape. Edna liked to do things like this, to make ordinary meals look and feel interesting.

"Because genetic make-up might be the reason some people were affected and others weren't." Buddy made a note on a small pad to look into the theory. Do you remember how all our classmates at Stanford used to complain about the flea bites? They'd break out in rashes from the bites, while you and I were immune to the effects of the bite. Remember? And it was because we grew up in San Francisco."

"Yeah," stated Edna recalling. She went over to the kitchen table where Buddy sat and picked up some of the documentation that he was reviewing. She browsed it, looking at the victims' nationalities. Some were Caucasian and others African American. She made a mental note to look at sickle cell anemia, a hereditary anemia characterized by the presence of oxygen deficient sickle cells, some episodic pain and leg ulcers. Edna knew that the African American population was disproportionately affected by this malady.

Several victims were Asian, two South Americans and a woman from the Caribbean. All were places that Hansen's disease was prevalent, noted Edna.

"If your assumption is correct, we have to look at family histories, stated Edna about to mess with her husband. "Also, because I see where a lot of the deceased come from nations where diseases like leprosy were prevalent."

"Don't even try it," stated Buddy. "I'm not suggesting a fishing expedition."

Edna went back and took the eggs off of the stove. Then she transferred them atop a buttered English muffin and brought it over to her husband.

"Here you go, dear," she offered, kissing him on the cheek.

"I asked for Eggs Benedict," said Buddy, "I don't see the ham."

"We don't have any ham. Now shut up and eat," Edna told him. "And about your theory, the victims come from many different walks of life. Faith seems to think the government won't pay Cimmerian any money. If there are more attacks, what do we do then?" Edna asked. "Test and compare the genetic make-up of everyone?"

"If we have to." Buddy swallowed his eggs. "But let's not get ahead of ourselves. We'll cross that bridge if and when we get to it."

CHAPTER 9

"The ball is rolling," Norton Burke told his detail man. "I received a call from my contact at the Center for Disease Control and Prevention. The bun is in the oven. I want you to go down to Washington, D.C. and visit with some of the doctors and pharmacists in the area."

"Am I promoting our new drugs?" asked Sterling Rayford. "Or am I just making friends?"

"You're doing both," stated his boss. "Let them know what we have in the pipeline. And try to get a commitment from them. You know the drill."

Yes he did, thought Sterling. He knew the drill very well having been a representative for Meyer-Burke for six years. He knew that Norton Burke was a cunning piece of crap. The only reason he still worked for Burke was because the man paid so well.

Sterling Rayford was African American, six-feet-four and extremely dapper; Just the right representative Meyer-Burke needed in the African American communities where most of the company's consumers were. Meyer-Burke was a fifty-year old company, founded by Norton Burke's grandfather and a business partner of his named

Meyer. Norton had acquired the Meyer family's shares in the pharmaceutical giant a decade ago, but didn't bother to change the company name because it was bedrock and consumers knew it.

He hired the chocolate-skinned smooth talker, Sterling, to push the company's high blood pressure medications, their diabetes drugs and their heart disease drugs. Their union had been very profitable in spite of the men having no personal relationship. Sterling's intelligent brown eyes always told Norton that he loathed him.

The two men never shared a smile, but this didn't bother Norton because this was business, and he could always appreciate a business relationship.

At two hundred and ten pounds, Sterling out-weighed him by thirty pounds. Personally, Norton didn't have a problem with him. He didn't like the fact that Sterling had short, silky, wavy hair while his was both receding and bald, but that was a small thing.

He disliked Sterling's kind; black men. To him, they all had a chip on their shoulder and came into the game and arena ill-prepared for battle. So, to keep things fair, Norton Burke kept two bodyguards and clean-up men around him at all times. This, he felt, was the preparation that Sterling Rayford lacked. He was armed with an attitude when a gun was needed, thought Norton Burke, as he sat staring at him.

"Why Washington, D.C.?" asked Sterling sensing that Norton expected him to ask that question.

The short, fat, white man, thought Sterling, was always browbeating him.

At five-feet-six, that was all Sterling felt he could do with him. His clever dark eyes knew this, regardless of what his loud voice said, thought Sterling.

"I like Washington, D.C. because it's mostly populated with black people," stated Norton sarcastically.

His remark caused both of his body guards to laugh. Pete 'The Pistol" Carpenter and Sergio Moshe.

"Why do you think?" asked Norton raising his voice. "It's a good location," added Norton, "considering that we can concentrate on their tri-State area of D.C., Maryland, and Virginia. Now does that answer your question?"

Sterling didn't answer him. It was a rhetorical question anyway, he felt. If the sarcastic remark could be considered a question at all.

Sterling stared at Moshe. The man was always staring at him, especially whenever he and Norton exchanged any words that could be considered hostile.

"We all stand to make a lot of money," stated Norton Burke. "The company cleared twenty billion last year, which will be just a drop in the bucket come this year."

Sergio Moshe was African from South Africa. He and Sterling were the same age, thirty-five. Sergio Moshe was an ex-mercenary. Two-hundred pounds, five-nine with skin so dark, it looked burnt. His eyes were also black, so he always appeared serious. Deadly, thought Sterling as he listened to his boss and watched his foot soldier.

It infuriated Sterling that he and Moshe, as he liked to be called, were both black men, but Moshe behaved like they didn't even have that in common. In Sterling's opinion, it was like Moshe and Norton Burke had more in common, and Norton Burke didn't like black men.

"I'm fifty-five years old," continued Norton. "I don't want to still be in the rat race like Jules Marceau when I'm sixty-six. Do you hear me?"

He wasn't addressing anyone specifically. The only people in the office were Norton Burke, Sterling Rayford, Sergio Moshe and the man's other body guard, Pete Carpenter. They called him, 'The Pistol.'

Sterling didn't have to guess why. The man was always armed and didn't have a problem flashing his firearm whether it be in a holster, on his hip, or up under his arm.

Pete Carpenter was forty-five years old, but in great physical shape at six-feet-one and two-hundred-thirty pounds. He had a barrel chest and heavily muscled arms. He wore a short crew-style hair cut and a goatee. His face was an olive color, like he frequented tanning salons. His blue eyes were shifty and very alert. He reminded Sterling of an old history teacher he once had. These two misfits, as Sterling thought of them, handled all of the pharmaceutical companies' security through a firm the two men owned. They knew each other prior to coming to work for Meyer-Burke. They'd been with the company for a decade.

"I can remember when that other New York drug company went through something similar to what we are experiencing now," stated Norton, refusing to say the drug company's name. Sterling knew who it was. Probably the same firm that was helping to keep his pecker up.

"That was over twenty years ago," he continued, "and they rose from the ashes. They lost investors and banks pulled out markers for investment capital from them. Pension funds panicked and dropped their holdings, I believe. The same thing will happen to us initially - when certain drugs stop combating infections. The only good thing about this is we won't be the only ones feeling the economic crunch. Every pharmaceutical company will be feeling it at the same time. But none will rise up except for us. It takes roughly ten years and about one hundred million dollars to produce a new drug. They won't have the time to produce anything effective, but we will."

Thanks to Jules Marceau, thought Sterling, who habitually leaked information to Norton Burke, Meyer-Burke kept research and development facilities operating around the clock.

"If you'd had the vision you have now," stated Carpenter, "you could have bought up all or a majority of your rivals' low stock in 1986."

Sterling knew for sure that Norton was talking about Pfizer and reminiscing about the good ole' days.

*   *   *   *   *

"Who died?" asked Faith, walking into her office and hearing the requiem that Edna always played when a colleague or fellow academician passed away.

"Francis Tally."

"What?" uttered Faith in a low tone, "How?"

"A bacterial infection," answered Edna.

Faith took a moment to listen to the hymn and reflect on Mr. Tally's life.

He was an asset to the medical community, thought Faith. He'd led the way in antibiotic research as the Chief Scientific Officer at Cubist Pharmaceuticals and brought drugs to the market that were effective against blood stream infections.

So to have one such infection take his life was puzzling to Faith. She felt that everything happened for a reason, but couldn't always figure out what that reason was.

"He actually passed away at the same age as Jules is right now," stated Edna. "So he's a little bit bent out of shape." Then she said a short *requiescat*, a prayer for the repose of the souls of the dead. To Faith's understanding, in Latin, it meant "Rest in peace.'

Faith looked at her stainless steel watch. It was nine-thirty and they had a brain-storming session scheduled for ten thirty. That gave her approximately one hour to read and review a 2004 report from the Infectious Diseases Society of America. She'd neglected to read it when it was published years ago. It was entitled, "Bad Bugs, No Drugs," and spoke about the shortage of antibiotics that could adequately treat the new antibiotic resistant super bugs that had been growing in recent years.

Faith got deep into the report. The number quoted, which spoke about bacterial infections killing tens of thousands of people every year, was dismaying. The report spoke about how during the last decade, antibiotic-resistant bacteria has been popping up in communities nationwide and away from hospitals where it originated. But no one seems to care very much; either that or they weren't paying attention, thought Faith. She felt more noise needed to be made. Pharmaceutical companies weren't working on developing any new antibiotics because of confusion over what types of clinical trials the Federal Drug Administration would be willing to accept. They didn't want to waste their money, thought Faith. That's what it all boiled down to.

The hour evaporated quickly, and when she looked up, Jules, Buddy and John were entering the office. It was a quarter to eleven.

Everyone took a seat in the office except for Jules, who usually paced during these types of sessions.

"Who had what?" Jules asked. "And who has found us something?"

"I examined the tissue samples that the coroner from Houston sent over," stated Buddy. "But I didn't find anything that wasn't listed in the original autopsy report. The mutation that occurred is somehow masking itself, almost like it knew we would be looking for it."

"It did. It's not just a super bug," Faith told them. "It's a soldier that became a supervisor. It was manmade. That's why it's able to hide its original characteristics."

"Are you saying that we won't be able to track it?" asked Jules.

"Maybe not with the information we presently have," John weighed in. "These were just the preliminary tests. More extensive tests are being conducted as we speak. So hopefully, something fruitful will turn up."

"I gotta be honest," stated Buddy. "I've never seen mutations take place so quickly inside a host. The replication is astounding."

"Calm down, Buddy," Edna told her husband. "We don't need you being alarmist. We're already on pins and needles."

"As you should be," stated Buddy. "Did anyone notice that one of the victims died from the West Nile virus?"

"Yeah, I saw that," said Faith.

"I saw it too," replied John, "I thought that it was interesting how the person killed was lacking the receptor CCR5 on his blood cells, which in itself is a genetic mutation that inhibits the AIDS virus from docking onto the immune system cells and killing them. Somehow, this plus became a minus because he was extra susceptible to contracting the West Nile virus."

"The man not having the receptor and contracting the West Nile infection doesn't alarm me as much as his catching a totally different infection, and having that infection mutate into the West Nile virus and kill him a day later."

Everyone was silent for a moment. Buddy had succeeded in doing exactly what Edna told him not to do, scaring the daylights out of everyone.

Edna decided to offset Buddy's paranoia with a little doubt regarding Cimmerian's involvement in the fatalities that were attributed to a pathogen.

"I'd like to say something," began Edna. "What if, we are supposing that Cimmerian has done all of this based upon faulty intelligence?"

"Like the Intel the Nation got on Iraq having weapons of mass destruction?" asked Jules, not trying to sound humorous, although his remark and example was.

"Exactly," said Edna. "I can see the first two attacks being orchestrated by a human entity, but not the germ infestations. How can someone manipulate microorganisms so well? I think this Cimmerian may be trying to take the credit for things that no one can control."

"I hear you, Edna," stated Faith. "And I've given that possibility some thought. But I keep coming back to the fact that these mutations weren't happening to the pathogens before, while they were in their natural environment. So why are they happening now, if they're not being influenced and manipulated?"

*   *   *   *   *

With his suitcase laid out on the bed and Smokey Robinson singing "Swept for You Baby," Sterling began to pack for his trip.

For some reason, the song felt appropriate for the occasion. Sterling lived alone in an elegant, pre-war loft building down on West 27th Street. Alone, but never lonely; having been an only child, he learned to appreciate his own thoughts. Occasionally, he invited a female friend into his home for an evening. Most didn't want to leave after only one night. They liked him and his maple wood floors, his eleven-foot ceilings, the beautiful French doors, two baths, and a very spacious bedroom. They loved it all.

Sterling took out several white linen shirts. Two were Brook's Brothers, solid sport made of Irish linen. Another was Ralph Lauren styled with Mother of Pearl buttons. The one he would wear for today was a J. Crew. He preferred the rumpled look occasionally, but only wore white shirts, dark slacks and very expensive shoes.

After all of his clothing was packed, Sterling removed his suitcase from the bed and replaced it with his aluminum case. It housed all of the revolutionary medicines that Meyer-Burke produced.

He checked to make sure everything was there, so that he could promote the new drugs in new markets. This was his job, one that he was damn good at, he thought, as he picked up a bottle of the company's new and improved Dapsone. The former was used in the treatment of leprosy - that dreaded tropical affliction. Dapsone was a strong anti-microbial agent that was tweaked. Meyer-Burke had found new uses for it.

Sterling dropped it back in the case. Then, he went to his walk-in closet to select which timepiece he would be wearing for his trip.

Sterling was a connoisseur of timepieces. He purchased a new one annually. He was big on craftsmanship; most of the watches in his collection cost several thousand dollars. He owned twenty-seven. The established luxury brands were the only ones he bought -- nothing too trendy. Platinum pieces took precedence over all others for their sophistication.

Sterling selected one without diamonds and with a leather band, not too flashy. He kept all of his investments, as he called them, in their original cases. He inspected his choice. Then began to wind it and gingerly wiped its face with a clean cloth, glancing up at his portrait of a smiling Billie Holiday as she stared down at him.

Sterling liked how the late singer wore the signature gardenia in her hair. Women didn't do that anymore, he thought. But they still sang the blues.

CHAPTER 10

"Fish can't drown, right Mommy?" Kimberly asked innocently.

"I don't think so dear," answered Faith hesitantly. "Why? Are you worried about them drowning?"

"No." Kimberly stared through the glass at all the exotic fish. "I was just curious."

"Let me get this," said Yvonne, jockeying for position next to Kimberly. They were having a family day out -- Faith, the children, Yvonne and Jeff. The venue was the new Atlanta Aquarium.

"I could be an aquarist," joked Yvonne to her sister.

"I gotta hear this," commented Jeff who was standing off to the side with Mel. Yvonne cut her eyes at him before she began.

"Kimberly," she said, "Fish are accustomed to living under water like we are to living on land. That is their natural habitat. But they do breathe oxygen too, Sweetie." Yvonne was pulling Kimberly closer while pointing to a fish right up on the glass in front of them. "Do you see those?" asked Yvonne.

"Yes," answered Kimberly, staring intently. Just like everyone else was, including Mel.

"Those are gills," explained Yvonne. "They allow the fish to breathe. If someone asks you, 'what is a fish?', you tell them that it is a cold-blooded, aquatic vertebrae of the Super class Pisces among other classes as well, such as the shark, rays, lampreys, and jellyfish."

Mel heard the word *jellyfish* and smiled while Kimberly was still stuck on the word Pisces, which was her zodiac sign.

"So, I'm a fish too?" she asked, dumbfounded.

'No, no baby," said Faith laughing. "Let me take it from here Yvonne before you scare my baby."

"Yeah," said Jeff and slapped Mel five. "Quit while you're ahead."

Yvonne rolled her eyes at them, and waited to see how Faith was going to explain the differences.

"Baby," said Faith. "The Pisces Yvonne is talking about pertains only to fish and marine life. Your Zodiac Sign is another Pisces that relates to the heavens and the stars."

"So, I'm not a fish?" asked Kimberly.

"No baby," replied Faith. "You're a star!" She told her daughter, making her smile brightly.

"Me too, right Mommy?" asked Mel. "I think my Zodiac Sign sounds kind of fishy too."

"Yeah, I know baby," stated Faith. "But it's not. You and your sister are related. You share the same space up in the stars. That's why your signs complement one another."

The children liked Faith's explanation, so Yvonne had to give her credit where credit was due. Kimberly was a Pisces with her birthday on February twenty-third, and Mel was an Aquarius. His birthday was on Valentine's Day, which made him Yvonne's little sweetheart.

"Who's ready to go get something to eat?" asked Faith. It was time to feed her babies. They had been out since early in the morning; and it was now a quarter to one in the afternoon.

"Me," replied Mel.

"Me too," joined in Kimberly.

"What do you feel like having, Kim?" asked Jeff.

"It's Kimberly," she corrected him.

"Oh, I'm sorry," replied Jeff. "What will it be, Kimberly?"

"I want a cheeseburger and some fries."

"Me too," said Jeff. "I knew you wanted that, Kimberly. That's why I asked."

"Stop encouraging her," Faith told her brother-in-law. "Mel, you want the same thing?" asked Faith.

"Naw," said Mel. "I want some fish and chips," he told her, trying to be funny.

Faith knew that Mel often referred to his money as chips, so she knew just what he was talking about.

"Come on, boy!" she told him, holding the children's hands as she navigated them out of the aquarium. Jeff fell in step with his wife as they walked briskly behind them.

"Baby, I didn't know you knew about marine life," Jeff told her, reaching for her left hand to hold.

"Yeah," responded Yvonne, sounding like a street smart young woman. "Prior to you, I swam with lots of sharks."

*   *   *   *   *

As John stood with his eye glued to a microscope he thought about the matter at hand in two ways: affliction and affection.

Since their return to Atlanta and the beginning of the investigation, Faith had avoided him as if he had the plague and she wasn't looking to catch it.

Across the room, he was studying sample slides with a contrast microscope. "You learn anything over there?" asked Buddy.

"Yeah, school's always open," John told him and laughed. "I might be more inclined to find what it is I'm looking for if I knew what it was."

"I know what it is." Buddy sounded focused.

John glanced over at his friend. "And what's that?"

"Something that shows a striking dissimilarity between each other, but at the same time, looks as if it is related."

"You make it sound so easy when you say that."

"It is easy, especially once you know what it is you're looking for."

"Kind of like you and Edna, huh?"

Buddy looked over at him, "if you say so." He hadn't actually been talking about relationships, but if John needed to compare, he was cool with it.

"Let me ask you something," stated John. "What's it like working with your wife? Do you ever get tired of interacting with her?"

"Tired? She's my honey bun. I never get tired of honey buns." Buddy laughed and patted his stomach. "The trick is finding someone that you're truly compatible with. Then you can be around them all the time and not be angry."

"Yeah, that's easier said than done," John told him. "Finding the pathogen that started it all may prove easier."

"I hope so," said Buddy. "What's the deal with Faith? You didn't pork her yet?"

"Whoa!" said John. "Be easy with that, good buddy. I don't like to talk like that."

"No disrespect," said Buddy. "It's just a figure of speech. I think it's kinder than the other word."

"Well, I don't like either one of them," clarified John. "So don't use them when you're referring to Faith."

"Okay!" Buddy moved away from his microscope momentarily. "I knew she had your nose open, but not your fly too."

John looked at him, exasperated, but he knew he couldn't make Buddy change his diction. John was beginning to regret bringing the subject up.

"You're approaching her all wrong, but you know what I mean?" continued Buddy.   "Not really," replied John, "but I'm sure you'll tell me."

"You damn right I will," responded Buddy. "It's kind of like the philosophy of Plato."

"Oh my God!" uttered John. Then Buddy stopped with the shenanigans.

"Alright," he said. "Seriously speaking, Faith to me is the type of woman that is looking for a relationship that transcends physical desire and leans towards spiritual and ideal love."

John listened. He could see that being true somewhat, in the way that Faith lived, her take on family and medicine. Yeah, he admitted to himself, Buddy had made a good observation. But he also knew that all women needed the physical part of a relationship, too. Unbeknownst to Buddy, he'd already seen and felt that part of Faith.

"I feel you," stated John, letting Buddy know that he was in agreement. "But it's still complicated because she's so reserved."

"Well, you've already let her know how you feel. You did, right?" asked Buddy.

"Yes, I did," answered John.

"So, now you have to do an about-dfcface when you see her move in widdershins," suggested Buddy. "You know what I mean?"

"The opposite direction," said John slowly. "Go at the situation in reverse."

"Exactly," said Buddy. "If she's interested, she'll approach you and you won't look so desperate."

"Who's looking desperate?" asked John, getting defensive. Buddy looked up at the ceiling, whistling softly.

"Shut up!" John said.

"That should work," Buddy told him, "unless she's exogamic."

"What's that?" asked John.

"That's someone who believes in the custom of marrying outside their social unit."

For the next half hour John and Buddy worked silently in the cramped laboratory. John found himself thinking about his own parents and how his father and mother had married outside of their own social orders. John's father had been a professor at a prestigious school. He taught science and John had inherited his love of science from him. His mother had been a streetwalker, to use a kind word; two people with completely opposite lives and social orders.

Yet, they connected and fell in love. John knew that his father appreciated the times his mother would educate him on certain fine points of life that he wasn't aware of because John could remember her many loud lessons. His mother was very loud and boisterous and she cursed like a sailor. Yet, she was still scholarly in matters that pertained to the streets.

"Hey," Buddy interrupted John's thoughts. "You know what those fools forgot to do at the location of that West Nile fatality?"

"No, what's that?" asked John.

"Test the birds in the area."

"Well, it's too late now," replied John. "And a single case wasn't probable cause for concern."

"Yeah, to a laggard," suggested Buddy, "but not to anyone with a rudimentary knowledge of mathematics. They'd know that anything has to begin with one."

Chapter 11

Sergio Moshe had never been to Washington, D.C. before so, it was with great pleasure that he accepted his present assignment. He'd read many books about the American Civil Rights Movement, and the fabled champions of it, Martin Luther King, Jr. being the first and foremost.

So, after he got situated and immediately following his first appointment, he visited the National Mall and tried to picture what King must have been thinking on August 28, 1963, when he delivered his most notable speech.

Moshe sat outside for a long time -- almost until the sun set, which was quite a while considering that he had gotten there early in the afternoon. Several women passing by took notice of the dark-skinned black man and wondered if he was a visiting dignitary. At times, Moshe could be very personable, at least around women. He nodded at the ladies politely until they were back on their way. Then, his disposition turned dark again. He hoped that he wouldn't be in Washington, D.C. more than seven days; he had several other stops on his agenda.

One inaugural week, he told himself.

Like King, Moshe had once had a dream. But his quickly turned into a nightmare.

* * * * *

There was no hotline or number for Faith and her co-workers to call in case of an emergency, but the sixteen missed calls recorded on Faith's phone was a clear signal that something was up. Faith was out in the field speaking with an expert on pandemics. She'd turned her phone off so as not to disturb the venue, resolving to cut it back on once she left. When she did this, she got all of her messages.

Five of them were from her director, Jules Marceau, one from her sister and the rest her co-workers. Her first call was to Jules.

"There have been two more attacks," stated Jules. "They're very serious. I need you back at the center A.S.A.P.!"

Faith didn't get a word in before he promptly hung up on her.

With no answers and nothing but curiosity on her mind, she raced back to the Center for Disease Control and Prevention. Speeding around on foot, she caught a run in her stockings and almost broke the heel on her shoe.

Getting out of the elevator on her floor she could see the entire gang was there. Everyone was piled up inside the director's office; that meant the matter was grave.

"Nice of you to join us, Ms. Millicent," stated the director as she walked into the office.

"I'm sorry, Sir." Faith was about to explain why she had missed his previous calls, but he cut her off.

"Check your phone, because there seems to be some kind of malfunction. I know none of my employees would turn their phones off during an investigation this grave." It sounded like a threat to Faith.

John was looking at her with a sympathetic face, while Buddy appeared dismayed.

"Will someone please bring Ms. Millicent up to speed?" Jules snapped.

"There was some kind of outbreak in Washington, D.C," stated Edna. "And there's another in North Carolina."

"You know people in Washington," Jules spoke directly to Faith. "I want you to go out there and see what you can find out."

"What was the nature of the outbreak?" asked Faith.

"They haven't determined that yet," replied the director. "For now, all we know is that several hundred people fell ill outside of the National Air and Space Museum."

"Several hundred?" repeated Faith. "But they haven't identified the cause?"

"No, and that's why I want you out there. I need to know if it's airborne, contagious or hereditary," he stated sarcastically. "Is that a problem?"

"No, Sir," replied Faith slowly. "John and I could get out there in the morning."

"Lovejoy has asked to fly out to Raleigh with Defoe, to the site of the second attack."

Faith looked at John and felt like he had slighted her. But she didn't know why. His idea that she'd been avoiding him was wrong. She was just working and trying to put some space between them so their tryst would become a distant memory. Now, it seemed, he was trying to do the same thing.

"Mrs. Defoe will have to stay here and man the ship," stated the director. "So, you're flying solo on this one. Buzz Shaw will meet up with you in Washington, Millicent. And Hunt Rhinehart, I believe, is headed out to North Carolina."

"Do you know why the museum in Washington was chosen to attack?" asked Edna. "The capital has so many other high profile targets - why choose that one?"

"My best guess would be the ten million tourists that pass through the facility. As targets go, terrorist couldn't pick a better one," stated the director.

"And North Carolina?" asked Buddy following his wife's lead.

"May I?" asked John, staring at the director.

"By all means," responded Jules, sitting back in his chair and closely watching all of his subordinates.

"I believe North Carolina was chosen as a strategic move - same for D.C. If you didn't know, the Raleigh Triangle area is located in the Research Triangle. It's arguably the country's largest and most influential research park, much like Washington, D.C. It is home to over one hundred government, corporate and liberal arts institutions. And to piggyback on what the director said, if the terrorists were trying to pick a better or perhaps equal target to Washington, D.C., I think they found it."

"Well put." Jules took control of the floor again. "I need everyone who's flying to be gone, if not tonight, by the morning at the latest. Any additional information that you need, Mrs. Defoe will fax to you. I want those birds in the sky," he stated forcefully. "We're usually the first responders, but I'll take second on this one."

He paused for a moment just to let the tension build. "That's it" he told them, and watched everyone pile out of the room.

"Oh, Ms. Millicent!" he called out as Faith was passing the room's threshold. "One moment," he told her.

Faith stopped and turned around at that point as everyone else continued to walk out.

"Yes?" she asked.

"I need you at your best," he told her. "This is the Nation's Capital. They're sending a message. You do understand that?"

"Yes Sir, I do," replied Faith. "Loud and clear."

"Good," stated Jules, "because an attack on Washington could affect our country's sphere of influence all over the world!"

"I understand Sir," stated Faith.

"I thought you would," replied Jules.

*   *   *   *   *

Faith went straight to her office, multitasking on the way. She had her cell phone out and the card with Buzz Shaw's number on it in hand. She wanted to speak with him before she flew out to Washington just to make sure that she wasn't about to fly into an area that was under quarantine. If anyone would know, thought Faith, it would be him. But while the phone rang several times, there was no answer.

She sat down at her desk. Edna was there, watching her closely.

"Faith, what's up?" asked Edna. "You look a little stressed."

"I'm trying to catch Buzz Shaw so I can see exactly what the situation is out there," answered Faith. "I don't want to put myself at risk."

"Good idea. Several hundred people, that's a lot." Edna paused for a second to think. "I don't think the director would send you out there if it was dangerous."

Faith glanced up from her computer and cut her phone off. Her look was one of apprehension with a touch of sisterly attitude.

"Edna, I hear you and I don't think that he would do that either. At least, not on purpose, but it's the inadvertent mistake that I'm trying to prevent. The government is trying to keep this entire extortion plot from the public. They just can't get on the news and announce that the Capital is under quarantine and all movement is restricted. Now, can they?" Faith logged onto the United Airlines site to check their flight schedule.

"I guess not." Edna found herself worrying about her husband's trip to North Carolina. "I'll keep you posted - I have some contacts down there. I'll ask them to let me know about any usual activity."

"Thanks," replied Faith, booking her flight online.

Edna, heading out in search of Buddy, passed John coming in on her way out.

"Hey." He spoke to Faith.

"Hey." She wasn't looking up.

"You're off to Washington." John spoke awkwardly, seeming to fish for something to say.

Faith looked up, then. He'd felt the slight too, she thought. She wasn't imagining things.

"You know that I would have gone to Washington with you," he told her. "But I have a lot of friends down in the Raleigh-Durham area. I studied at the University of North Carolina at Chapel Hill School of Medicine for a few years."

John was trying to take Buddy's advice about acting nonchalant to win her over, but he had reservations. Too much self-restraint, he thought, could cause him to lose what little ground he had with her.

Faith felt his discomfort and was satisfied. She wasn't really upset with him. She didn't want a relationship with a co-worker. It would just be too awkward, she told herself.

She could just see it now. Edna would want to double-date and have dinner parties where the four of them could talk shop-talk. Not! She told herself adamantly.

"It's okay." Faith cut him off. "You don't owe me any excuses, John." She saw the expression on his face, and added, with a laugh, "You're standing here like you're going through a random walk or something."

John nodded. She was right about him not owing her an explanation, but the fact was, he felt compelled to give one. And he wasn't sure why.

He thought about the random walk that Faith suggested he was taking. He hoped that she was talking mathematics and not life; in math, a random walk was a series of sequential movements in which the direction and size of each move is randomly determined. That didn't sound too bad, thought John. He was sure she could clearly see that he was nervous and feeling his way around.

If she was talking life and not math, though, he was afraid she might see him as a weak and unsure man. He wasn't that and had never been. But beautiful women and that four letter word that he dreaded had a funny way of making a man into a fool...

"Is that it?" She cut her computer off and stood.

"Yeah, I guess so." He turned and headed for the door. As he reached it, he stopped and looked back at her. "You have a safe trip," he told her and walked on.

"Yeah, okay." Faith stared after him and mumbled under her breath, "You too."

*   *   *   *   *

"I can't stay." Faith was standing in the living room of her sister's apartment in Greenridge. This part of Lithonia, Faith rarely got down to. So Yvonne wasn't even listening to her pleas of being in the middle of an emergency.

"Yvonne, please!" said Faith. "I have a cab waiting outside for me to take me to the airport and I want to say goodbye to my children."

"Oh, all right!" snapped Yvonne, walking off with her slippers dragging. She glared at Faith over her shoulder. "You don't have to get all snotty."

"Kimberly!" yelled Faith. "Come here!"

She sat down carefully. The chair looked ancient, although Yvonne swore that she had just bought it. It was rusty with duct tape strategically placed on its arms and back support section. Yvonne said that the chair came like that from the Jason Miller Collection and cost several thousand dollars. Faith strongly doubted that and didn't believe it was trendy.

"Kimberly!" called out Faith again.

The kids didn't get to stay at their aunt's house much. So when they did, they always got lost in all the eclectic furniture and secret hiding places the Kincaid's home held.

"Mommy!" Kimberly ran into the living room. "Mel disappeared! He's not in his usual hiding place."

Faith bit back a laugh. "He's not?"

Kimberly shook her head and her freshly braided hair was banging against her cheeks.

"I'll help you find him," said Faith. "But, first Mommy wants to tell you something okay?"

"Yes," said Kimberly, paying close attention.

"Mommy has to go on another trip. I'll be gone for maybe a week, two at the most. You can call me if you need to talk, okay?"

"Yes mommy." Kimberly gave her mother a quick hug.

"Okay," said Faith. "One more thing, do you remember what Mommy said about anyone touching you in the wrong way?" Faith asked looking over her daughter's shoulder at Jeff and Yvonne in the kitchen.

"Yes," replied Kimberly. "No one is to touch me like that, if they do, I should scream and tell you."

"That's right, baby," said Faith, hugging her daughter again.

Faith hated to have to be like that. She loved Jeff and trusted him, but it wasn't just about Jeff. It was about all adults, men and women. The world was a very violent place for adults, violent and scary. And if it was that bad for adults, thought Faith, it had to be ten times that for children. An ounce of prevention went a long way.

"Baby," she told her daughter. "Go over there and hide while I call Mel for you, okay?"

"Okay." Kimberly, smiling, ran off to hide behind another tattered-looking chair.

"Mel!" called out Faith. "Come here, Mommy has to leave!"

Faith smiled at her daughter as Kimberly peeked out from behind the chair. Mel came quicker than his sister did and Faith didn't have to call him twice.

"Mel, I have to go now," she told him. "You know what that means, right?"

"Yeah, I'm in charge and it's my job to look out for Kimberly."

"That's right baby," agreed Faith and planted a kiss on his cheek. "Mommy loves you." She looked over his shoulder giving Kimberly the signal to come out. "Mel, call me," she told her son. "I want a progress report."

"Yes mom," said Mel, tensing up as he heard the pitter-patter of his sister's little feet as she ran up on him.

"I got you!" she yelled, hitting him on the back. As Faith made her way to the door, she could hear her son arguing that he and his sister had been on break.

The cab was waiting. On the doorstep, Faith paused to thank her sister and brother-in-law. "Thanks," she told them. "I had to give Mommy a break. Call me if you have any problems and remember what I said about strange situations and people around you experiencing health problems."

Faith didn't normally discuss CDC business with her family. This time, things were different. It was imperative that her family be aware of the potential health crisis that the extortionist 'Cimmerian' was posing to the common folk.

"Don't worry," Yvonne told her. She looked very domestic, with an apron fastened around her waist. "Ain't nothing gonna happen to your precious babies; I got this! You got me in here playing Susie homemaker with this cooking and stuff."

"That's right," said Faith. "My babies need home cooked meals and easy on the condiments and fried foods. I got enough stress to deal with; I don't need an obesity issue also."

"Didn't I just say, I got this!" Yvonne repeated. "You just take care of yourself and be careful. We can't do like Grandma used to do when one of us got sick. There are too many animal rights groups today."

"Shut up," said Faith, laughing. "You believed that stuff?"

Their grandmother would always talk about an old ancient southern treatment for whatever ailed her grandchildren. It consisted of her taking a dead black cat and burying it in a grave yard at night. The remedy and story was so scary that Faith and Yvonne hardly ever got sick because they always pictured their sweet old little grandmother doing that for them and maybe even killing a cat.

It wasn't until Faith became an adult and began to study medicine that she learned such stories were a form of psycho therapy in the psychological treatment of mental, emotional and nervous disorders. At that point, she discredited that her grandmother had actually ever really done that. In any event, it kept her and her sister from getting sick so she wasn't mad at all.

"I'm out!" she yelled. "I'll call you from Chocolate City."

CHAPTER 12

"Excuse me," asked Sterling. "Is this seat taken?"

"No," replied Faith, looking up at the tall, dark, and handsome man. Faith had a window seat but the one next to her, the aisle seat, was open.

"Thank you," replied Sterling, smiling at the pretty woman.

He'd changed his seat because a heavyset man, whose hygiene wasn't up to par, had commandeered the seat next to him. Sterling sat down and got comfortable. He glanced at Faith's lap and read the title of a book she was holding.

"*SHE*," he said, reading the title out loud. "I suppose it's about women?"

"What gave it away?" Faith asked, sharing the charm. He sounded very charismatic.

"I've read it," said Sterling. "It's a very good read."

"Well I've just started," confessed Faith. "But the author is a friend of mine."

"That's nice," replied Sterling. "I'll let you get back to it."

As Faith got into her book, Sterling took out a book of his own, an encyclopedia of medical drugs, articles on the drug preparations and use. The book, 'Pharmacopoeia', was huge.

"I've read that," Faith remarked, getting his attention again.

"You have? Why?"

Faith laughed giving Sterling a view of her pearly white teeth. "I'm in the medical profession," she admitted. "And you?"

"I just like all of the big words," replied Sterling, looking very serious.

"Surely you jest?" Faith asked.

"How did you know?" Sterling asked, using the same line that she had used on him. Faith, smirking a little, waited for an answer.

"The name's Sterling Rayford." He offered Faith his hand. "I'm in pharmaceuticals."

"Pleased to meet you," she told him. "Faith Millicent, the Center for Disease Control."

"You don't say, in what capacity?"

"I'm a research expert" stated Faith. "I'm on my way to Washington."

"Me too," replied Sterling. "Actually this is my second time there in under a week. I was in Washington last week."

"You said pharmaceuticals?" She questioned. "Are you in manufacturing or the actual research and development?"

"I'm the detail man for Meyer-Burke."

"Okay," Faith was familiar with the pharmaceutical juggernaut. They were into the manufacturing of countless old and new drugs and were a major institution in the field. He being a representative of theirs was a prestigious position. "You must stay pretty busy; being that Meyer Burke is constantly on the cutting edge of things"

"Busy is an understatement," corrected Sterling. "I never sleep and I hardly ever complain, so it evens out I guess."

"If you say so," Faith laughed. "But I need my beauty sleep and things stay pretty busy over at the CDC."

"I can imagine," commented Sterling, "but I doubt you require much sleep. What drives a woman to work for an agency that chases diseases? I mean, most women run away from such things."

"I'm not trying to catch any in my hand, trust me," replied Faith. "Actually, I find it fascinating. I like to solve complicated puzzles and improving the quality of life for people is a bonus."

"I like that answer," stated Sterling. "The next time someone asks me why I went into my line of work, I'm going to use that."

"Why, don't you have your own words?"

"I do, but they're not as politically correct as yours."

"Is that so?" she asked. "Can I hear them anyway?"

"I wanted to be a doctor, but I couldn't stick to the regimen; the system of no parties while I was in school and all the constant studying did not work for me."

"You're not a man for a diet and therapy?" Faith offered. She understated the sacrifice involved because she did it.

"I can get with that now," confessed Sterling, "but as a young man, I couldn't."

"You talk like you're eighty!"

"I'm thirty-five," confided Sterling. "That's close enough. But yeah, I always wanted to do something in the medical profession. My mother had Charcot disease and she passed away from it."

"I'm sorry to hear that."

"It's okay," replied Sterling. "I was very young, five years old to be exact. My father raised me from there. He recently passed too, from cancer. So since I couldn't be a doctor, I figured that selling their health care providers the drugs that would have saved their lives was the way to go."

"That's a contribution," offered Faith politely, then she remembered something. "Didn't Meyer-Burke patent an effective drug in the fight against Charcot disease?"

"Yeah," said Sterling, smiling. "They called it their multiple sclerosis miracle drugs in the press. That was the reason I chose to work for the company, that was several years ago. I thought it was a sign." He stared off for a second. "But everything that glitters is not gold. Anyway, you probably don't want to talk medicine. I imagine you get that all day, every day."

"I do," conceded Faith. "But then, if I didn't enjoy medical jargon I wouldn't be able to do what I do."

"I can't argue with that," said Sterling. "Not in my line of work."

"Can I ask you something?" Faith lowered her voice to an almost conspiratorial tone.

"Not if it's gonna get me into trouble," replied Sterling, raising one of his eyebrows.

"It won't." Faith paused. "Are you traveling all over, in the midst of an acquisition?"

"No." Sterling stated. "If I were, I wouldn't be on my way to Washington. The only firm worth acquiring out this way was ICOS and Eli Lilly already acquired them."

"I know," stated Faith. "I've been reading about all of the big acquisitions, so I just thought that I would ask. There are still others that are ripe for the picking."

Sterling smiled. He realized Faith was very well informed. Acquiring biotech facilities have been all the rage, he thought; for the last several years, Meyer Burke had looked at a few acquisitions themselves.

"To be honest," Sterling told her, "Acquisitions aren't my department. If it was, I would have brokered that deal with the California vaccine company, Chiron, and cut Novartis out of that deal. But, like I said, that's not my department."

"Well, what is?" Faith asked boldly.

"Monitoring websites like Medzilla.com, to see what's cutting edge. My job is to advance Meyer-Burke's interest."

"I like all of the mergers that are going on within your industry," offered Faith. "Like the GlaxoSmithKline partnership with Sirna Therapeutics. I think these collaborations are good for both industries -- the biotech companies and the pharmaceutical companies. Hopefully, they'll result in more life saving drugs. If you can put a word in at Meyer-Burke, you might want to tell them we need more antibiotics. The super bugs are gaining on us.

"I'll see what I can do," offered Sterling, smiling.

The conversation moved easily from there becoming a discussion about the possible ramifications the merging of biotech and pharmaceutical companies could have.

"I heard about a few friends of mine being displaced over at Johnson & Johnson," said Faith.

"Yes, I know," conceded Sterling. "That's the unfortunate part of the growth and development. I can't lie, in the beginning I anticipated that many people would lose their jobs. Everyone can't benefit. Downsizing is always a part of mergers."

"I know. Thank God medicine allows a person to find work in a wide range of capacities," stated Faith.

Sterling nodded, digging out and opening a leather carry-on bag. He pulled out a small book, 'Nature's Cure for the Common Cold' and dropped the 'Pharmacopoeia' in the bag. He was about to put the smaller book away as well, when Faith stopped him.

"May I see that?"

"Sure," said Sterling, handing her the book.

Faith read the subtitle: *Powerful, drug-free remedies proven to work*. She gave him the book back and watched him put it away.

"Why would a man that peddles drugs be interested in the holistic approach?" she asked. "Don't you believe in Meyer-Burke's treatments?"

"A friend gave it to me. I haven't read through it yet and yes I do believe that Meyer-Burke does have some very beneficial medicines. I just don't use drugs myself," admitted Sterling.

"Ah ha!" said Faith. "So you can sell the stuff, but you refuse to use it?"

"I'm from the old school," said Sterling, "The one that believed that you should never get high on your own supply."

"If Meyer-Burke has good medicine like you say, why wouldn't you use it?" Faith asked. She suddenly realized that she found him enchanting. She wanted to understand more of what made him the man he was.

Sterling lowered his voice. "Here's the skinny," he said. "Most people don't need the medicine that pharmacies sell to them. But Big Pharma is not going to tell them that because it would hurt their pockets. So they sell it and it has a placebo effect. I'm not talking about drugs that treat serious conditions, just all of that other crap out there on the market."

"Oh my," said Faith, pretending to be shocked. "That's unethical and they could hurt someone."

"They could," admitted Sterling. "And they probably have in the past. But that's just the nature of things and how the game is played. I didn't make the rules when I got drafted into this league. The rules were already set and in place."

Faith had to credit some of what he was saying. She herself hated the fact that when most women went to go see their healthcare providers they always left the office with a prescription for something, even if it was a runny nose. "So you also support what's advocated in the bestseller?"

"What bestseller is that?" Sterling asked.

"*The Natural Cures that They Don't Want You to Know About*," answered Faith.

"No," said Sterling. "I don't subscribe to that."

"Whoa," said Faith. "You scared me for a moment."

"I don't want to do that," stated Sterling. "If anything, I'd like to pique your interest. Maybe we can get together sometime in the future. Are you a native of Atlanta?"

"Yes," replied Faith. "I am."

"I get out that way quite often. Maybe whenever I'm in town I could take you out to dinner and tell you some more secrets about the pharmaceutical industry."

"I'd like that." Faith watched him as he fished out a business card.

"Can I give you my card?" he asked her, finally locating one.

"Sure," replied Faith. She was glad to accept his information. "I think I have one here too. Here you go."

Sterling took the card noticing that she wasn't wearing a wedding ring. As it happened, Faith had already checked out his fingers the minute he sat down next to her. She also searched for a light spot around his finger that would indicate the removal of a wedding band. But he appeared unattached at the moment.

As the plane landed and taxied towards the arrival gate Sterling thanked Faith for the wonderful conversation they shared.

"I really appreciated our talk," he told her.

"Me too," replied Faith politely. "It was very…" she paused while searching for a word. "…insightful."

"Ditto," replied Sterling, shaking her hand. "Take care - until we meet again," he added and walked away.

CHAPTER 13

"Thanks for coming down." stated Hunt Rhinehart.

"No problem, Mr. Rhinehart," said John.

"Call me Hunt," he stated. "It keeps me focused."

"Okay, Hunt." John corrected himself. "This is my colleague, Buddy Defoe."

"Good to meet you," stated Hunt while shaking Buddy's hand. "Are you both ready?"

Hunt immediately led the way to his vehicle. Buddy and John, both traveling light with one carry-on bag apiece, had no trouble keeping up with him. John, watching Hunt Rhinehart move like a leopard, a large feline, dressed in all black and track shoes.

"This is me, right here," stated Hunt directing them to a black BMW X5. "You can throw your bags in the back."

"I hope you fellas have been inoculated against the flu because that's what my people say is going on down here."

"It's an influenza outbreak?" Buddy asked. "That's it, right?"

Hunt glanced at Buddy from the side. "You must be immune to the flu."

"Well no." Buddy was puzzled. "But I thought the situation was much more grave."

"Any graver than this," remarked Hunt, "and we'll all be digging a mass grave."

"How many people with flu-like symptoms are we talking about?" John asked. "Do you have a roundabout number?"

"Yeah," replied Hunt, "it's approximately two thousand, that's all," he said while looking at Buddy again, this time sarcastically.

"Two thousand," repeated John. "All reporting flu-like symptoms at the same time?"

"Yeah," said Hunt, "and it's not even flu season yet."

They drove in silence for a while, finally ending up in an area just outside the city.

"What's this?" asked John.

"It's a make-shift treatment facility that we set up," stated Hunt. "Many of the people had to be hospitalized. We couldn't place them in regular hospitals because we don't know the exact nature of their illness and we don't even know if it's contagious."

Or newsworthy, thought John, but he kept that to himself. He looked out at the military vehicles and make-shift tents and thought, they were hiding these people.

"This was put together rather quickly, I'd imagine," said Buddy.

"Yeah, they're pre-fab," replied Hunt. "Your government has gotten pretty good at their response to natural disasters."

"Have we determined this one to be natural?" John asked.

"Well, that's what you're here to tell me," replied Hunt, and brought the car to a stop. "For the sake of the gentle folk of North Carolina, I sincerely hope so. But Cimmerian has already taken credit. We received correspondence yesterday claiming responsibility for this and the outbreak in D.C. I'm not sure how this entity could spread a virus," confessed Hunt. "So I'm hoping you will tell me. You know, answer this little Koan. You do know what a Koan is?" Hunt asked turning the engine off.

"That's a riddle in the form of a paradox," stated Buddy, "used in Zen Buddhism as an aid to meditation and a means of gaining intuitive knowledge."

"That's right," replied Hunt, exiting the vehicle first.

"Are you a religious man?" John was speaking to Hunt as he stared out at the makeshift hospital, hoping it didn't turn into a hospice for the terminally ill.

"Everyone needs some religion in times like these," said Hunt.

The magnitude of the situation suddenly became clear. Thousands of lives hung in the balance.

"Gentlemen," continued Hunt, as he began to walk toward the facility. "I am a fantast, a dreamer and a visionary. I sincerely believe in good and evil, so I know that we are going to win this battle. What I don't know, and am concerned about, is the number of casualties that we'll suffer along the way. I recently saw a book that I personally am afraid to read. It speaks about the one thousand places a person should see before they may die. I sincerely hope Raleigh, North Carolina wasn't on the list."

CHAPTER 14

"The outbreak has been contained." The physician was giving the Associated Press an update. "We don't normally prescribe antibiotics for influenza but this strain seems to be a very virulent one. It's not a new strain and nothing the public needs to be concerned about. Its genetic blue print has been mapped out. I would be remiss if I didn't admit that this bug is extremely antagonistic. But, we have its number. There's nothing to worry about."

Faith stood off to the side of the podium with the other members of the medical community on hand. She hoped the physician, Dr. Peterson, didn't call on her to give credence to his assertions. Not that he was deliberately lying to the press; he was rather just not telling them everything.

Faith had been in town for two days and hadn't seen Buzz Shaw yet. She had, however, treated several of the patients who had taken ill outside the museum. The common bug among all six hundred of them was definitely a flu virus; it wasn't any the medical community had seen before. So that had been a misstatement, thought Faith.

The second misstatement had been the fact that the public need not be concerned.

Faith thought that they should be very concerned, if not terrified. What alarmed Faith was how the strain had very similar properties to the deadly H5N1 strain of bird flu. It wasn't H5N1, but it was too damned close for comfort. It also displayed properties from several animal diseases; one that had jumped to her attention was Newcastle disease, which had been mistaken for H5N1 flu several years ago in Nigeria. Another was East Coast Fever located in African livestock and Rift Valley Fever, which was identified in those that fell ill, and is endemic to Ethiopia, Somalia and the Sudan.

No one, but Faith, seemed overly concerned that potentially deadly diseases and viruses had been found amongst the American population, just because several antibiotics proved to be effective in treating the problem. Never mind the fact that the pestilences named weren't suppose to infect a human host, thought Faith.

"I have time for a few questions," stated Dr. Peterson, "but please make it brief."

"Isn't it true that there are representatives from the Centers for Disease Control and the World Health Organization here?" The question came from the front row. "If so, why is their presence needed if everything is under control?"

"They're here to ensure public safety," stated Dr. Peterson. "You should be grateful for their participation, not alarmed by it. Next question."

"Were there any fatalities?" Female reporter asked. "Because there have been rumors." "The rumors are false. No one has died as a result of this outbreak," stated Dr. Peterson, as he glanced to his left. Curious to see what he was looking at, Faith peered off in that direction and saw Buzz Shaw standing there with two military types. Although he was secreted and she hadn't seen him before, Faith was sure that he had seen her.

"Last question," stated Dr. Peterson.

"Allen Taylor - Associated Press. I'd like to know why this flu strain is making an appearance now. Was something done to the environment to bring it out of hibernation?"

"Are you suggesting Global Warming?" The doctor asked. "Because we just don't know. If my memory serves me correctly, you did a report last year concerning the public disposing of their old medications by flushing them down the toilet."

The reporter smiled. "I'm guilty, but are you alleging that was a contributing factor?"

"It's a possibility," the doctor told him. "Everything is a possibility at this point. I'm curious about the cause and effect relationship of the residue that we're finding from antibiotics, depressants, hormone supplements and countless other drugs that are consistently showing up in the nation's streams, rivers and lakes. We need an alternative disposal procedure."

"You may have a point there," conceded Mr. Taylor. "One of my colleagues ran a story about fish that were found in the Potomac River with both male and female characteristics."

"That's my point exactly," stated Dr. Peterson. "We have to look at every contamination, in situations like this. Something roused this bug from its sleep and we won't rest until we find out exactly what it was. And I'm afraid that's all the time we have. Thank you."

Dr. Peterson walked off the podium. Faith looked back over at Buzz Shaw and he signaled to her. When she got over to him he was just dismissing the two military types that had been standing with him.

"That's it," he said, "keep me in the loop."

The men went on their way. It sounded as if Buzz Shaw was in charge of military personnel. Strange, thought Faith, if he was a police officer.

"Ms. Millicent - Faith," he added. "I trust you had a chance to go by one of the medical centers and have a look for yourself what we are up against?"

"Yes, I did," said Faith. "And I must admit I'm alarmed."

"So am I, Faith," he replied. "You think that I am not up late at night, thinking? Because trust me, I am."

"Thinking's not enough," Faith told him. "This virus is mutating. They found traces of the bird flu in it. I don't have to tell you how this thing has catastrophe written all over it."

"No you don't have to tell me," stated Buzz. "This thing is a chiller, but I have it under control. Who do you think thought up that Royal Flush campaign?"

"The public won't believe that just because some people flush medication down the toilets, a superbug was born."

"They don't have to. All I need is some time to catch the Cimmerian person, then the attacks will stop and the public can go back to worrying about hospital-borne infections."

"You have a catbird seat," said Faith, "but I don't see why if you are afraid to tell your commander and chief that he needs to come to a compromise...."

"What kind of compromise?" he asked.

"Pay the money," pleaded Faith. "It will relax Cimmerian and give you a chance to really catch them."

"Were going to catch them anyway," stated Buzz. "Nothing this diabolical goes unanswered. It's just a matter of time."

Faith didn't argue with him. What he was saying had a ring of truth to it. She just hoped that their time didn't run out.

* * * * *

"What the hell is this?" John placed another culture sample down on the counter for Buddy to look at next. "We're in trouble."

"You don't have to tell me," agreed Buddy. They had been in a makeshift lab for three days, testing people who had turned into gravely ill patients overnight and taking numerous biopsies from those that had broken out with unexplainable rashes all over their bodies. Buddy and John attributed it to immune systems forced into overdrive to combat a flu infection that was proving difficult to treat.

"This has to be psoriasis," concluded Buddy, looking at the skin specimen that they had removed from a man's shoulder area.

"Yeah, that's what I'd say," concluded John. "If I really didn't know what it was."

Buddy thought about a person's immune system, silently. He knew that it was divided into two basic branches. The cellular immunity, which consisted of the T-Lymphocytes, which were divided into at least three subtypes that were T-helper cells (the CD-4 cells), T-Cytotoxic cells (TC cells), and lastly T-Suppressor cells or CD8 cells as they're called.

The T-helper cells, thought Buddy, activate B-cells to produce antibodies and activate T-Cytotoxic cells against invading organisms. These were the two cells Buddy thought to be working over time. T-Cytotoxic cells kill target cells by connecting with antigens on the target cell surface and producing toxin, thought Buddy.

T-Suppressor cells down regulate the immune system by decreasing B-cells antibody production, he recalled and suppressing T-helps Lymphocyte function. The Lymphocyte being a white blood cell, formed in lymphoid tissue constituting between 22 to 28 percent of all Leukocytes in the normal adult's human blood. A lot of T-cell function thought Buddy was able to be done by production of soluble proteins called Lympokines. Buddy was very proficient in immune system function. He operated with expert correctness and facility. Therefore John didn't have a problem deferring to him on the matter.

"Tell me something." John was exhausted. "Most of these people came in contact with a strange strain of influenza. It mutated and took on properties of several different viruses, West Nile being one of them, like the subject in the other attack. That's how we know that the attacks are related. Then it mutated again, and the strain began to resemble H5N1, the Bird Flu. That's what really knocked these people off their feet, but what about the psoriasis?"

"Their immune systems were overwhelmed. Their Humorial immunity branch was stimulated, so the B-Lymphocytes that regulate this particular branch began to produce antigen at an alarming pace. The plasma cells began to form and large numbers of antibodies were produced. Now you must remember although only one micro organism entered these people's bodies, it quickly mutated and began to appear as many. So many different proteins formed to combat the numerous foreign proteins that the initial invader possessed. This virus, if invented by man or not," stated Buddy, appearing to be in awe, "is genius and I am very afraid of it. Cimmerian has to know that he is playing with fire because if it gets out there will be hell to pay."

John thought in-depth about what Buddy was saying, as he stared off at their three Fungi cultures that sat on a nearby table. The Candida Albican, which was pathogenic yeast like imperfect fungi, made him think. These fungi made him think about the virus that they were chasing and researching. Although it was certainly deadly now, thought John, he knew it was still imperfect, that's why it kept on mutating. It was trying to become something else. Another fungus culture was the microsporum canis, this one didn't conjure up any visionary thoughts.

And, their third one, the Tricophyton Mentagrophytes, didn't give him insight. It was only the first one that made him pause with concern.

"There are some young kids out there," stated John, cutting his daydream short. "Do you think we can give them anything besides the antibiotics to ease their discomfort?"

"I suppose we could give them anti-febrile to bring their fever down," suggested Buddy, looking through the medicines that they had and finding an antipyretic. He passed John the medication. "Here, take this. I'm gonna go call Edna and give her an update."

"Cool," replied John. "I'll go and find a nurse to give this to, so the kids can receive it today."

John left the lab as Buddy began to pack up what he was using. He was ready to call his lady when a nurse stormed into the room.

"I'm sorry," she said, mistaking Buddy for a doctor. "But, we have several patients that are experiencing bouts of violent turmoil," she told him. "We can use some help," she added.

Buddy, who was a natural prankster and would have loved to tell the woman how he wasn't a doctor, but had played one on television once, was all out of jokes and witty responses at the moment. So, he turned around and looked back through the medications that he had just consulted, looking for a convulsion suppressor. He saw one and grabbed the anti-convulsant, walking toward the door, not bothering to ask the nurse anymore questions. "Lead the way," was all he said, walking steady on her heels.

CHAPTER 15

As Pete Carpenter stared off at all the pretty women, he began to understand why they said Paris, France was for lovers. A man in his opinion could very easily fall in-love with one of the beautiful women he saw. The atmosphere and scenery to him was even romantic.

"Can I give you a hand?" He asked a petite woman, who was struggling to board the shuttle train with a large carry-on bag and several children.

The woman answered him in a foreign tongue that sounded like silk to his ears. Since she clearly neither spoke English nor understood him, Pete gestured at her bag. The woman understood and allowed Pete to help her onto the train as she rounded up her kids. Once everyone was organized and safely inside, Pete returned the woman's property and nodded his head. The woman smiled and said something to him in her native tongue that Pete thought to be words of appreciation.

"You're welcome," he replied, walking off through the train car. An American watching him, thought to herself -- *And they say chivalry is dead.*

Pete didn't know why he had suddenly felt courteous, because personally he didn't subscribe to the quality. It had to be the atmosphere, he told himself. It was like the learned minds said in the States; music soothed the savage beast.

Pete was in Paris, aboard a mover train at Charles de Gaulle airport, staring out at a flower trail, which displayed white wisteria blossoms, magnolia and Japanese azalea plants along the train line. The flowers and the women were beautiful, but the truth was, Pete wished to handle his business and get back home. He was there for one thing only.

He began to think, focusing again on his task.

France had given the United States the Statue of Liberty, he thought. The statue was a symbol of the right of people to engage in certain actions without control or interference. Pete had to laugh at that as he thought about a country reaping that which they themselves had sown.

*   *   *   *   *

"Yes, I know," replied Faith, over the phone. "I told him, but you know these government types."

"He's government?" Edna asked.

"Yes," replied Faith. "I believe so. Everyone in the law enforcement community is."

"Just like us," concluded Edna. "The governmental bureaucracy affects us sometimes too."

"Yes, but, we're not as pigheaded as them."

"Phooey!" exclaimed Edna, being as charming as ever. "I've seen the same stubbornness around here."

"Edna!" stated Faith, cutting her off. "I didn't call you so that you could defend their position. I called you to vent."

"Okay," laughed Edna. "My bad, go ahead and vent."

"Thank you," replied Faith. "This thing is mutating. We don't know how it's spreading. Is it airborne; is it disease or just an abnormality caused by infection? Is it viral, or sexually transmitted?"

Edna wanted to tell her to calm down, but she didn't because Faith was the one out in the field and she didn't know what horrors or sickness she had seen. Buddy had called her hours earlier relaying the same kind of distress.

"Faith," Edna told her. "Listen. Do as your name suggests, just have a little faith. We'll find out what is going on and cure it. We always do, well most of the time."

"You think so?" Faith asked, sitting down on the edge of her bed in her hotel room.

She was butt naked, just got out of the shower and put lotion on her entire body. She stared into the large mirror across from the bed admiring her own body, while thinking about activating her gym membership again.

"Trust me," stated Edna, over the phone. "You call me because I have the Wisdom of Solomon right?"

"I didn't say that. I mean, you're smart," replied Faith, hesitantly. "You have wisdom teeth," she said, making Edna laugh. "That's gotta count for something."

"I'm slapping you as soon as you get back here, Faith."

Faith laughed and laid back on the bed. "Just crunch those numbers for me Edna, I will need to see them when I get back. I gotta go," she stated. "I want to call my babies, so bye."

Faith sat up and grabbed her black note pad. She liked to write down facts, opinions and guesstimates on her research, when she was out in the field.

From outside and across the rooftop, Sergio Moshe wondered exactly what Faith was writing. He couldn't see the page, only the pad and the pen working.

She had a nice body he thought, very shapely, her buttocks curved just right. She wasn't distracting him with her nudity. He was just merely making an observation, he told himself.

Moshe glanced at the photo of Faith that he held in his left hand while removing the high powered binoculars from his eyes. There were photos of Faith and her family, John Lovejoy, Edna and Buddy Defoe, Jules Marceau and Hunt Rhinehart. Moshe was briefing himself on all of them, but one at a time. Tonight Faith was the target, so he placed the photo back down and brought the binoculars back up.

Faith was still writing; she paused for a moment and bit on the back of the pen, then she ended the notation by writing: *Pathogenic, which is very parasitic. It could be any number of submicroscopic pathogens consisting essentially of a core of a single nucleic acid initially surrounded by a protein coat, having the ability to replicate itself very rapidly inside of a living cell.*

Faith felt a slight chill. She put her pen down and closed a nearby window. She also pulled the shade down; she hadn't realized it was up that far. Then she put on a big fluffy white robe and picked up the phone. She dialed her sister's number and listened as the phone rang several times.

"Hello, Kincaid residence."

"Yvonne, what's up," said Faith. "It's me!"

"Hey," replied Yvonne. "What's going on over there?"

"You don't want to know," replied Faith.

"It's that bad?" Yvonne asked. "Well, go by Rock Creek Park and tell my old boyfriend, Edward, to get out of town. You know they made that song about us, right?"

"What song?" Faith asked, realizing that the question was a setup, but unable to resist asking.

"The one where the chorus talks about the couple doing it in Rock Creek Park, silly," answered Yvonne, laughing.

"You're silly, where are my children?"

"Your daughter's right here and Mel is in the bathroom. Be quick too, because I'm reading a story to Kimberly."

"Give her the phone; I'll be all day if I want too."

"Hi mommy."

"Hi baby, what are you doing?"

"Me and Auntie are reading a book together. It's called '*Dainty Little Dancing Feet*'. It's about a little girl who wants to dance and she's the same age as me."

"That's nice, baby. How's Mel?"

"He's okay, he's in the bathroom, and he stinks. Mel! The phone, it's mommy."

Faith continued to talk to her daughter for about ten minutes, while she waited for her son to come to the phone. When he finally did, he was laughing hysterically.

"Mel, what are you doing?"

"They say that I'm stinking up the place, mommy," still chuckling. "But, I told them, using the toilet for a number two is like creating art. Everyone's a masterpiece."

"Stop that, Mel. That's nasty baby, you don't put everyone in your bathroom business like that," she advised him.

"Mommy, I'm trying not to, but they're bothering me."

Faith changed the subject. Mel filled her in on the other events of his day. Faith said her goodbyes and asked for Yvonne.

"What?" Yvonne stated, answering the phone rudely.

"If you had this much attitude in school," said Faith, "you could have been a doctor."

"The world doesn't need two of us," countered Yvonne, "running around doing goodwill work. You do your thing and let me do mine."

"Just finish entertaining my daughter. Can you do that?" she asked, sarcastically, hanging up on her sister before Yvonne had a chance to respond. She threw the phone down on the bed and was about to get up when it began to ring. She picked it back up, figuring that it was Yvonne calling back, not satisfied with not getting her rebuttal in.

"You want to entertain me now?" Faith asked, answering the phone.

There was a short pause over the line, then Sterling said, "I was thinking about dinner maybe some music and dance, but if you have something better in mind, I'll listen."

"Oh," uttered Faith. "I'm sorry." She wasn't sure who the party calling was, but it certainly wasn't Yvonne. "Me and my sister were having a moment," she explained, "and I thought you were her calling back. Who exactly is this anyway?"

"Hopefully, your evening entertainment," Sterling laughed. "We met on the flight into Washington the other day. Remember? The name's Sterling Rayford, you gave me your card."

"Oh yes," remembering him now. "Tall, dark, and criminally handsome, I remember you. Are you back in Atlanta? I'm still in Washington." she said.

"So am I," replied Sterling. "I know I said I would give you a ring when I was in your neck of the woods, but I finished my work early and thought maybe we could have dinner. That is, if you are free?"

Faith looked down at the notes and documentation she was preparing to read over tonight. "I'm free - I'm not working tonight." She touched her forehead with her free hand in a gesture that said *what are you doing?*

"So would you like to grab something to eat with me? I know my way around Chocolate City, so you couldn't find a better guide."

"Sure, where shall we meet?"

Faith was familiar with Washington D.C.'s national landmarks and she'd visited several historical sites as she traveled the city, but she'd never heard of Blue's Alley. She took down the information from him and drove her rental car to the heart of Georgetown excited to see what one of the top jazz and supper clubs in the nation looked and felt like. She parked a block away and followed a couple up the block to the club. She could tell that she was in the right place even before she saw the simple white sign, which hung over the club's entrance that read *'A Jazz, Blue's Alley'*. Right under the sign, she got a pleasant surprise: Regina Belle was performing there tonight. Faith was a fan of Ms. Belle's.

When she got to the entrance, Sterling was there waiting for her. He wore a black suit, and dark shoes. No tie, just a crisp white shirt.

"Glad you could make it," he told her; smiling seductively, thought Faith.

"I'm glad that I could also. You didn't say there was a performance here tonight."

"It was a surprise. Do you enjoy her music?"

"I love her," bushed Faith. "I didn't know what to wear, not that I had a lot of choices with me. But, is this alright?"

"That's fine," replied Sterling, loving the golden simple cotton dress that she wore, and the open toed gold stilettos. She looked radiant and golden herself, he thought.

"Are you ready to go in?"

"Yes," replied Faith, pointing at the line that extended down the block.

She was about to suggest to him that they get on line, when Sterling took her hand and led her straight past several people in the doorway and into the club. Obviously, he knew people there, thought Faith.

The stage sat in the middle of the room with tables surrounding it. Sterling got them a nice table with a great view of the stage. He pulled her chair out for her before taking a seat himself.

"Thank you. You enjoy jazz music a lot?" Figuring that question would be a good ice breaker.

"Very much," he replied. "Culturally and aesthetically, it eases my mind."

"This is a nice club." Faith, looking around, noticed several prominent patrons.

"I make it my business everywhere that I travel to stop off and enjoy the craft. That is if the city I'm in has a jazz venue. I've got my favorites: Dizzy's club, Coca-Cola up in New York City's, Frederick P. Rose Hall. Are you familiar with New York City?"

"Yes," answered Faith. "But not the clubs."

"Chicago is cool too. They have the Green Mill Jazz Club up there. Al Capone was a jazz lover. He even had his own booth in the place."

"Prohibition must have been a damper." commented Faith.

"Not really - that's what trap doors were built for. How'd your business go up here?" Sterling asked, abruptly changing subjects.

"It's really too soon to tell," replied Faith, not wanting to talk about the patients she had examined over at Howard University Hospital.

"Okay," tacitly accepting her reticence. "You know, you're good at masking your discomfort."

"How so? I mean, why do you say that?"

"Well, it's easy to tell that certain things about your work disturb you. But, still you are able to put on a charming face, glow and emit sporadic joy."

"You can see all of that from one or two smiles?"

"Yes, because I'm the same way at times too."

The show opened up and Faith looked toward the stage. A minute or so later a waitress came over and asked Sterling and Faith if they would like to order anything.

"May I?" Sterling asked.

"Please do - you know the club."

They watched the show quietly for a while. Suddenly, Sterling interrupted Faith's thoughts with a personal question.

"Faith, can I ask you something?"

"Sure, just as long as it's not my age or weight."

"Why are you single? I'm curious. I can see why you're successful at your work. Because you're intelligent, but that should not make you being single difficult also."

"I'll have to make no questions about my status, my third. No question in the future," stated Faith. "But, I'll answer it this time. Men are intimidated by me. If you hadn't wanted to change your seat on our flight, you probably wouldn't have spoken to me either."

"Is that so? And why do you believe that men are intimidated by you? Not just because you're beautiful, either, because men jump over other men to get next to beautiful women."

"I don't want to sound conceited, but you asked. Intellect. Most men just can't handle a successful woman. They can't deal with a woman who can change a tire on her own and manage her own affairs."

Sterling shook his head, feeling her approach to the subject. "That's a shame, it's a good thing I don't consider myself to be like most men or we may have never met. And I don't like changing tires myself, so, can I call you if I get a flat?"

"Not from New York," laughed Faith. "And a big part of the demographic picture of America is singlehood. Single people live very fulfilling lives. I have a great family."

She took out her wallet, "this is my daughter Kimberly," passing over a wallet size photo.

"She's adorable," how old is she?"

"She's seven now, but she was five in that photo. This one's of my son, Melvin. He's nine years old," said Faith. "That's my little man."

Sterling looked at the photos and noted the stark differences in the children's features and Faith's.

"You're divorced?"

"No, I was never married. I adopted," Faith informed him. "I love children and couldn't wait for the falling in-love process to happen before I had a family. So I got my wish for two beautiful, healthy children and, I also did my part as a woman concerned with the fate of the nation's orphans."

"That's beautiful," replied Sterling, handing her pictures back.

"Thank you," putting her pictures back.

"Supposing you're not married and looking for a little criminal conversation?"

"Why not?"

"Simple, I'd rather be single than settle. I must admit, though, I don't like being single all the time. I really feel it at tax filing time and when I have to shell out those extra fees when I fly and going to dinner alone on too many rainy nights. It's awful, but I take the good with the bad."

Faith didn't have a witty reply on hand. She was too busy wondering about just how many rainy nights he was talking about. Fortunately, their food arrived, so she didn't have to say anything.

Sterling thanked their waitress and waited as Faith smiled and said her grace. Then she dug in the tasty morsel that set the tone of her meal.

"Um, this is delightful!"

Not as delightful as you, Sterling thought, and smiled.

As they ate, they spoke about, laughed over and pondered the political landscape of the nation's capital, with Faith suggesting that many elected officials were more concerned with bedding interns than governing the country.

"That's a bit harsh, don't you think? Isn't there time to do both?" he asked jokingly.

"Apparently not," answered Faith. "Look at the state of affairs the country is in."

"The problem is deeper than who's bedding who," Sterling told her. "Sex is good, but powerful people covet money, not sex. The only booty they're looking for is that which has been plundered from an enemy and can be made into a valuable commodity, an article of trade. You know, gold, silver, assets, property and the ever elusive negotiable paper note."

"Well, you'd probably know." Faith took the kid gloves off. "Meyer-Burke is in bed with our elected officials."

"I think I might regret this," stated Sterling. "But, I'm going there anyway. Why do you believe that? Pull the sheets off for me, will you?"

"I'd love to," stated Faith. "Want to tell me why Congress has no problem with pharmaceutical companies manufacturing generic brands of their own branded drugs? Could it be that someone's palm is being greased? I mean in-house divisions at major pharmaceutical companies whose only job is to manufacture authorized generics."

"You don't like knock-offs?"

"Not when it smells like a monopoly or when it appears to only be about making more money. If you have a successful drug that is extending a patient's life, why do you need a cheaper generic? Why not just lower the price of the brand name drug? And, what are they doing with the generic anyway; lowering the medication's potency, because it's supposed to cost less. So, instead of curing you, it will only get you halfway cured."

She sounded like a tempest in a teapot, thought Sterling, as she made her point, whistling everywhere. "You're only looking at it one way, Faith. Regardless of who makes the generics, the consumer will benefit. They'll be able to buy an affordable drug. If the drug is an authorized generic, they have the best chance of getting a drug that's close to the original."

"You're good," said Faith. "You know how to highlight everything that a consumer might want to hear. But, I know all of that. What peeves me is the fact that Big Pharma is so greedy. The billions that Meyer-Burke makes for its original, branded drugs aren't enough, they have to monopolize and squeeze a few more billion out of the sick. You're not slick," added Faith. "I see how Meyer-Burke ups the price on their top brand so their generic looks like it is a real discount. That's deceptive marketing."

"Is it? Or is it just how business is done nowadays?" He looked at Faith's hands. Her nails were beautiful, manicured. "How about the Korean nail salons? They operate throughout the lower economic neighborhoods. They hoodwink the residents, they open salons facing each other, they try to make it looks as if the salons are in competition, because the one on the left hand side of the street is one dollar cheaper, which is Tommy Rotten because they're both owned by the same person. Under your definition, that would or should be a monopoly too."

"It is," agreed Faith. "I haven't attacked that yet and come on; they're not making billions of dollars like Big Pharma to get next to Meyer-Burke. Each shop would have to do every person in America's nails."

"I can't win this argument, can I?"

"No, you can't," replied Faith. "But, I'd enjoy it if you would try."

"All I can say is what I've already said," stated Sterling slowly. "The competition will only make all drugs affordable."

"How much is the generic drug market worth in the States?"

"Twenty billion dollars; and your point?"

"That's a lot of money. I see why the original patent holder of certain blockbuster drugs wants in on that cash cache. Those who make unauthorized generics can't be happy with Big Pharma cutting into their profits."

"America is about promoting healthy competitive business environments," argued Sterling.

"Well, I hope Congress stops allowing Big Pharma to circumvent the 180-day exclusivity law that grants new generics this window to sell their new knock-off exclusively without Big Pharma coming at them. I might consider that 'healthy'."

"You can't be mad at Big Pharma for following the letter of the law," stated Sterling. "Their generics being authorized aren't new drugs. The 180 day rule doesn't apply to them."

"Not 'them'," countered Faith. "Don't exclude yourself from the equation. You're probably in Washington lobbying for that old Congressional influence that Meyer-Burke enjoyed, not too long ago."

"Lobbying is someone else's job, I don't do that and I don't grease palms. That's not to say that no one's doing it," he added honestly. "Just not me and, for your information, I'm here, or was here, to participate in the American Enterprise Institute think tank's discussion on designer drugs. You know those that are genetically developed."

She let him off of the hook. She finished her meal and drank some wine hoping that she hadn't gotten too aggressive on him. Men liked to pursue beautiful women, just like he said. But they stopped chasing the very aggressive ones.

"Thanks for the entertainment," stated Faith sweetly, after the jazz set was finished. "I really don't get out much like this."

"I can see why," looking straight at her.

"What's that supposed to mean?" ready to defend everything she had said and her position.

"It means that sometimes you have to leave your work at work," he told her in a smooth, non-threatening voice.

"We were just talking, Sterling," she offered. "You know dinner conversation."

"I know," he replied. "And, I enjoyed the debate. I'm just trying to tell you that sometimes, I enjoy other things." Sterling ended his statement by offering her a sly smile. Then he took a sip of wine, allowing the nectar to wet his lips partially. As she watched him, Faith imagined that his lips were sweet chocolate Hershey kisses. Candy, she thought. I could go for a piece of candy right now.

The night came to an end and the show was over. Sterling walked Faith to her rental car; he had a rental of his own. "Hopefully, we can do this again, and not too far in the future," he told her.

"We'll see," said Faith. Sterling was holding onto her hand, so Faith thought that he might kiss it. But he didn't. He leaned in aiming for her cheek, but managed to fool her and touched her lips gently. It was unexpected, yet just delicate enough not to feel intrusive. His lips felt very soft, thought Faith, and her thoughts of candy returned.

"Goodnight," he said, turning around and walking off into the night.

Sergio Moshe had to smile at Sterling Rayford's pretentiousness.

His graciousness tickled the woman, Moshe could tell. Things were about to get very interesting, he told himself; in a macabre sort of way.

CHAPTER 16

Relaxing was something that Norton Burke very rarely got to do, in spite of having several thousand people working for him. And not having any more children in his home, after divorcing his third wife and giving her a large multi-million dollar severance package.

That was what Norton Burke called all of his divorce agreements: The money his ex-wives got was severance pay, money based on their length of employment. Norton Burke never loved any of them. They were his personal whores, he thought. The fact that he had children with all of them meant nothing to him either. He never fought over custody or visitation because he didn't have time to raise a child, or help entertain one. Money was all that he was able to provide and no one ever asked for more.

Today, his phones were turned off. He was trying to escape and relax for one day, if he could. Soon things would be hectic. Another chance to relax might not come for a good while.

Norton had over a dozen homes, including luxury condos in every major city. But his home in Neversink, New York was his favorite. It was so tranquil that he did his best thinking there. The house was only ten years old. And no one was allowed to enter it but Norton himself, his own private retreat.

He'd chosen to have it built in Neversink because the town fit his motto for life: *Never sink, never give up and during a negotiation, never give in.*

The house wasn't an original thought. Few of Norton Burke's ideas were. But, he didn't care. Capitalizing on the shortcomings of others was his forte and he excelled at it.

Ceiling to floors, this particular house was made entirely of glass. Anyone in close proximity could see Norton during his most personal moments, sleeping in his bed, eating breakfast or using the bathroom. It was modeled after the late Phillip Johnson's glass house, now in a museum in New Canaan, Connecticut. Just like the Johnson's, his was a single large room, fifty-six feet by thirty-two feet and had floor to ceiling glass set between black steel beams.

Burke had a small brick home next to his glass house, where he kept a support system for the glass house. Business associates called him a copy cat behind his back.

The townspeople of the Catskills, where the home sat, not knowing Norton Burke's name or position only saw the electric fence that enclosed the forty-seven acre estate. They thought he was a kook and called his home the Ghost House. It made for very interesting campfire stories when they took the children in the region camping.

Norton Burke felt a sudden urge to cough and quickly brought his left hand up to cover his mouth, while simultaneously looking over at his virus killer. He hated getting sick and to prevent that, he used hand sanitizers constantly and placed what he called his 'biohazard surveillance system', wherever he worked and slept. This system was a small fan that operated without any moving parts, but created a flow of ions. That's what Norton thought about now, as he imagined the influenza virus being ripped apart before it could get to him: the makers of his fan, Kronos Advanced Technologies, had assured him that he would be safe if he installed a safety net. He took that to mean the fan, hoping that they weren't talking soap and water.

The fan, Norton believed, could rip molecules apart with its electric field and kill pathogens like the influenza virus.

Norton Burke coughed several more times as he looked at his fan, feeling protected, yet cautious.

*   *   *   *   *

"What do we know and who do we need to call?" asked Jules. "Don't everyone speak at the same time," he added, when the information he requested didn't come immediately.

"All of the Washingtonians say that it began with a simple cough," stated Faith. "I examined a few of them at Howard University Hospital. They were all suffering from the same strain of influenza. It had their bodies feeling battered and bruised."

"We compared the information Faith brought back," stated John. "And her strain looks like it's the same as ours, but the people in North Carolina seem to have been in much worse shape."

"Do you know why?" asked Jules.

"I think that it had something to do with their treatment, Sir," answered Buddy.

"Explain," Jules stated. "Well it is my understanding that both groups were treated with Tamiflu, as well as other antibiotics."

"That is correct Sir, but the group in North Carolina had their treatment delayed by the government authorities who quarantined them and tried to contain the situation." John stated.

"You mean the press," said Jules.

"Exactly," confirmed John. The group in Washington went to their area hospitals and received treatment right away."

"So, early treatment made a difference?" asked Jules.

"Certainly, without a doubt," answered Faith.

"What were Tweedledee and Tweedledum doing?" asked Jules.

"Buzz Shaw was making sure the press got as much misinformation as possible," said Faith.

"And Hunt Rhinehart looked like his chief concern was keeping the people under quarantine." noted Buddy, shaking his head. "I wonder who is out there looking for Cimmerian?" he asked.

"They probably have people on it," offered Jules. "But, they want to control everything. That includes effect, not just cause."

"I think the public should be made aware," Faith said. "That way they can protect themselves and take precautions."

"Americans know that influenza is a seasonal bug," stated Jules. "And, most know that it kills approximately thirty-six thousand people a year. In the United States, that is," he added.

"Maybe and maybe not," argued Faith. "It's not even flu season, so that information doesn't help them."

"We don't want to start a panic. We also gave the Secretary of State and the Department of Homeland Security our word that we would not leak any information that was made privy to us."

"That was before we knew what we were actually dealing with."

"We still don't know, Ms. Millicent. Or, do you?"

"I know it's an extremely aggressive and virulent strain of influenza. I know it has characteristics of the Avian Flu."

"Don't leak that, Ms. Millicent," stated the director. "We are going to follow protocol on this one."

"This isn't protocol, keeping quiet?"

"That's enough, Ms. Millicent!" Jules' voice had risen.

Faith looked at John first, and then Edna and then Buddy, hoping for their support, but no one said anything.

"Let's focus on what we can do to protect the public," states Jules.

"You know," John spoke up suddenly. "During that S.A.R.S. outbreak in China in 2003, the Chinese government's initial cover-up cost hundreds of people their lives. The mayor and the health minister were fired."

"It's a good thing that there's no cover-up going on here," said Jules. "And being the mayor of Beijing wasn't all people thought it to be. But thank you, Mr. Lovejoy, for that information. This isn't Severe Acute Respiratory Syndrome, am I correct?"

"No," stated John.

"Then I don't want to know about ancient Chinese history," snapped Jules. "The public isn't stupid. They don't need us to sound the alarm; they will sound it on their own, at the appropriate time.

Buzz Shaw and his cockamamie story about pollutants in the nation's streams aren't going to wash. The U.S. Geological Survey has been on that for years. Now, can we let everyone else do their job so that we can get back to doing ours?"

Jules paused, to give everyone present a chance to digest what he had said. Aside from Faith, John, Edna and Buddy, there were close to fifteen other CDC personnel present at the briefing. They had moved into another stage of the investigation.

A virus had been identified and samples collected. More research experts had to be brought in and the scope of the investigation broadened.

"Normally, how many flu vaccines are produced globally?" asked Jules.

"About three hundred and fifty million annually," answered Edna.

"Of which how much does the United States purchase," asked Jules, "to combat seasonal flu outbreaks?"

"Somewhere in the ball park of twenty million," stated Buddy.

"We're going to have to ask the pharmaceutical companies to make more than that available," stated Jules. "We may also need to set up a pre-emptive strike."

"By vaccinating people against this new strain now?" asked Faith.

"Yes," replied the director. "We could do so, without letting too much information out. People are already afraid of the Bird Flu - you say this new strain resembles it. Technically, we wouldn't even be telling a tall tale. The Bird Flu has infected close to three hundred people worldwide, killing half of them. If this new strain has similar properties, we may be looking at the mutation everyone feared."

"You want to use Tamiflu?" asked John.

"Tamiflu is working against it, right?" asked Jules.

"Well, yeah," said John. "But what if the virus mutates because it's changing rapidly in each host?"

"We'll cross that bridge when we come to it. We have to use what we have for now. No one knows how effective any drug will be against a mutation." Jules spoke somberly. "That doesn't mean that they stop producing and stockpiling it. You have over 80 nations stocking up on Tamiflu today because it's better to be safe than sorry."

"We really have no choice," offered Faith. "Because if this thing mutates to something resistant to everything we have now, it would take up to four to six months minimum to develop another vaccine."

"And by that time," added Edna solemnly, "this thing could turn into a global pandemic just as devastating as the one in 1918. And that one killed tens of millions."

It was the bleakest assessment yet. All eyes were on Jules.

"I don't know what to make of the animal viruses that were detected," he told them. "But I will pass that portion of the data on to the U.S. National Institute of Allergy and Infectious Diseases. Maybe they will have an answer. They're also working with several pharmaceutical companies trying to develop something consumers can buy to protect themselves against a possible influenza outbreak."

"I hear that the European Medicines Agency has approved a vaccine for the Avian Flu." stated Buddy. "Maybe we should see what that is?"

"Yes, do that," agreed Jules. "And, we need to find out what pharmaceutical companies have what in the pipeline. In the event of a major outbreak, we need to know who to go to. So if any of you know people who know people, now is the time to call them."

Speaking of calling people up, Jules knew that it was time for him to brief the Center's Coordinating Center for Terrorism Preparedness and Emergency Response. He had held onto the information in house long enough, only briefing his department because any leaks would rest squarely upon his shoulders.

But the time for preparation was upon them. And, although he didn't entertain his subordinates' theories on a pandemic occurring, he knew one was on its way.

He was walking a tightrope, trying to balance the concerns of the public and the United States Government who didn't want the terrorist Cimmerian to get any news coverage. He or she was thought to be a sensationalist, craving having the name Cimmerian on everyone's lips.

"How about contacting the University of Rochester?" suggested John. "They've been studying rapid test response to influenza for years. I think they were funded by the NIH. We may be able to learn something from their study."

"Okay," stated Jules. "Look into that also."

If they got a hold of the new strain during the initial infection, thought Jules, they might be able to curb some of the mutations.

"Isn't the University of Rochester one of the six centers of excellence for influenza research and surveillance that the Department of Health and Human Services established last year?" asked Jules.

"Yes, that along with Mount Sinai School of Medicine in New York," stated Faith. "The University of California, in Los Angeles, the University of Minnesota, Emory University and St. Jude's Children's Research Hospital in Memphis."

"Let's see what data they have compiled," asked Jules. "That's it for now, and I suppose that I don't have to tell any of you that we needed this information yesterday."

CHAPTER 17

Allen Taylor couldn't believe his luck. He had stumbled upon the story of the century, he thought. When he reported this, they would probably give him a Pulitzer Prize; the federal government was quarantining Americans stricken with a deadly flu virus that resembled the dreaded Avian Flu.

He had seen some of the patients who were afflicted. Their complexions were abnormally pale. One doctor had spoken to him, in confidence, on the condition of anonymity: those patients were terminal and on their last breath. And the doctor had heard about other patients in North Carolina, who had also fallen ill.

Allen Taylor, investigative reporter, flew down to Raleigh, North Carolina to have a look for himself. It took two days of scouting around, but he found the quarantine facility. It was just as the doctor had described it: a makeshift palliative care facility, out in the middle of nowhere, nothing like the ordinary end-of-life care facilities around the country.

Allen Taylor had been to them all: The University of Washington Medical Center, Duke University Hospital, Westchester County

Medical Center, Robert Wood Johnson University Hospital and New York Presbyterian Hospital. He had interviewed and spoken with terminally ill cancer patients in those facilities, but not one of them had such a dark cloud over the place as this makeshift center did.

Allen Taylor stood outside of his vehicle looking at the facility through a pair of field glasses that allowed him to focus with both eyes.

Someone was coming. He quickly put the field glasses away and walked back toward his vehicle. It was a man, carrying a bed roll in his hand. Allen thought bindle stiff, as the man got closer; probably a migrant worker traveling from one area to another looking for work.

"Can I get a lift?" asked the man once he got in shouting distance of Allen. "I'm going whatever way you are."

"Yeah," stated Allen. "But you better hurry along. I think that we're in a restricted area."

The stranger looked across at the facility, then back at Allen. "What is this place?"

"A secret," stated Allen, still standing outside his vehicle, smiling at his find.

The stranger walked toward him and dropped his bedroll on the floor.

"Come on," Allen told him. "Pick up your stuff and go around to the other side."

The stranger smiled, reached out very quickly and struck him across his throat.

Allen grabbed for his own neck, momentarily caught off guard. The man grabbed him and spun him hard until he was standing directly behind him. He clamped one hand over Allen's mouth and nose, pressed a fragrant cloth against his face: chloral hydrate.

Allen struggled and Hunt applied pressure, apparently a little too much. Hunt Rhinehart felt the thin man's neck break in his hands. Allen Taylor's body slumped to the ground with a loud thud.

Quickly, efficiently, Hunt searched the dead man's pockets and car. Then he hauled the lifeless body over and threw it down on the back seat. There was no one else around; he'd made sure of that when he first spotted Allen's car.

Pausing before he started the engine, he looked at the reporter's identification. The Associated Press, it read. Associated with whom, Hunt wondered, as he started the vehicle. There wasn't one assignment that he could recall where he had remained clean-handed. He didn't expect this one to be any different.

* * * * *

"Mom, have you ever thought about re-marrying?" asked Faith.

"Not since my last one night stand," answered Fanny.

"AH!" uttered Faith. "Mom, that's too much information. Could you just answer the question?"

Fanny saw that her daughter was serious, so she relaxed a little. "No, not really… I mean, what for, I've been there and done that. I don't have time for anyone but me and my grandchildren, occasionally. Why? Are you thinking about marriage?"

"No not marriage, but maybe companionship."

"What's wrong with meeting a companion, every now and then? You don't need a partner for economics. You're not running for political office, where you might need a marriage of convenience. You're not running, right?"

"No Mom," glancing over at her children, as they played a video game.

"So there's no social benefit to your being attached," continued her mother. "If I were you, I wouldn't look for love; I'd just live my life. Love will find you, if it's meant for you. This is the age of independence baby. Just live and let live."

"Thanks Mom," said Faith thoughtfully, rising from the couch. "Excuse me a minute, okay? I have to make a phone call."

Faith didn't want to get married; she was just curious and wanted to know what her mother thought of the institution. She'd been there and done that, but not Faith. Faith had been a bridesmaid for Yvonne, but that was it.

John Lovejoy, in spite of his last name, was the marrying kind, thought Faith. He looked and behaved like a man that would respect the institution. Sterling Rayford didn't look like he would violate it, but he didn't look like the kind. He looked more like that Rolling Stone, to Faith. He wasn't the kind to pick up any moss. So, many questions and so little time, thought Faith, as she dialed Sterling's number.

It rang for all of ten seconds before he answered. "Hello?" He sounded groggy.

"Sterling?" asked Faith. "Hi, this is Faith. Did I wake you up?"

"Yes, but it's cool. What's up?"

"I need to speak with you about some things, they're…" Faith paused, remembering their conversation at the jazz club.

"They're what?" asked Sterling, sounding more awake. "Personal?"

"No," replied Faith, laughing a little bit. "They're work related," she told him.

"Don't you ever stop?"

"I'm working on it, but not today. So, can we talk?"

"I guess so," replied Sterling. "You've already got me up; you might as well tell me why."

"This is confidential," began Faith. "But, being that you and I see eye to eye on so many health care issues, I think we can talk."

"Ha!" exclaimed Sterling, responding to her observation. "We both can see, but I don't know if we're eye to eye."

"We're close enough," remarked Faith. "Sterling, I know that you are familiar with the influenza virus."

"I come in contact with it throughout my travels. Why? What about it?"

"Well, at the CDC, we're working on a few strategies to combat a pandemic. Not that we see one developing in the near future, but we are doing what you could call mock drills."

"Okay, I follow you. How can I help?"

"Well, last year," continued Faith. "We issued new guidelines that were detailed in a 108 page report. They advised each state, municipality, business and community what steps they should and could take in the event of a pandemic, seeing that it would take several months to develop a vaccine to combat whatever strain of influenza we may face."

"I read the report."

"Very good, we didn't include the pharmaceutical companies in that plan."

"What do you mean?"

"We didn't include information concerning what drugs the major pharmaceutical companies had in the pipeline," said Faith. "We would like to know about possible drugs to see if our proposed timeline for a suitable vaccine is adequate. Not to delve into trade secrets – I'm not asking you to talk about any potential research. But, I would appreciate it if you would."

She sat on the edge of her mother's bed. This was a habit of hers, during in-house telephone conversations. This was her comfort zone.

"That depends," sitting up in the bed himself. "Are you using our friendship to steal trade secrets?"

"Certainly not," replied Faith. "The CDC was going to have someone call over to Meyer-Burke and speak with your Chief Executive Officer. But, I offered to call, because I have a friend over there. I do, right?"

"Certainly," replied Sterling.

"Okay, so that's why I'm calling. Of course, anything discussed would be completely confidential. Who knows, I might be able to even point you in a certain direction."

"Why does it feel like you're dangling a carrot in my face?"

"I guess that's because, in our line of work, we are used to the quid pro quo approach for everything. But, honestly I'm just speaking as one friend to another."

"Then I'll speak the same way," he told her. "We have several drugs in the research and development stage, Faith. Some that I'm very excited about and quite a few are being developed to combat influenza."

"That's very reassuring," said Faith.

"Now tell me, how was it that you were going to point me in the right direction?"

Faith thought quickly, wondering how she could tell him what the CDC was looking for in terms of a vaccine, without telling him too much.

"Well, we studied the S.A.R.S. outbreak in 2003. Some two hundred thousand people had to be quarantined. I believe one hundred and fifty-three thousand in Taiwan, twenty-three thousand in Toronto and several thousand more in Hong Kong and Singapore. We don't want it to get that far. The President has detailed and set aside nearly eight billion dollars for a pandemic preparedness plan, which focuses on stockpiling influenza drugs. Now, between me and you, I don't believe that is enough. I like the Department of Health Services plan – it's more specific and extensive. But the CDC believes that if the pharmaceutical companies are not made privy to every bit of information the health care community has, nothing will work, or be adequate. The pharmaceutical industry is our last line of defense."

"So, why doesn't the government make us aware?"

"Because there is a small sticky issue of national security," Faith offered Sterling a bit of truth. "Government officials are very concerned about terrorists compromising imported vaccines and waging biological warfare."

"I see."

"You do understand there are no major pharmaceutical companies within the United States that can produce the amount of vaccine that we need annually? Meyer-Burke is only recently getting into the vaccine production market. I don't know why the powers that be would leave the American people open for such an attack -- you'd think they'd have stopped it with the nuclear weapons race. Maybe open some labs, so that we wouldn't have to import our vaccines. It might be a stretch, but that's what I think, especially in the age of terrorism."

"You're one hundred percent correct, Faith," stated Sterling. "That's food for thought; you need to serve it up on Capitol Hill and make them eat it."

Faith laughed at his analogy. "If only logical inference were that easy, I'd be up on Capitol Hill tomorrow giving my take on bioethics."

"It's a shame," remarked Sterling. "You have me ready to lobby for you."

"That's good to know, but getting back to our discussion," Faith replied. "The CDC thinks extra emphasis should be placed on developing a vaccine that could combat the Avian Flu; something more potent than Tamiflu. I'm not dismissing Tamiflu - Roche Pharmaceuticals has done a good job with production and they say that they can produce four hundred million treatment courses annually. That's twice worldwide demand. That would be great, if Avian Flu stays in its present form or a strain close to it. But if it jumps from human to human and shows up in the United States, the CDC's worried that Tamiflu won't be enough to combat it."

"Faith, you do know it's extremely difficult, if not impossible, to perfect a vaccine before a strain has mutated."

"I know," said Faith.

"Then what are you asking me?"

"I really don't know." Faith found herself a little confused. The director wanted to know what was in the pipeline and that was all he wanted. But Faith, fearing for the public's safety, was stepping out of that scope. The first wave of a pandemic was the most crucial. She knew something, from the Cimmerian attacks. And she wanted to share it badly.

"I do know," she corrected herself. "The CDC wants to advise the pharmaceutical industry to prepare for a strain similar to the Avian Flu, but also leave room for a strain that may mutate and adapt to accommodate certain animal diseases." There, thought Faith. It was out.

Sterling was quiet for a moment. Faith feared that she might have said too much. Sterling was a very bright man. He would know to read in between the lines.

"Sterling?"

"Yeah, I'm here," he said. "I was just thinking. We have a drug like that in the pipeline. We're just conducting tests and doing the research at this point. But, we definitely have a potential vaccine like that on the horizon."

"Why?" asked Faith, curious.

"It began with one of our researchers asking the question 'what if?' Sterling told her.

"What if what?"

"What if viruses began to conspire," answered Sterling. "We were studying the White Fly, actually the Bemisia Tabaci, for the agricultural industry. Are you familiar with the insect?"

"Yes," said Faith. "It's not really a fly, but it's related to the family Aphididae. Go on."

"Well, our friends in the agricultural industry were having a hard time with the White Flies in China. Then the problem spread to every continent except Antarctica. They were spreading disease at an alarming rate and infecting dozens of species of plant life. So, we sent a team of researchers to take a look, to see how we might be of assistance. That's when we discovered a new species of the fly. And this one's learned to extend its life expectancy up to six times its counterpart, by living on infected plants. They reproduced more, almost a dozen times more."

Faith was quiet, listening and mentally taking notes.

"The pathogens that the White Fly spreads are tomato yellow leaf curl virus and tobacco curly shoot virus. Plants infected with these two viruses began to extend and strengthen the White Fly. We wondered why and what other viruses might form a pact. We looked at influenza."

"Okay," stated Faith. "So, that includes animal diseases that might make the jump to humans as well?"

"As you would say," said Sterling. "Certainly."

"That's wonderful!" Faith was elated. "So each one, the insect and the two viruses, are essentially working together to extend one another's life?"

"Exactly. Just like we suspected multiple viruses would do. It's a new day, Faith. These pathogens want to live and they're looking for new ways to do it."

Ain't that the truth, thought Faith, as she thought about the influenza strain the CDC was investigating.

"Mommy!" Kimberly was yelling from the other room. "Come here Mom!"

"Sterling, my daughter's calling me, so I have to go. Thank you for hearing me out, and I'm sorry I woke you."

"It's cool," he told her. "Wake me up anytime you need to talk. You can always have my ear."

"Okay," replied Faith, with a great big smile on her face. She looked at her watch and saw that it was only eight o'clock. "You always go to bed so early?"

"No," he replied. "Didn't we just hang out the other night?"

"Yeah, but it's only eight o'clock. You were asleep way before I called."

"I have a trip that I'm resting up for," he told her. "I leave in the morning."

"Where are you off to?"

"Las Vegas," he told her.

"Sin City," stated Faith. "Business or pleasure?"

"Business. Although, I might get in a little gambling."

"I hope you win." she told him.

"I feel like I already have," stated Sterling and she felt herself blush.

"Mommy!" shouted Kimberly again.

Faith stood up. "I have to go," she told him. "But, thanks again and have a safe trip."

CHAPTER 18

Jules Marceau was distressed. Something resembling the virus the CDC was chasing had emerged in his homeland of France. The newspaper, Le Parisien, which he had delivered to himself daily, was reporting what they called a 'Black Plague', an obvious reference to the form of plague known as the Black Death pandemic throughout Europe and Asia for many years following 1353.

Hundreds of people had been stricken, reported the article. The French were making a lot of noise over it, alerting the international community to maintain comity of nations and seeking assistance, just as China did from the international community with their scare.

Jules read the article, indulging his coffee cravings -- popping chocolate-covered espresso beans into his mouth one after another.

The article was a long one, twenty pages. According to the report, many people had been hospitalized, including key figures from the Socialist Party. They were some of France's more prominent citizens. Jules crunched his coffee beans wondering if the afflicted, the country's rich and superrich, had been shocked by finding themselves susceptible. As he remembered them, they thought themselves immune from the pestilence that plagued the poor. They were probably asking themselves right now why their wealth tax, paid routinely, wasn't protecting them from common folk calamities?

When Jules finished reading, he reached for his desk phone. Sitting beside the phone was his gold lucky cat. The tiny statuette, thought to bring good fortune, had been a gift from a friend. Right now, Jules wondered when the good fortune would come.

*   *   *   *   *

"I'm afraid we have several more outbreaks on our hands." The director spoke to a room that was packed with close to three dozen of his subordinates.

"Paris, France is reporting an outbreak of residents experiencing flu-like symptoms and aches accompanied by excruciating pain. We're getting similar reports from Las Vegas, Denver, Philly, Ohio and Rhode Island. I want to send an exploratory team to each one of these locations to collect data and compare the information collected to what we already have on file.

"Ms. Millicent," asked Jules. "How does Paris sound to you?"

Faith loved Paris; what woman didn't, she wondered. Under any other circumstances she would have wanted to go, but not now.

"I'd prefer to go to Las Vegas, unless you need me to go to Paris."

"No," replied Jules. "You can be just as useful in Las Vegas. Defoe, you can take Paris, and take your wife with you."

Jules scanned the room for John Lovejoy, who wasn't yet present, although the meeting had been taking place for close to half an hour. The director doled out several more assignments, before he remembered that the U.S. Geological Survey had called. They'd asked the CDC to send someone to the Great Lakes. They were tracking a deadly Ebola-like virus that was killing freshwater fish in the lakes. Whatever this virus was, it was causing hemorrhaging in fish, much as the Ebola virus did in human beings.

131

"I also need someone to go down to the Great Lakes area," stated Jules. "It seems that V.H.S., the ugly viral hemorrhagic septicemia, is killing our freshwater friends."

Jules selected two candidates for that assignment, instructing them where exactly the virus had been found.

"Lake Erie, Ontario, Huron, the St. Lawrence river and the Niagara river. We're concerned about it making its way into Lake Michigan and Lake Superior. Check it out and will somebody please track down Lovejoy for me?"

Across town, John Lovejoy was walking around the Atlanta Aquarium, hoping he wasn't wasting his time. He checked his watch and saw that he had already missed the meeting at the CDC; the director was going to be furious, so this meet needed to pan out.

John had received an e-mail from someone who said that they had been part of something terrible and were responsible for the flu-like plague that the CDC was investigating. The e-mail had come half an hour before the meeting.

The email had told John to be at the aquarium and told him when. So, here he was, in a dark blue suit and a royal blue tie. He was here to meet a woman who called herself Rosa Klebb. She told him she would be wearing a pink summer dress.

John was intrigued for two reasons. One being the clandestine way that he received the message: the second being the woman's choice of alias. He recognized the character's name right away. It was from the James Bond film "From Russia with Love," and had belonged to a secret agent from an Intelligence Community called SPECTRE.

He had seen several women dressed in pink shirts, some wearing pink shoes, but no pink dresses. Then one approached him, walking slowly, and looking around. John, standing directly in her path, didn't move.

She walked over and stood next to him. She seemed to be admiring the aquatic animals that swam in the tank directly before them.

"Mr. Lovejoy?" asked the woman.

"Yes," answered John, turning towards her.

"Please don't look at me." Her voice was distinctively Russian. "Please watch the fishes, so you do not draw attention to us."

John felt a little foolish, but he did as the woman asked.

"I read your e-mail," said John. "You said you were responsible for the flu-like virus. How?"

"I, along with some colleagues of mine, engineered it. We did so, anonymously, at an undisclosed location."

"Why? And who asked you to do this?"

"We did it for money, a very large sum; I was paid two million dollars. I believe all of us were paid the same amount. I don't know the identity of the person that paid for our services. The only name that I was ever given was Cimmerian. But I believe that to be a pseudonym. The offer to work on the project came through the mail to me. In Russia, once I agreed, I was brought to the United States and placed in an apartment in New York. I was told to go to a warehouse each day. There I was blindfolded by a tall, white man and transported to a very sophisticated laboratory, some forty minutes away from the warehouse. Three other men were also brought there each day; a German, a Chinese man and an American. We worked on the project for six months, mixing and mutating influenza viruses, until we could get one that had the ability to mutate within a given host to something totally different."

John glanced at the woman in horror, not understanding why she would do such a thing. No amount of money in the world, he told himself, could persuade him to do something so diabolical.

"You do know that what you have created is killing people," John informed her.

"I do," she acknowledged. "That is why I am here, and the fact that all my fellow contributors are dead."

"Dead? Why? What has happened?"

"I think our former employer wishes to tie up loose ends. We all collected our money and exchanged our personal information secretly, just in case one of us ran into trouble. The German man was smart; he anticipated something like this happening. Double-cross is what he called it."

"And, they're all dead?" asked John again.

"Yes, answered the woman. "I'm afraid so."

"You must go to the authorities, they can help you."

"Not after what I have done. I only wish to help the people. I contacted you after seeing the report on the news in Washington D.C. I know that it is our virus. I liked your name, so I contacted you once I learned that your department within the CDC was spearheading the investigations."

"Rosa Klebb," stated John. "That's not your real name."

"Of course not, no one used their real names. I chose that name, because it was my favorite villain and a fellow countryman - the character, anyway."

John thought for a moment, not knowing what he should ask the woman first.

"Why did they pick you?" he asked the woman.

"I don't know how they knew about me," she said. "But, I was the top in my biogenetics class back in Russia. Each one of us was an expert in biology and infectious disease."

"How do you think that you can help now?"

"I don't know, but I want to do something," replied the woman.

"Would you consider coming down to the CDC with me?"

"No, I won't go anywhere with you."

John thought about forcing the woman and she seemed to sense his desire to because she moved slightly away from him.

"Do you want my assistance or not?" she asked him.

John looked at the woman. He thought about the patients: the children he had seen in North Carolina, the pregnant woman who had died in Texas. This Rosa Klebb was a monster, he thought. Far worse than the cinematic agent who attempted to kill with a poison-tipped spiked heel.

"Tell me about the virus," asked John, controlling his voice.

"Its ribonucleic acid changes rapidly. It attacks just like the common cold, starting with inflammation of the mucous membranes of the nose, throat, eyes, and the Eustachian tube. We called it a rhinovirus, for months, because it moved like the common cold and could be treated as such. Then they brought us a number of animal diseases to mutate it with and several viruses - the avian flu, S.A.R.S. and, the last one, the one that gave it a life of its own."

"What was that?

"The 1918 Spanish Flu, the one that killed fifty million people."

CHAPTER 19

Faith got into McCarran International Airport a little after eight in the evening. She rented a car and drove down the strip on South Las Vegas Boulevard. It was amazing, she thought, everything was lit up. The streets had such an airy, light and friendly effect. She didn't want to stay at a hotel directly on the strip. Let the gamblers do that, she thought as she drove past Caesar's Palace and the Bellagio. She wondered where Sterling was staying and decided she'd call him in the morning. On the surface she was in Las Vegas to do a job, but deep down inside she knew that she'd picked Las Vegas because Sterling was there.

There weren't really any small, quiet hotels in Las Vegas - the place itself was bigger than life, thought Faith. She laughed to herself as she drove, thinking about a friend of hers back in Atlanta. The woman had a phobia of being near any objects of great height. It was funny to Faith but quite serious to her friend. She never came to Vegas; there were just too many skyscrapers there for Faith's friend. Faith chose the Tropicana because it didn't look very crowded. The outside didn't look that way, at least, she thought as she searched for a place to park.

Coming to Las Vegas, Faith had wondered why Cimmerian had chosen to attack there. It was quite obvious to her now that she'd arrived herself: there were just so many people there coming and going. Those coming in would be at risk. Those leaving, returning home to other states, would possibly be taking something unwanted with them.

*   *   *   *   *

"So, she won't be coming in?" asked Jules.

"No, she won't," replied John. "I tried to persuade her, but she wouldn't budge. As one of the architects of this thing, this super rhinovirus, she's afraid. And she should be."

Jules sat very still and stared at John. "We know most of its parts now. Maybe we can come up with a vaccine."

"There are still many variables." John wasn't convinced. "This thing is extremely aberrant."

"Yes, I am aware of this, but your Bond girl has undoubtedly put us a step closer to beating this thing. I want you to assemble a team of microbiologists, the best we have at our disposal. Get our top virologists on this as well. The Rhinovirus, Pico Rhinovirus, and enterovirus, none of them alarm me. The common cold has been around since 1786 and we have its number. Avian Flu and SARS, that is something different, as are the animal viruses that they have mixed and matched. But, the real threat is that myxovirus. I told our colleagues, back in 2005, that resurrecting the Spanish Flu was a bad idea, but no one listened to me."

"I'm not privy to that. I'm very curious. What happened?" John asked.

"Well, in October of that year some of our colleagues pieced together the virus's genome, from the lung tissue of a female victim."

"Where did they find a female victim?" John asked in disbelief. "We're talking about a ninety-year-old outbreak!"

"She was found in some frozen sub-soil in the polar regions of Alaska."

"Jesus!" exclaimed John. "So, they brought what killed her back to life?"

"Yes, all in the name of science. They wanted to study a real pandemic, the most deadly one recorded. And it's still around."

"But, how did these terrorists get the virus?" asked John.

"It's the Information Age, Lovejoy. America, the great democracy, has laws that let the sunshine in. Once the virus's genome was pieced together, the genetic information was published. Anyone could have gotten their hands on this information."

"Didn't they put up any safe-guards?" asked John.

"Of course they did," replied Jules. "They even have a vaccine that combats the deadly virus."

"They do?" asked John incredulously.

"Yes, but I don't know how good it's going to be if the virus mutates or if the mixing that your contact and her colleagues did proves to be successful. Whoever Cimmerian is, I fear that he or she knows about our vaccine and is multiple steps ahead of us."

Both John and the director were quiet for several moments, gathering their thoughts on the subject. Then John asked, "Do you think there's any way to compare the strain that's loose to the resurrected strain?"

"You want to send a sample to the department that has the resurrected virus?" Jules asked.

"No," John told him. "I want them to send us theirs. I want to conduct the test in-house."

"That can be arranged."

As Jules dialed the bioterrorism department's number he had a thought and looked up at John.

"In that Ian Fleming movie," he stated, "what happens to the Russian woman that your contact fancies?"

"She gets shot and killed." answered John.

* * * * *

"You're following me," stated Sterling over the phone. "You can tell the truth."

"No, I'm not. It's just a coincidence that I'm here. I'm working, just like you."

"My work is finished. I was about to catch a flight back to New York tonight," he told her.

"Oh." Faith made him aware of her disappointment. "Well, do you think that I could see you before you leave?"

"Sure, I have several hours, where are you staying?"

"The Tropicana."

"I'm at the Mandalay. Do you want me to come over there or what?"

"Can I come to you?"

"Yeah, that's cool too," he told her. "Are you alright?"

"Yes, I'm fine. I'd just like to talk to you."

"Okay, come on over, I'll meet you in the lobby. Say half an hour?"

"Yes, that will be fine," replied Faith.

She hung up the phone, grabbed the keys to her rental and headed out. She had taken care of her business earlier that day, visiting two medical facilities where patients were being treated for the influenza strain she was monitoring. She'd spoken with the physicians treating them; that was all she could really do, short of contracting it herself. Of course precautions were taken as far as protective equipment, but nothing was foolproof and Faith knew it. She had enough sense to be worried.

The Mandalay wasn't far from the Tropicana, just down the strip. Faith took her time getting there. She even stopped off to call her mother and check on her children. When she finally got to the Mandalay, forty minutes had passed. Sterling was right there, waiting for her in the lobby: Dark slacks, crisp white shirt and a broad smile.

"You're late," he told her, as she approached admiring how she always looked carefree and breezy, even when she was feeling otherwise.

"Thanks for waiting," said Faith.

"New York's not going anywhere, regardless of how many times it is attacked."

Faith raised her eyebrow and wondered. What made him take it there?

"Nice blouse," he told her, changing the subject and bestowing her with a compliment. Women loved those, thought Sterling, looking at her gold ruffled top and gold Capri pants that fit oh-so nicely.

"Thanks," replied Faith, giving him a smile. Is there someplace we can talk?"

"There are a million places and a great one nearby." Sterling guided her to the elevators and pressed the top floor.

"You like gold, don't you?" he asked her.

"And silver," she replied. "I like them both, but I love diamonds," added Faith casually.

"Me too. Why the long face?" he asked her, when she didn't return his smile.

"Not yet," she replied. "I'd like to talk about you for a minute. What are you doing out here? Enjoying yourself some European bathing?"

"Actually, no," answered Sterling. "But it sounds like you know the drill."

"I might," replied Faith. She followed him off the elevator on the top floor. She smiled suddenly. "But a lady never tells. What a view!"

Sterling had led her into the Foundation Room. The view from there was breathtaking, thought Faith, as she looked cross at the Vegas skyline.

"This is beautiful," she told him.

"Yes, it is." Sterling wasn't looking at the view, he was staring at her. Faith caught his gaze and the implication.

"I'm out here trying to find a buyer for a new prescription drug that Meyer-Burke has developed." stated Sterling. "It's a lot like Armodafinil, but ours can keep a person fresh and alert for up to six days. That's significantly longer than the 48 hours Modafinil promotes."

"You're trying to sell a generic?" asked Faith. "To challenge Cephalon's drug?"

"Not really. Ours isn't a knock-off, it's an advanced therapy. It treats sleep apnea and narcolepsy. It was really designed for the military, but the military beat us to the punch and came up with their own no-sleep remedy. DOD's Advanced Research Department has a drug called CX717 that I hear can keep a soldier up four days, with sleep breaks up to four hours, every day. I believe our drug is significantly better, but it's still a tough sell."

"I wouldn't want to be up for six days," Faith told him. "I love to sleep, so I couldn't see not getting any."

"Well, you could work longer." Sterling was fishing for a plus side.

"I don't think so. I'm still upset with the makers of the electric light bulb. They messed up our half-a-days." She took a deep breath. "You're probably wondering why I needed to speak with you."

"A little bit," replied Sterling.

"Well, when I told you the other day that the CDC was concerned about a rogue virus, I left something out of that discussion."

"What was that?"

"The fact that a deadly strain of influenza has been discovered in the nation. I'm one of a team of researchers tracking it."

"Okay," replied Sterling, as if he'd suddenly had a revelation. "So, it's out here in Las Vegas?"

"Yes," replied Faith, "as well as almost a dozen other places."

"Are we at risk?" Sterling asked. Almost like he was a layman in the field of medicine, thought Faith strangely.

"Anywhere we go in this country and abroad, we're at risk," replied Faith. "Are we more at risk by being in Las Vegas? I don't know."

Sterling stared at her. "Do you think it can be contained?" he asked.

"Now, that's the question," said Faith. "If I could honestly answer that, I'd be the best in the profession. We're hoping."

"Then I'll hope too," offered Sterling, reaching out and taking hold of her hand.

A minute later, after standing still and holding hands like two school kids, he asked her, "Why you, Faith? Why'd they send you out here alone?"

"Well, there were a couple of sites. I could have gone to Paris, but I chose Las Vegas because I was hoping to see you again," she confessed.

Sterling smiled. "Thanks for coming. But I was asking, why'd they send you alone, why not with a partner? You were in Washington alone, also."

"I had a partner," she told him, thinking about John. "But, my partner's investigating somewhere else, with another colleague of ours, in a place where he had friends. He chose the buddy system, so I had to go it alone."

"You're okay with that?" Sterling asked.

"Oh yeah, it's cool, there isn't much work to be done. Mostly observation, which I'm good at. Look, what time does your flight leave?"

"I'm not sure," replied Sterling.

Faith frowned. "You don't know what time your flight leaves? How do you know that you haven't missed it?"

"I don't care," he replied calmly. "I think I'd like to catch a later one, anyway."

Again, they fell into a comfortable quiet. Faith realized that he hadn't let her hand go yet.

"Does the virus you're chasing have the characteristics that you asked me about?" Sterling asked.

"For the most part," confirmed Faith. "It mutates a little differently in each host. That's what makes it so tricky and sophisticated."

"I see," said Sterling.

'Sterling, listen," asked Faith. "Do you mind if we discuss the trials and results Meyer-Burke has had with that new drug you were telling me about?"

"You don't have to butter up your voice," stated Sterling letting her hand go.

"I'm not!" uttered Faith. "I'm just talking."

"No, you're not," said Sterling. "Talking only requires that you move your mouth. You have your eyes, lips and entire face working. You sound like the American Medical Association, wanting to know all of the steps we're taking."

"What's wrong with that?" Faith asked. She was laughing, now.

"I'm not sure. I'm just not used to providing a registry of our hit and misses."

"Oh, come on," said Faith sweetly, rocking her body and bumping her shoulder up against his. It's just me and you here."

"That's the same thing that Delilah told Samson," remarked Sterling, laughing.

"Oh, stop it," replied Faith. "You don't have long hair anyway. Seriously, I just need to hear a little bit. I can't mess with that ten to fifteen years it takes for a drug to reach the market. We don't have that long."

"That number's inflated," Sterling told her. "If you say that something takes longer to make, you can charge more for it," he told her. "Of course, that doesn't mean that drug production isn't a tedious task. Thousands of test compounds don't make the cut while you're searching for the Holy Grail. We're not using Petri dishes anymore."

"I should hope not," replied Faith.

"We passed the *in vitro* studies, testing the compounds in both human and animal cells," Sterling continued. "That went well. About seven thousand compounds were eliminated at the pre-clinical stage. Then we began phase one of the first of our three clinical trial stages. We tested healthy subjects and monitored their responses. We checked their aches and pains and looked for any toxic effects. There were no percussion cap explosives there."

"And...?" She was listening carefully.

"We filed about six I.N.D.'s, the Investigational New Drug applications, with the Food and Drug Administration, within thirty days. Those went through with flying colors," he informed her.

Had anyone been watching them or listening to their conversation, they would have been puzzled by the look of delight on Faith's face. Very few people could understand how the process of creating a new drug could be so exciting. But Sterling understood it well; he got the same rush from the same things.

"At phase two of the clinical trial, we determined the adequate dosage. We also looked at whether it should be taken orally or intravenously. About two years later, we were ready to move on to stage three," said Sterling.

"You've been developing this drug for a while," concluded Faith.

"Since before the avian flu was even discovered," he nodded. "We gave out thousands of placebos during the height of the flu season to folks suffering from influenza. "And we gave hundreds of people the real deal. The blind test checked out well, also. If a test subject's recovery-time wasn't cut down to one day, they began to feel better immediately. He paused. "And that's where we are right now."

"How much more is there to do, or go?"

"Not much. It's proving safe. We'll definitely be sponsoring it. We're testing it in different parts of the world right now. After its effectiveness has been gauged, we'll be ready to submit a N.D.A., a new drug application, with the Food and Drug Administration. We anticipate that this last application will be three thousand pages - it has to include both animal and human test results, along with every compound that makes up our wonder drug. How it's processed and made to undergo the necessary changes."

"Metabolism," cut in Faith.

"Exactly," agreed Sterling. "But, this will still take roughly two years."

"We may not have that long," said Faith grimly. "We may have to put a word in for you, I mean Meyer-Burke, with the F.D.A. to speed the process."

Sterling nodded his head in approval. "We wouldn't stop you."

"I bet you wouldn't!"

"Now, if you or the CDC could extend our patent protection longer than the standard seventeen years," he told her, with a smirk on his face. "So that generic drug makers would not be able to come after us so quickly, then you might be saying something."

"Don't push it," Faith warned him.

She decided to speak with Jules as soon as she got back about Meyer-Burke's possible addition to the fight against influenza. If anyone was going to fast-track a drug, or give the F.D.A. a recommendation, it would have to be Jules.

They sat on top of the world, lost in their own thoughts. It was so peaceful she could have sat there and talked forever...

"Hey." Sterling interrupted her thoughts. "You like it here?"

"Yeah," answered Faith, "It's real nice."

"I know someplace better," said Sterling. He was smiling. "You want to see it?"

Faith looked at him for a few seconds. She smiled back at him.

"Yeah, sure," she replied. "Why not?"

CHAPTER 20

"This isn't at all what I expected my first trip to Paris to be like," said Edna. "This stinks!"

Buddy tried a chuckle on for size, but couldn't muster up a hearty one. Paris was depressing, it was true, but then, the depression he and Edna felt had began back in the States.

The trip had been fraught with problems. First, neither of them had been able to find their passport. Then they had to wait on exceptionally long lines to obtain a *laissez-passer*, which was a pass that could be used in lieu of a passport. Three hours after obtaining the necessary papers, they'd boarded a flight bound for the capital of France, not knowing what to expect, but hoping for the best.

Charles de Gaulle was partially shut down; it was the location identified as being the origin of the outbreak. The French Government wasn't officially cooperating with the CDC, even though they had reported the outbreak to all the international media outlet. They didn't believe they were in the throes of a terrorist attack.

The citizens, on the other hand, felt differently. Everyone in the country, it seemed, had run out and brought a respirator and was wearing them everywhere they went. Buddy and Edna, not wanting to look out of place, also sported the lightweight polypropylene masks.

"This reminds me of how China was during that S.A.R.S. outbreak." Buddy's voice was muffled by his mask.

"Yeah, I know," agreed Edna, as they rode the mover train through the airport. They'd been in Paris for two days and had already made several trips through and around the airport.

Today, Buddy was taking notes of the airport's ventilation system, noting the level of international traffic that came through the place. He and Edna were prohibited from interacting with the passengers or citizens of France who'd fallen ill, but they had confirmed that there had been three deaths, all elderly people. It was likely that the victims' immune systems weren't strong enough to fight off the virus until medical attention could be provided to them.

"Are you ready to go meet up with that Rhinehart fellow?" Edna asked, looking at her watch. It was four o'clock and they had a four-thirty appointment.

Hunt Rhinehart had flown into town a day after them. He'd seemed surprised to learn that Buddy was in town. John called Buddy to tell him about the developments in Atlanta. He'd suggested that he call Rhinehart, who was also in Paris.

Buddy and Edna left the airport and hailed a cab. As they drove toward the city, Buddy tapped the driver on the shoulder.

"Pull over for a minute," stated Buddy. The cab driver, who spoke broken English and understood it even less. "I'll just be a minute," he told Edna, climbing out. "I need to use the bathroom."

There was a *pissoir* on the street, a public toilet that Buddy found to be much cleaner than any public toilets he had used in the States.

Buddy handled his business quickly and came back out, but Edna and the taxicab were gone.

*   *   *   *   *

"Who are you really?"

147

"What do you mean?" asked Sterling. He was grinning from ear to ear.

"I mean, how do you know where all of the truly romantic hideaways are in every city? Faith asked as they walked along the lake.

"I travel a lot, and I get lucky occasionally. It's just that simple, it's amazing, but I think that I'm blessed."

"That's what I used to say," Faith told him. "I haven't said it in a long time, but that was one of my favorite sayings."

They were seventeen miles away from the strip, walking along Lake Las Vegas, finding out that they had a lot in common.

"Tell me something personal, something that no one else knows about you," asked Faith.

"Well, let me see," Sterling considered the question. "I would say that I used to wet the bed, but that's not really a secret."

"You? That doesn't sound like you," she told him. "And, why isn't that a secret?"

"Well, first of all, what do people with weak bladders look like?" He asked her.

"I don't know," uttered Faith. "Older, I thought."

Sterling laughed and waved her off. "I was a kid," he told her. "And it's not a secret because my entire family knew. They even clowned me at family gatherings and holidays."

"Okay, then that doesn't count," agreed Faith.

"How about my shoe fetish?"

"You like women's feet?"

"Shoes," he corrected.

"You like their shoes?" Faith asked.

"Forget it," said Sterling. "I'm not confiding."

"Alright, alright," said Faith. "I don't understand, explain it to me."

"I like men's shoes," he told her. "I have owned close to three hundred pairs, myself."

"For real?" Asked Faith. She saw Sterling nod. "You're like a male African American, Imelda Marcos," joked Faith.

"Oh, you got jokes," he told her, giving her a little friendly push. "I've given many away to charity, though. I don't horde them like I used to."

"You can't clean the secret up," stated Faith. "Just leave it as it is."

"Cool," replied Sterling. "I was tired of talking about me anyway. Now, you tell me something."

"I have no secrets," replied Faith. "My life's an open book."

"Knock it off," he told her. "Everyone has secrets. It doesn't have to be the dark skeleton in the closet or the comedic 'I used to wet the bed.'"

"That wasn't funny," interjected Faith.

"Can I finish?" He asked her.

"Continue…" acquiesced Faith quietly.

"Okay, you can tell me an insecurity or an injustice that you suffered that no one knows about. Maybe another little girl gave you a knuckle sandwich in the third grade. But, no one saw it or felt it but you."

"A knuckle sandwich?" repeated Faith. She was giggling. "Well, there were these two girls, Leslie and her sister Rhonda, but Yvonne and I gave them knuckle sandwiches. So that's not it, right?"

"No."

Faith didn't really have any secrets she could think of at the moment. She had brought the game up. The suggestion to share had been hers. It was her turn and she felt obliged to speak about something.

"You know," she said, "There is something, but I don't necessarily look at it as an insecurity. To me it's more of a slight concern."

She was coming around, thought Sterling; trying to sugarcoat it. He didn't interrupt her.

"I have two beautiful children. And my immediate and distant family is great, but sometimes I do wonder about my soul mate or significant other. I'm not worried about becoming an old maid or any derogatory term like that. It's just thoughts, you know what I mean?"

"Yeah, I can relate," said Sterling. "I'm afraid of becoming an old man myself. But you know, getting back to you, I don't see you ever becoming anything like that. You're too intelligent. Honest and independent. Old maids didn't have those attributes. They were just older unmarried women who really didn't become mothers or anything else, career-wise. And, don't forget our other discussion," he reminded her; "about how the single people rule now!"

"Okay," replied Faith. "I'm sold, you're a great salesman. But I'm a little confused. What exactly are you selling?"

"Me," he confidently replied.

*   *   *   *   *

With nothing left to do, Buddy continued on his way to the eatery, where he was supposed to meet up with Hunt Rhinehart. He was very upset and worried about Edna, but he needed help.

When he got there he saw Edna sitting down, directly across from Hunt. She didn't look pained or upset, so this calmed him somewhat.

"What… what's wrong?" Edna asked as he approached her.

"Why'd you leave like that?" He asked her.

"It was the cab driver," she explained. "He didn't really understand that we wanted him to wait. So, he took off. By the time that I explained it to him, we were already here. I figured you'd follow."

Buddy nodded, with his heart rate slowing down.

"Mr. Rhinehart," he said, reaching out to shake the man's hand.

"You had a scare?" Hunt asked.

"Yeah," confessed Buddy, taking a seat next to Edna, as she rubbed on his shoulder.

"My phone!" Buddy suddenly remembered "I left it in the taxi."

"I know," Edna handed it to him. "I tried to call you and the damn thing started ringing on the seat next to me," she told him, laughing.

"You don't have a respirator?" Buddy asked, looking at Hunt, who was dressed in black slacks and a black shirt. His eyes looked…

thought Buddy. What was the word? He asked himself. Feral...yeah, that was the word.

"No, I've always taken my chances when out in the field," he told them both. "Besides, I checked out the National Institute for occupational Safety and Health. They advised me that those disposable paper-like masks are deceptive because they're being represented incorrectly."

"It's a barrier," said Edna. "Nothing's completely safe, but it may reduce transmission somewhat. It beats doing nothing at all. I like the fact that the people are informed and taking precautions."

"I doubt if the health and human services department would want to hear that," joined in Buddy. "Seeing how they just spent, or pledged to spend, close to thirty-five million dollars to stockpile these respirators in case of a full-fledged pandemic. The French were prepared," acknowledged Buddy. "They brought close to seven hundred million masks when avian flu first became a concern."

"Here." Edna reached into her bag and tossed a protective mask on the table in front of Hunt. "That's me and my Buddy's private stock. It's an N95 respirator. We use it while we're treating flu victims. It can block about ninety percent of all particles which measure 0.3 microns or larger. The influenza virus is miniscule, but not that small."

"Thanks," replied Hunt, picking the mask up and placing it in his pocket.

"Just be careful," added Buddy. "If you're wearing it and running down the street, the mask is resistant to fluids, but it can't handle airflow above the rate of eighty-five liters per minute. That's about ten miles per hour. So, if you have to pursue someone and they're running faster than that, I'd let them go."

"Duly noted," stated Hunt. Not even cracking a smile and no change in his poker face.

"Okay, *quid pro quo* time," he told them. "I don't have long, but I need to know what new developments you have. Then, I'll share mine."

Buddy was thoughtful, but only for a moment. Hunt knew something; or rather he knew that Buddy and Edna knew something; and it wasn't the information that had been picked up in Paris.

"We have the virus's genome," stated Buddy. "And, there's a woman that calls herself Rosa Klebb that states she was one of the architects of the virus. She's back in Atlanta, and contacted one of our colleagues, John Lovejoy. You met him."

"Yes, of course. Can he turn her over to me?"

"She contacted John by e-mail," said Buddy. "But, she refuses to come in. I believe that she is a Russian national."

"Okay," replied Hunt. "We'll see if we can track her down. Is that it?"

"Basically," replied Buddy. "If there's more, we haven't figured it out yet. We're here to assist and monitor the French situation, but somehow I don't think that you are here for the same reason."

A faint trace of a smile crossed Hunt's lips. It was very subtle, but Buddy saw it.

"Actually, I'm not," replied Hunt. "I'm here chasing down a lead. Recently, the French government detected an American mercenary entering their country. They didn't intercept him, or obstruct his entry, because at the time, they didn't have any cause for concern. But, after the outbreak, they lost track of the man and they notified our state department. It could be something, or it could be nothing. That's what I'm here to find out."

"Why would a mercenary be involved in something like this?" Buddy asked. Then, he remembered the billion dollar demands. "Forget I asked that," he said, before Hunt could respond. "But tell me this, why did he raise a red flag? And, you said he's American?"

"Yes, he's American," answered Hunt. "As to your red flag inquiry, since the days of Carlos the Jackal, the French have been on edge about mercenaries and men who kill for money."

"I'm not sure why this man was in the country." Hunt opening a dossier handed Buddy and Edna a photo each. "Have either of you seen this man before?"

"Can't say that I have," said Buddy.

"No," replied Edna firmly.

"He has connections within the United States," continued Hunt. "But we really don't know where. He drops off the radar quite often and pops back up occasionally. His name is Pete Carpenter and they call him *the Pistol*."

"You say that he was here in Paris recently?" Edna asked.

"Yes, we are certain of it."

"Do you know where he went or what he did?" Edna asked.

"The French tell me that he visited two small clubs, one called Pulp and the other, Le Paris, before that they lost him. And since I don't think he came all the way to Paris to visit a sweat box, I must assume that he went to these clubs with the intention of losing his tail."

"You're the expert," stated Buddy, probing, a bit. "So we have to defer to you, but tell me this -- How does a mercenary put together a team of scientists to mutate a gang of deadly viruses right up under the government's nose?"

"Negligence, I would imagine," answered Hunt. "I was summoned after the fact - my job is the clean-up. I don't do prevention. But since this is the only lead we have to go on at the moment, I'm following it until it proves incorrect. At this point, however, it has not. So I must treat this target as though he is the Nidus I am looking for. Do you follow me?" Hunt asked.

"Loud and clear," answered Buddy, thinking about the man's characterization of the mercenary as the seat of bacterial growth in a living cell.

CHAPTER 21

John had a sense of dread as he hurried down the street. He'd tested the ninety-year-old strain and compared it to the new and improved, manipulated mutation and he'd noted the similarities.

He needed to speak with Rosa again, so he e-mailed her. Three hours later, she got back to him and they set up a meet. This time, Rosa specified the High Museum of Art.

John went online to find out about the place. There he learned that they were having an exhibit through the summer that focused on the artwork of Annie Liebowitz. He enjoyed her work, so that was cool, he thought.

He got there half an hour early, so he waited out front for her after checking inside initially. It was hot outside and the exhibit was crowded. Many of the nation's photogenic were in attendance, but he didn't see Rosa among them.

Rosa Klebb had been preparing to return to her native Russia when she'd gotten the email from John.

Her first reaction was to ignore it and not reply, but her conscience wouldn't cooperate, not after reading and seeing the news reports about a new influenza strain that was slowly making its way around the country and abroad. She needs absolution, she told herself, before she could leave. All she could hope for was that the man from the CDC would give her this.

She was approximately a block away when she saw John, standing out in front of the museum, apparently waiting for her. Their eyes met, even from this long distance away, and he kept watching her as she brought her arm down and her body fell to the ground.

She's tripped, thought John. Instinctively he began to walk towards her. Several passersby stopped and attempted to help her back up. Rosa remained slumped on the pavement.

His heart began to race as he realized that she had injured herself. She wasn't a young woman, he figured her to be in her early fifties. John began to run towards her, pushing his way through the crowd.

"Excuse me, excuse me, I've got her," he told a short, heavy-set man that was kneeling over her. "Let me help." He placed his hand on her back and looked into her face. She appeared to be having a difficult time breathing, gasping for air.

"Rosa! Rosa, what is it?"

She began to choke, and coughed up a wad of blood. "I'm sorry" she managed to say, and died right there in John's hands.

Several people standing around got their cell phones out and called for help. Others snapped pictures. John was completely perplexed until he saw a large puddle of blood pool up beneath her. He moved her body slightly and saw that his hand was covered with blood.

"Help!" he involuntarily shouted. Realization had hit him. "Someone call the police!"

Someone had shot Rosa in her back, multiple times, John thought. On a crowded street, in the middle of the day and he nor anyone else had seen or heard a thing.

*   *   *   *   *

"It's just the truth," said Sterling. Too many people are afraid of being alone, so they settle for less."

"When they should hold out until they meet that special person that will appreciate them for who they are," replied Faith, repeating his exact words.

"That's correct. Tell the truth, doesn't it feel good when you're appreciated?" He asked her. "Not just by a significant other, but in any situation."

Faith nodded her head slowly. "But what happens if life passes you by while you're waiting for that special person?"

"Then it just passes you by," he told her. "What will you have really lost, if you have lived a good, loving and fruitful life?"

"Companionship?"

"I don't think so, friends and family are companions. It's all in how you look at things. If by chance, you don't connect with that special person that will appreciate you, know that you didn't settle for less. And you appreciated yourself enough not to."

This was Faith's kind of conversation, the kind she didn't get to have that often. Sterling took her mind off of the troubles of the world and she appreciated him right now, she thought.

They were sitting in a restaurant called Big Mama's Rib Shack and Soul Food, which was right off the beaten track, enjoying a fried chicken and baked macaroni and cheese meal.

"Look at this one," stated Faith, laughing and passing Sterling the menu, which he took and immediately began to read. The menu was full of short southern sayings, like *bon mots*, which were cracking Faith up. Since she'd finished eating, she continued to read the menu as Sterling finished up.

When he was done, he asked her, "Would you like to get a drink?"

"Alcohol?"

"Yeah," replied Sterling.

"No, I'm good. I don't need anything else."

Sterling didn't believe her, so he continued to look right at her. "What?"

"I wanted to ask you something else, but now I'm not sure."

Faith felt warm all over, so she knew that she didn't need any spirits. She felt like she was psychic and could read his mind.

"You want to offer me an indecent proposal?"

"That depends on your definition of indecent."

"Something immodest," said Faith. "Coming from your lips, it sounds sweet, but it's still scandalous."

"Is that a no?" He quietly asked her.

Faith licked her bottom lip and then she bit it a little. "I need to hear what it is that you want to do with me exactly?" She wasn't batting an eye.

"Nothing too outlandish," confided Sterling. "I simply want to touch you in all the right places."

*　　*　　*　　*　　*

After the shooting, Pete quickly crossed the street and doubled back. He placed the Hi-point nine millimeter in his pocket and proceeded up the block towards the crime scene with the crowd.

The researcher from the CDC was still sitting on the floor next to the dead Russian woman, but the police were here now, taking statements from a bunch of people.

Pete would have smiled to himself, for committing the perfect murder, had this been his first. But it was more like his twenty-first and he no longer took any real pleasure in it. It was just another contract honored. A person had to have honor, thought Pete. They must always keep their word. He'd offered his word to kill all four of the people who'd brought the deadly flu virus to life. That contract had been fulfilled. The Russian woman had been the last one.

Pete had been a hairsbreadth away from her when he had pumped four shots into her back. He always outfitted his guns with silencers. That enabled him to kill quietly and very discreetly, even in a crowded place.

The guy Lovejoy looked distraught, Pete thought. He was speaking with the police officers, pointing back towards the museum. Pete had walked right past him after the shooting. He walked so close to John as he'd run toward the woman, that he could have touched him.

Pete gripped the gun in his pocket. This was the last time that he would use it, provided he wasn't accosted while leaving.

It was now a throwaway; just like the Glock .40 caliber, he had used to kill the German and Chinese scientists who had worked with the Russian woman. The American hadn't been his problem; Moshe had taken care of that one.

Pete thought about how much he loved low budget firearms, because they were all over the streets. Once the ballistics had been run, the police would attribute her death to nothing more than an ordinary street shooting, regardless of what the researcher from the CDC said.

He turned his back on the scene, and walked away.

*   *   *   *   *

Sterling hadn't lied, Faith thought, as he touched and kissed and tickled her all over. *You're a greedy lover*, she whispered in his ear, as he pleasured her repeatedly.

Sterling nibbled on her ear. "That which we savor," he told her in between tender kisses, "we enjoy with great zest and zeal. I've thought about loving you from the moment I saw you."

"Loving? Or making love?"

"Tell me what the difference is?" Sterling rubbed and caressed her caramel skin.

"When you love something or someone," whispered Faith, breathing hard and trying to control their rhythm, "it takes a long time. But when you make love, the way we're doing right now, it can be over in a heartbeat."

Faith thought of the two of them as making love because she hated to think that their experience was cheap and something else. She loved his chest and the muscles in his arms and back. His tailored clothing hid all of this masculinity, as she felt him all over her lower extremities.

She was an eyeful, thought Sterling. "If we continue throughout the night," he asked her, "will I have proved to you that love and making love can sometimes be the same thing?"

"Just because you happen to be a good lover," Faith told him, "that doesn't change the definition of the words. It still is what it is."

"What about tomorrow? Will our code of conduct today affect our behavior tomorrow?"

"You just spoke about keeping me up all night, then you jump to what tomorrow will bring. Honestly, I don't know. But I'd like to finish savoring tonight."

CHAPTER 22

"That your only bag?" Buzz Shaw reached for Faith's globetrotter bag.

"Yes, that's it," replied Faith, tossing her light weight carry-on over her shoulder as they made their way out of Hartsfield-Jackson Airport.

"I'm sorry I wasn't able to connect with you in Las Vegas," Buzz told Faith. "I was busy chasing down a couple of leads."

"That's okay. Hopefully, you have learned more than me about this thing we're fighting."

"There were some developments." They stopped in front of a black Avalanche pickup truck. "This is mine right here." He waited for Faith to get settled in her seat. "So you didn't discover anything out there in the desert?"

"Not really," she remarked as Buzz started the vehicle up. "I just made a lot of observations."

Her mind drifted back to the heavenly view from the top of Sterling's hotel. The walk by the calm and serene lake. The delicious and humorous eatery. And, last, but not least, the sweet spot he had taken her to in the end.

As they drove, Faith noticed that Buzz was seething a bit. "Is there something wrong?"

"Several things, as a matter of fact," he told her." First of all, I thought we had more time, but this thing is out of control now. We can't contain the press coverage anymore. And we can't quarantine anyone quietly. Also, we had a lead on a woman, a foreign national who had direct dealings with Cimmerian. She helped the virus mature. She was shot and killed on her way to meet your colleague John Lovejoy."

"What! When was this?"

"Yesterday. She made contact with him previously - she'd given him the virus genome. Apparently, he had some further questions for her and she agreed to meet with him again. I wish he would have called me, I would have liked to bring her in, charge her with conspiracy and see what information she gave us then. Damn!" A car cut in front of them. "They killed her on a crowded street, right in front of Lovejoy and he didn't see a thing."

Faith listened wide-eyed, as the fake healthcare worker spoke about murder and placing people under arrest. He hadn't even asked her if she wanted to stop at her house first to drop her luggage off.

"I believe that everyone is waiting for us," stated Buzz. "Hunt picked your colleagues, the Defoe's, up from the airport earlier. From what I hear, Paris isn't as merry as it used to be."

Faith didn't speak to Buzz anymore on the ride over to the CDC. She was lost in her own thoughts, thinking about the information from all of the outbreaks that she had taken the time to review on the flight home.

Ten minutes later, she and Buzz Shaw were walking into a strategic meeting at the CDC called by Jules Marceau. He looked up as they entered the packed room.

"Ms. Millicent," stated the director. "Nice to have you back and thank you, Mr. Shaw, for retrieving my colleague. Will someone please bring Ms. Millicent up to speed?"

As Faith looked around, she counted forty people, including her team and Hunt Rhinehart. John nodded his head at her in a private greeting. So did Buddy, followed by a warm smile from Edna.

There was a large blackboard set up in the room. John stood in front of it, writing down formulae.

"We have the genetic makeup of the virus," he informed Faith.

Edna came over to sit next to Faith, providing her with documentation, as well as notes that she and Buddy had taken on their trip. There were also notes from John in the pile, which pertained to his studies, tests and conversations with the deceased Russian architect of the virus. Faith, with her passion for multitasking, had no problem reading listening and taking notes herself at the same time.

"Unfortunately," continued John, after he dissected the virus for them, "this thing was homespun by someone with an extensive knowledge of medicine. Yes, they brought in experts to perfect the viruses mutation, but that doesn't mean that they themselves didn't understand every procedure that was taking place."

"I would like to interject something at this point," Hunt interrupted. "We lost a woman the other day, as all of you are aware. She had pertinent information concerning this investigation. In the future, if any of you are contacted by an outside participant, please notify me at once. That way, sources and information won't be lost."

He stepped back over to the side of the room. It was obvious to Faith that the man was upset that the Russian woman had been killed. But his tone of voice and his words made Faith wonder if he was upset with John and the rest of them.

John caught the inference, but ignored it. He was there to fight the virus. It was someone else's job to do the police work.

"As you all know," continued John, "the strain from 1918 is a killer and no one born after 1930 is immune to it."

A young intern at the back of the room stood and spoke. "How do we know that this new virus didn't just escape out of some top secret pathogen storage government facility?"

"Because we're the only agency that keeps dangerous pathogens around." stated John, raising his voice. "If something was missing, we'd know, believe me. And stop watching the science fiction channel!"

Laughter erupted, easing up the tension, but only for a moment.

"There is a vaccine that thwarts this reconstructed virus, at least in mice, when taken along with antiviral drugs." Buddy spoke up. "But we don't know how well they'll perform in human subjects, or how well it could perform against this new strain. It's being tested right now, out in the field, but as you know, we have no containment."

"Did anyone consider that the Canadians could have let this thing loose?" asked a bioterrorism expert from the Federation of American Scientists.

"Please!" Jules had taken the floor. "We're not here to point fingers at legitimate nations or agencies. This is a brainstorming session, designed to come up with a counter-strike. Right now, our priority is combating this virus, not chasing down its maker."

"Why can't we do both?" asked Hunt. "I'm interested in thwarting the spread of the virus, but I'm also concerned about bringing the masterminds behind it to justice."

"That's what I'm trying to say," agreed the bio-terrorism expert. He was nearly shouting. "The Canadians were doing their own study on the 1918 strain!"

"Why don't we scientists and doctors let Mr. Shaw and Mr. Rhinehart handle that aspect of the investigation?" Jules asked calmly. "So that we can combat this silent killer? Those who plot and scheme will make noise. I'm sure they can be tracked down and brought to justice. But this virus, this plague, won't shout when it comes through, it won't even make a whisper. It could be here in this room right now, silently killing someone. So you tell me, which suspect do we make our priority to catch?"

Jules watched the magnitude of the situation register on everyone's face. "I need to know what drugs we have out there on the market or in production that will assist us."

Several people began to speak at once. The name Tamiflu was thrown out. Someone spoke of Pfizer, Merck and Bristol-Myers Squibb. For all of the drug hunters and scientists that worked high up in Ivory Towers, thought Hunt, and in centers of excellence, as they called their laboratories, not one concrete solution, treatment or drug seemed to be available.

He looked over at his colleague Buzz Shaw, who stood on the other side of the room with a smirk on his face. He was obviously thoroughly amused and it made Hunt angry.

"People!" Hunt shouted, quieting the room down. He was suddenly furious. "Is this what you all get paid for in here, to bicker and not solve a damn thing? Maybe after this thing is over, I'll see if I can get this industry some regulation. Because don't think I don't know that many of you are in bed with these pharmaceutical companies, benefiting from the unrestricted pricing of these drugs. Maybe I'll look into that next, see who the other conspirators are."

He stalked to the door, but stopped and tossed over his shoulder, "If any of us are still here tomorrow."

Buzz smiled and shook his head at all the perplexed faces.

"You have to excuse Mr. Rhinehart," he told them. "He has a problem with the way your industry cosseted and its costly research centers. He's learned a great deal about the industry that he didn't know prior to this case."

During the discussion and the outbursts, Faith had been finishing up; reading all of the notes and documentation Edna had given to her. She wanted to speak about the new drug Meyer-Burke had in the pipeline, but Hunt Rhinehart's statement about strange bedfellows gave her reservations that took her a minute to shake off.

"Sir?" she said, getting the director's attention. "May I have the floor? Before you sent me to Las Vegas, you asked us to check with big pharma's that we knew to see if there was anything in one of their pipelines."

"Yes?" She had Jules' attention now.

"Well, I recently had a conversation with a representative from Meyer-Burke Pharmaceuticals. He informed me about a drug they're working on over there. It's specifically designed to combat the 1918 influenza strain, but it also targets avian flu, SARS and several animal diseases -- the ones they anticipate may one day make the leap to human hosts, or conspire with a virus that infects human beings."

"Are you serious?" Jules sounded disbelieving; giving everyone in the room the impression that he felt what Faith was saying was too good to be true.

"Yes, Sir. I was just as surprised and shocked as you."

"Where did they get the inspiration for such a drug?" snapped Jules.

"From a study they conducted on the spread of viral diseases and the whitefly," answered Faith, shrugging her shoulders. "My point is, I've been informed that the drug shows potential. It began as a study in rhinoviruses and expanded to cover the rest. And it sounds like they're right on the money, in light of the information John received about how the virus was put together."

"Yes," agreed Jules. "It appears that way. But how far along are they?"

"They've completed all clinical trials and applied for a new drug application approval notice. I suspect they're also getting their scripts together to see which certificate holder will be entitled to what share of stock in the new drug, if it's all that they're saying."

"That may still put them a year or so out of the loop."

"I know," Faith nodded. "That's why they'd like us to put in a special recommendation with the FDA to fast track their drug, outlining the urgency."

"So, in essence," stated Jules, "they need a sponsor?"

"I guess so," said Faith. "I'll put my recommendation down."

"I'll endorse it," said John.

"Count us in," called out Edna and Buddy nodded.

"Yes," Jules told her. "But I'll need an expanded access protocol. We need to be able to get our hands on this miracle drug right now and run our own tests."

"That shouldn't be a problem, sir. I'll pass your request along."

"Good. Then if there nothing else, let's get to work, people." Jules, looking over at the door, noticed that Buzz Shaw was gone. He must have just slipped out, thought Jules. "And by the way, don't let what

Mr. Rhinehart said get you out of kilter because this is how progress is made. Brainstorming is how great minds glean their knowledge."

CHAPTER 23

During the course of the following week everyone was extremely busy, doing their jobs and assisting one another where help was needed. The recommendations were sent to the Food and Drug Administration. And a nationwide bulletin was put out for Pete Carpenter.

It wasn't an arrest warrant because, technically, they didn't have any proof to charge him with a crime. The notice was more of a detaining order.

Things held steady during the course of this week. Then the winds of change swept across the United States and all hell broke loose.

The new strain of influenza popped up in thirty-seven states and sixteen countries. The pandemic had begun.

*   *   *   *   *

"How bad it is?" asked Yvonne. "Can Jeff and I still travel?"

"Yvonne!" yelled Faith. "You just don't get it, do you?! People are dying, Yvonne. No one's traveling, unless they're in route to a hospital. You need to sit in the damn house and wait this thing out."

"Alright, calm down," Yvonne told her sister. "I only asked because I see people outside in the neighborhood and on the news."

"People are going out," agreed Faith. "Not everyone has the luxury of being able to work from home. Or be self-employed, but you and Jeff do. So you just stay there!"

"That's what I told her." Jeff's voice was no surprise to Faith; she'd suspected he was listening in. "But your sister's hardheaded."

"I know she is," agreed Faith. "But this isn't the time to be. You need to hold her butt down. Because if you let her run around and she brings that bug back home, you're done off too."

"But what can I really do?"

"Hold her, make love to her," suggested Faith. "I don't know - that's between you two. Just don't let her go out, unless it's absolutely necessary. And if you do, for god's sake stay away from crowds and wear the masks I gave you."

"Not a problem," stated Yvonne. "You made your point, but I hope you're happy because you're scaring me now."

"Good! Join the rest of the world." She hung up. Why couldn't Yvonne be more like Fanny? Their mother took instruction without any argument. All Faith had to say to her was, 'Mom if you do this, or such and such, it could have very detrimental consequences," and Fanny stopped going out. She told her friends to call on her in six months, after the first wave of the pandemic passed. She even told all delivery men to leave her packages at the curb; she'd get them when the air cleared. The fact that she was a retiree was significant. Still, Faith found herself considering that, if things got any worse, it might be a good idea to get the entire family together at one location. That way, everyone could look after each other.

"Mommy?" Kimberly interrupted Faith's thoughts. "We're not going outside again today?"

"No, dear," replied Faith. "Mommy will let you know when."

"Alright," said Kimberly, with her surgical mask dangling around her neck.

Faith had made it a game in the first days of the pandemic. She'd had the children wear their respirators all day, even though it was only her and them in the house. Faith wasn't taking any chances. She remembered Jules' remark about the silent killer sitting in the room amongst them. Faith didn't want to bring anything home to her kids.

She stocked up on respirators, the official ones and the cheap ones. The N95's were for when she left the house; the others were for in the house. She distributed the respirators and Tamiflu to her family and friends. And she was waiting for Sterling to get his company's drug to her, before it hit the shelves. The CDC had an expanded access protocol for it and was currently testing its compounds.

The miracle drug was called 'Trivium-1' and reminded Faith of the lower division of the seven liberal arts in medieval schools.

Grammar was one of them, which Faith felt fit. So much written work had to be submitted to get the drug pushed through.

The next was logic, which gave everyone hope. The drug's beneficial affect was no longer a proposition. It was now a godsend, accepted by most in the medical community as being in accordance with nature and logic. So, Faith felt good about that liberal art as well.

It was only the last one of the three that related to the drug's name that upset her and gave her pause. That one being rhetoric, only because she sincerely prayed that all of the acclaim the drug had been given, was not pretentious hyperbole. *If you take this, you'll never get sick again!* If she had a nickel for every time she'd heard that statement, Faith told herself, she and Oprah Winfrey would have the same accountant.

The children were watching her and she shook off her thoughts. "Who wants a sandwich? Ham or turkey?" Faith had her family living on the bare necessities, but she wasn't going to starve them.

"Mommy" yelled Kimberly. "There's a scary movie coming on, do you want to watch it?"

"If you and Mel want to," replied Faith, from the kitchen. It took her five full minutes to prepare three sandwiches and some iced tea. When she got back in the living room and handed the food out, the movie was in full swing. She was three bites into her sandwich when she recognized exactly what the children were watching and promptly lost her appetite.

It was an old film from 1971, one she'd seen back in school and had done a book report on: *The Andromeda Strain*. And it was about a small team of super-scientists chasing a virus that had come from outer space. They were in a race against time, trying to save the world from not only a killer pathogen, but from a nuclear war as well. There was nothing else to think or say, she told herself. Finally, it was a case of life imitating art.

* * * * *

"They say that a period of anestrus doesn't apply to human beings." Norton Burke spoke loudly and boisterously. "But I hadn't had sex for two years prior to them polemics changing the name of their drug from Sildenafil to Viagra. Now, I'm knocking down them working girls left and right."

Both Pete Carpenter and Sergio Moshe were present. Sterling could hear them laughing on the other side of the door. He waited another five seconds or so and then he knocked.

"Who is it?" asked Burke.

Sterling didn't answer. Instead, he turned the door knob and entered the room.

"What?" Burke snapped. "Does *who is it* sound like *come in* to you?"

Sterling walked further into the room with an angry look on his face. "You want me to go back out?" he snarled.

Burke, Moshe and Pete all wiped the smiles off of their faces. "No, you're here now, so what's up?" barked Burke.

"I just heard that the patent and approval by the FDA went through," stated Sterling.

"Yeah," replied Burke. He was smiling again, raising a glass of wine. "We're celebrating, you want a drink?"

"You're celebrating?" repeated Sterling. "What are you celebrating; the fact that women and children are dying?"

"No, we're celebrating my birthday!" Burke shouted sarcastically. "It's a little belated, but I didn't get a chance to celebrate back in April."

"That's funny," replied Sterling, cutting his eye at Moshe and then Pete. He knew he was about to tread on thin ice, but didn't care.

"You guys are a real piece of work," he told them. His voice was very cold. "I didn't sign up for mass murder."

"Quiet down!" Burke lowered his voice to almost a whisper. "What do you want to do, include the entire company in our talk?"

"People are dying, Burke!" Sterling shouted.

"You knew the risk!"

"No, I didn't. You told me you were going to bring in top scientists from Russia, China and Germany to perfect the strain, not make it even more deadly."

"That's what we did, but it mutated. What did you think that we could control it one hundred percent? Well, news flash! We can't! Resurrecting deadly viruses isn't an exact science. Am I upset that lives are being lost? Of course I am! But this is science and with science comes a degree of risk, casualty and now conscience. I feel bad, but 'Trivium 1' has been approved. I'll be able to help the people. Avian flu was coming, Sterling - it was just a matter of time. Those lunatics over at the CDC brought that 1918 Spanish Flu back from its final resting place. Sooner or later, it would have gotten out. Then what? The world would have been faced with repeating history."

"So, what's your point? By releasing it yourself, you're single-handedly saving the world? Is that what Meyer-Burke's great purpose is?"

"Sterling, I anticipate catastrophe, plague and disease. I'm good at it. That's why I'm in the business of cure. I'm trying to make the world a better place. Our drug will provide the world with a defense to the Avian Flu, SARS and the Spanish Flu. Mark my word, history won't forget us!"

"No, history won't and you better be correct, because history has a funny way of constantly being rewritten."

*   *   *   *   *

After Sterling left, Moshe turned to his boss.

"You want me to take care of him?"

"No," replied Burke. "What is he going to do? He's not going to tell anyone, he wants the money just like everyone else. He was in from the beginning, ever since he set his price of fifty million dollars. He knows the projections we have for Trivium 1. One hundred billion is a small number compared to its potential. He just has a weak stomach, but he'll be alright. Show him the extra security we have, that will calm him down."

"I saw him with that woman Faith Millicent in Washington, DC," Moshe said. "They seem to be real chummy."

"Is that so?" Burke was smiling. "I knew following and keeping our eye on the CDC would prove fruitful. Dangle her in his face also, that should touch his bleeding heart."

"Do you want me to see what the Russian woman told the black guy?" asked Pete. Moshe looked at him, wondering why he wasn't using Lovejoy's name.

"No," replied Burke. "She can't point a finger at us; the most she could have said was that someone named Cimmerian retained her to resurrect a virus. She only saw one face and it wasn't any of ours. So leave that alone. Not an oar points to us, so I say don't rock the boat."

CHAPTER 24

"Yes, for at least three months! All schools, daycare facilities, and anyplace where children congregate are under strict orders to remain closed for a period of at least three months."

Edna was on the phone with the state representative. She hung up and took her next call.

Edna was in charge of coordinating and enforcing the CDC's guidelines for the pandemic. It was her job to notify every state capitol, contact their representative and instruct them on the proper procedure needing to be followed. The bottom line was that all schools and community centers were closed. Anyone experiencing flu-like symptoms was asked to remain at home or face the chance of being forcibly confined under a civil commitment order. Justices across the country were issuing those orders by the hundreds, daily. They were running out of places to confine the people.

All large public gatherings were cancelled. All sporting events had been shut down. This had a major impact on the economy and the ramifications were being felt around the world.

China, Japan, the Middle East, Europe, Russia, Germany, France and Great Britain were all experiencing the same thing: Pandemonium, during the early weeks of the world wide pandemic.

Antiviral drugs, including Tamiflu, were being distributed worldwide. But it was like playing Russian roulette because the virus mutated and changed, depending on its host. The drugs were a gamble that might work for one person and not the next.

No one in the free world ventured out of their domicile without a respirator on their face. Crime skyrocketed; people went hungry, for fear of leaving their homes to obtain food. Sometimes the fear proved to be more fatal than the actual virus.

"Where's our help?" asked Edna, when Jules entered the office.

"I'm trying to get some more people to come in," he told her. "Ms. Millicent may have to come in from home. The work she's doing from there needs to be coordinated with us."

"She needs to be with her children, sir."

"I understand her situation," replied Jules. "But I have people calling in sick everyday; so either we bring the healthy people in or we let the ones with only a runny noses work. It's your choice."

*   *   *   *   *

"The odds are against us." John sounded bleak.

"I know," conceded Buddy, piloting the car. "But we still have to proceed."

They were on their way to a meeting with several health advocacy groups. The groups were getting together to coordinate their efforts, and get advice from the major health officials on how to best aid the indigent citizens of the nation by providing at least the bare necessities: food, water, a portable radio and a flashlight. Some medicine was also being distributed, but there was hardly enough to go around.

John glanced over at Buddy. They looked like a pair of emergency room doctors, he thought, dressed in scrubs and wearing N95 respirators, rushing towards a community in need of cardiopulmonary resuscitation.

*   *   *   *   *

"Hello?"

"What's up, Miss?" Faith heard Sterling's voice through the phone. "How are you doing?"

"Oh, hey!" replied Faith. She hadn't spoken to him since Las Vegas. "I'm good, I'm managing. Did you just call here, about twenty minutes ago?"

"Yeah, but no one answered. So I waited and thought I'd call back. Did you step out?"

"No, I was in the shower. My children are sleeping. I had a half-hour window before my next series of phone calls, so I decided to try and wash some stress, strife and worry off."

"Did it work?"

"Nope, but it was worth a try. I smell good," she added.

"I bet you do," replied Sterling, laughing.

"So how have you been?" Faith adjusted her bath towel. "I thought you forgot about me after sinning with me in Sin City."

"No, I don't think I'll ever do that. I've just been working hard and trying not to fall under the weather."

"You're not feeling sick?" asked Faith, concerned.

"No, I was talking emotionally."

"Is there anything that I can do?"

"Just pray for me," Sterling told her.

"Ok." That she could do, she thought, being that she and God were on a first name basis. "Do you want to talk about anything? Women like when men show their emotional side; hint, hint."

Sterling needed to laugh, because his heart felt like it weighed a ton. "Thanks for offering, but I don't want to really bring you down. I've just seen a whole lot in the last week, thats all."

"I can imagine," sighed Faith. "I've been indoors, so I haven't seen anything. And I stopped listening to the news because it's just too much."

"Yeah, I know. Yesterday, I found myself thinking about tautologies. Such as either things will get better tomorrow or they won't. And guess what?"

"What? Unable to guess, I'm listening."

"We got the letters patent, now we can move forward with getting the medication to the people."

"Sterling! That's great!" Faith's towel fell to the floor. "So it will be on the drugstore shelves within a week?"

"Tomorrow, if it's up to me," answered Sterling. "I just left the company's headquarters, where I spoke with the operational chief. He advised me that one hundred thousand treatments would be shipped to the CDC, Washington and The Department of Health and Human services; as well as several other grassroots organizations."

"Thanks, Sterling, really, I mean it. Thank you and tell everyone over at Meyer-Burke also." Sterling was very quiet. "Are you there?"

"Yeah, I'm here." He was trying to process her blind trust, to make sense of it. She sounded as if she might be weeping. "Are you ok? Are you crying?"

"Yeah, I'm okay." Faith wiped away a few solitary tears. "These are tears of joy. There's a difference, trust me or I wouldn't be standing here in my birthday suit doing it."

"You are special," feeling enchanted once again.

"Believe that," agreed Faith. "And you better not be talking special education," she added, laughing harder.

"No, special… like in there being only one of you and God breaking the mold once he was finished." It was her time to stay silent. "Faith, are you there?"

"I'm here."

"So, what happened? No witty rebuttal?"

"I was trying to think of one, but my heart got in the way."

"That's what usually happens during relationships like this," he told her. "The mind stalls and the heart take over. Hang on a minute, okay?"

Sterling was in the back of his apartment, but he'd heard something up front. Walking towards the front of his home, he could hear one of Faith's children, calling her: *Mommy!*

"Hold on one minute, Sterling, " stated Faith, as he got to the front of his apartment and his front door swung open. Sterling dropped the phone, and threw himself against the door, trying to push it closed. But it was too late. The intruder was already in, pushing the door against him, slamming it into him, knocking him to the floor. Then the intruder entered, closing the door behind him.

*   *   *   *   *

"Why are you naked, Mommy?"

"Mommy's towel fell." Faith bent and picked the towel up, wrapping it around herself. "Why are you so nosy?"

"I'm not nosy," Kimberly laughed, as Faith touched the tip of her daughter's nose in a friendly gesture.

"Yes you are." Faith picked the phone back up. "Sterling?" She waited a moment and then hung up. He probably hadn't heard her when she told him to hold on. He'll call back, she thought; if I'm really special.

"Mom, I'm hungry," said Kimberly. "But I don't want a sandwich."

"What do you want?"

"Cereal would be cool."

"What, you want to eat breakfast again?"

"Yeah, you said it was the most important meal of the day, so why can't we eat it twice?"

"Oh, you're a smart aleck?" Faith chased her daughter, running throughout the house. They woke Mel up, and he joined in on the shenanigans.

Faith had both of them pinned down on the floor and was tickling them when the phone rang again.

"Ok, ok," she said. "Let me answer the phone. We'll continue this later." Faith smiled, and fixed her towel. She figured it was Sterling calling back, anxious to finish their special conversation.

"Hello?"

"Ms. Millicent?" It wasn't Sterling. It was Jules Marceau.

*   *   *   *   *

"What are you doing?" Sterling was yelling, not much liking the high-pitched tone that his voice had suddenly taken on.

"Shut up." Moshe stepped directly on Sterling's chest with his right foot.

"Get off me!" Sterling was about to panic as he saw Moshe remove a large knife from a sheath hidden inside the black leather jacket that he wore. Sterling was holding on to Moshe's leg, around the ankle and shin, about to try and free himself from the floor. The shiny blade made him abruptly stop struggling.

"What's the matter?" The African mercenary sneered and bent down over Sterling and rubbed the blade across his face. "You only know how to handle pretty women?"

It was a very sharp knife. It cut him slightly, nicking as Moshe dragged it across his left cheek and around his left eye.

"Make me cut you," he whispered to Sterling, staring into his eyes. Moshe's eyes looked black as coal. Sterling lay very still. He didn't move, but his mind raced. Moshe was a highly skilled assassin. Sterling didn't think he could disarm him, not from the position he was in, laying on his back. He wondered if Moshe was even sane. The man was salivating from the mouth like a mad dog, allowing the drool to fall onto Sterling's face.

He wants me to move, jerk, or do something, Sterling kept telling himself. If I do that, he'll have his excuse to cut me. When Moshe saw that Sterling wasn't going to fight anymore, he wiped his mouth and placed a knee on Sterling's chest.

"I want to kill you," he told Sterling. "I am a murderer, you are not. Yet, you look at me daily with contempt in your eyes. Am I supposed to fear you? Or feel inferior to you? This is how most of you American blacks look at me."

Sterling stayed quiet.

"It is only your women that see the real black man underneath. Not you American men. I am a Kaffir," stated Moshe. "Do you know what that is?"

Sterling didn't answer him.

"It is a Bantu, but you probably thought that it was a curse word because of your American movies." There was contempt in Moshe's voice. "I've been asked to come here and explain the crude truth to you. You agreed to spread the plague for fifty million dollars. You were paid five million dollars up front. For fifty million dollars, you thought no blood would be shed?"

With a sudden movement of the knife, he cut Sterling below the chin.

"You don't have to do this, Moshe." Sterling's voice was tight. "I understand."

"Do you?" Moshe stared into his eyes. "Because if I have to come back and explain it again, we won't talk." Moshe didn't move away or get off of him, either. "If you make a big stinky over this, not only will I visit you, I will also visit your lady friend from the CDC and her two little ones."

Moshe moved his knee. Then he stood up and stepped away from him. He looked down at Sterling, lying on the floor, paralyzed by fear and anger. Moshe nodded. "Remember who it was that flew to all of the cities, where the outbreak occurred. Then think about who the authorities will believe. Who was the most instrumental in getting our plague out there, to the masses?"

He dropped a scroll on the floor beside Sterling and walked back towards the door. He was gone a minute later, leaving as quietly as he had come.

Once he was gone, Sterling began to function a little. He sat up and placed his back against a nearby wall and picked up the papers that Moshe left. He pulled the rubber band off and rolled the papers down, so that they were straight and readable.

It was his itinerary from Meyer-Burke, the one that showed all the trips he had taken during the past three years. It was five pages long and very detailed. Also attached to that were several flight manifests confirming he did actually travel to the places highlighted in the itinerary.

Not every place on it was a place that Meyer-Burke had released their super Rhinovirus slash influenza bug, but most were. They were showing him that if push came to shove, they were prepared to place all of the weight on him.

That was why Moshe hadn't just killed him, he thought. They were saving him in case they needed a fall guy. Sterling sat back and began to bang his head against the wall. *You idiot*, he thought. He had ruined his life. Not the best life, but a damn good one. And it was all over money. Money he didn't even really need.

CHAPTER 25

"Mr. Burke?" His receptionist's voice sounded through the intercom. "There's a man here to see you by the name of Hunt Rhinehart."

"Tell him that I'm in a meeting," Norton Burke told her, as his office door burst open. "What's the meaning of this?"

"I'll only be a minute." Hunt looking around the huge office, which was empty except for Norton Burke and some very expensive furniture. "Telephone conference?"

"What?" Burke, seriously confused, wasn't following him.

"Your meeting, is it over?"

Burke didn't answer the man, but he did stand up.

"I'll have to ask you to leave," stated Norton Burke, walking out from behind his desk and over to Hunt. "Who are you, anyway?"

"I'm here on official business by authority of Homeland Security, The Federal Bureau of Investigation, you name the agency," Hunt told him, "and I am here by their authority."

"What is this some kind of a joke? What do you want with me?"

"Nothing," replied Hunt. The little man, he thought, was behaving very nervously and downright belligerent. "I just need to ask you about a man that is employed by you. We're interested in an ex-mercenary named Pete Carpenter - white male, forty-five years old, six-feet tall and goes by the nickname 'Pistol'."

"Doesn't ring a bell," stated Norton Burke. "Is that it?"

Hunt stared at the man and suddenly got a revelation.

"Yeah, that's it." He walked back towards the door and stopped at the threshold and turned back, meeting Burke's eye. "By the way, I heard about the new vaccine and treatment. Congratulations."

"Thank you", replied Burke. He was anxious for Hunt to leave so he could call Crossbones, a critical contact of his.

"How is it that you had the perfect compound in the pipeline to combat this plague?"

Hunt's question caught Norton Burke off guard, but only momentarily. "Catastrophe, plague and disease is my business, Mr. Rhinehart. I anticipate these pestilences, so I stay with something in the pipeline to combat them. It just so happened that this one made the jump to human beings faster than anticipated. But I'm on it now, so I guess you could say that in a lot of ways, we got lucky."

"That's what I thought," Hunt told him. "Thanks for your time and cooperation."

The moment the door snapped shut behind Hunt, Burke ran to the phone. He needed to call Pete and tell him that the authorities were looking for him. And he needed to call his ace in the hole and let him know that a clean-up might be in order. Crossbones would know what to do.

*   *   *   *   *

Out in the hallway, Hunt waited for the elevator, he went over his conversation with Norton Burke in his head.

Norton Burke had lied about not knowing Pete Carpenter. The New York Bureau of the FBI had called Hunt once they matched Pete Carpenter to the all-points bulletin that Hunt had put out. Carpenter was closely affiliated with Meyer-Burke Pharmaceuticals,

Hunt was told. That's why he had flown out to New York in the first place. Lying about that had been Norton Burke's first mistake, thought Hunt, as the elevator came and he got on.

Next, Burke had gotten very nervous and never asked to see any identification. Why? Because he had anticipated Federal Agents coming to speak with him sooner or later, Hunt told himself.

The last thing Norton Burke did was remember and repeat Hunt's last name after only being told it once prior, over an inaudible phone system that Hunt could barely understand. *Rhinehart* was not a common name.

Norton Burke didn't have to ask his name twice either because he already knew it, or had at the very least heard it before. The elevator door opened in the lobby and standing right there in the building's vestibule was Pete Carpenter, waiting to board the elevator to go up to the office, thought Hunt, as he stared at the man.

"Mr. Carpenter? Mr. Peter Carpenter?"

That got the man's attention. They locked eyes for a brief second. A moment later, Pete Carpenter pushed a woman standing next to him toward Hunt and ran.

"Ah!" yelled the woman as she slammed up against Hunt. Hunt steadied the woman and took out his firearm. He sprinted through the lobby and headed outside. He didn't like Manhattan's streets for hot pursuits.

Carpenter had about half a block distance on Hunt, who began to run down the block at top speed. Carpenter looked back several times, and then he reached a corner and turned. Still sprinting, Hunt reached the corner and almost ran into a barrage of gun fire.

Two pedestrians walking by were hit and immediately dropped to the ground. Hunt ducked down himself, looking down the block.

This *son-of-a-bitch*, Hunt thought. Carpenter had just shot and killed a middle-aged man and injured a woman. Pete fired two more times, and then fled down the midtown street.

Hunt jumped up and chased after him. He was tempted to return fire, but he couldn't risk hitting an innocent bystander. Up ahead, Pete ran smack into a uniformed policeman.

Hunt smiled as he gained on him. "Hold him right there!" He yelled, pointing his firearm at Pete. Pete managed to swing the dazed and confused policeman in front of himself and put his own gun to the policeman's head.

"I'll kill him!" Pete yelled. "You better back up!"

"What is the story with you guys?" Hunt asked. He had his gun aimed at Pete's head, and he was continuing to approach. "Why does everything have to be a matter of life and death? All I wanted to do was talk!" He told Pete, who looked wide-eyed and extremely desperate at the moment.

Hunt glanced at the police officer who couldn't have been any more than twenty-three or twenty-four years old. Probably a rookie, he thought.

Pete held the Austrian-made Glock .40-caliber pistol. Hunt would recognize that make and model in the dark. He'd killed many men who carried it.

Hunt's gun was also a .40 caliber, but his was made by Smith and Wesson as part of the American Pride series. Hunt trusted in that, as he squeezed off two shots.

The first shot hit the police officer in the arm and traveled straight through him. It tore into Pete Carpenter's chest and lodged an inch away from his heart. The second shot hit Pete in the neck. He dropped his gun and fell.

"You shot me, you shot me!" screamed the panic-stricken police officer.

Hunt walked over and kicked Pete's gun away.

"My God, you shot me, and killed him!" The officer stated.

"I'm a federal agent. I did not want him to kill you." He went through Pete's pockets for any clues that would explain Pete's actions. He found another gun on him and two full clips. There were several thousand dollars, two passports in different names and a phone book. Hunt stood up as several police officers approached him with their guns drawn.

"I'm a federal agent." He put his own gun away and looked down at the police officer he had shot. The police officer looked furious.

"Tell me something... are you, left or right handed?" Hunt asked.

CHAPTER 26

By the time Faith got down to the CDC, the press conference had begun and was in full swing.

The director of the influenza division at the CDC had deemed it necessary and crucial that they hold a press conference and address public concerns. There had been a rash of melee-like situations all over the country, at first thought to be the conduct of the nation's mentally deficient. But, as it turned out, these were the country's ordinary citizens: the professionals, blue collar workers, and lower economic work force. They were afraid and looking for answers.

It was happening everywhere: in China, Germany and Africa. That was surprising; the world thought these countries were used to plague, but there had been mass rioting and many deaths as a direct result of the world wide pandemic. The United States was hell-bent on not letting the situation get out of control like that.

"Ms. Millicent." Buzz Shaw greeting Faith, as she exited her vehicle. "Nice to see you again; I'm glad you're here. I was worried about you." Faith locked up her truck and turned to greet him. "I thought you might have taken ill," he added.

"No, I'm fine, how are you?"

"I'm great," affirmed Buzz. "Everyone's up at the podium, the director is addressing the media now. I'll escort you up - the crowd has been a little unruly at times."

She saw people standing around everywhere -- on the top of parked cars, hanging out of city bus windows that had parked near the center, all hoping to get information. There were even empty sleeping bags scattered all around the place.

"What's this?" Faith asked, pointing to about a dozen bags that were lying on the floor in a row.

"Oh, the people have been sleeping out here, night and day hoping to get their hands on some medicine. It's been the same way outside of most hospitals and health care facilities. Last night alone, once the temperature dropped, there were ninety reported fatalities - hypothermia."

Faith nodded, acknowledging what he said. She had seen many people sleeping in the streets as she drove around collecting her family and dropping everyone off at her mother's house earlier in the day. She had asked them to wait out the storm there, together. But, she hadn't attributed what she saw to despair. No, for some strange reason, she had incorrectly assumed these people to be the nation's homeless and she had said a silent prayer for them.

The director was still speaking when Faith got up front and onto the podium. She and Buzz took their seats and tuned into what Jules was saying.

"Please, allow me to address one question at a time. You… ma'am, in the pink shirt. Your question was…?"

"Why is the public being forced to go at it alone?" The woman asked. "And why isn't there one media station that has constant coverage and updates?"

"No one wishes for the public to be uninformed. This is why we are holding this conference. As you know, the first wave of this pandemic caught us by surprise. So, we had to go it without vaccines and without an adequate supply of antiviral medication. But a new treatment has been approved and is currently being distributed. It is called Trivium 1, you can find it at local drug stores. Your healthcare provider should have it and area hospitals too. If you are currently feeling ill and have not had any form of treatment, you can sign up for treatment at any one of the white medical trucks that you see parked outside and driving throughout the community. On behalf of the United States Government, we apologize and we are regretful for not having a more comprehensive plan in place."

"But-"

Jules raised his voice. "Then there has been much talk of a nascent pandemic. But no government can truly anticipate what such a pandemic will bring, or the exact makeup of the pathogen. We anticipated it to be something similar to the avian flu, and we prepared for that. But it mutated and we had to go back to the drawing board. Our friends in the international community are looking to us to set an example. Therefore, I ask everyone to maintain a degree of civility."

He held up a hand and cleared his throat.

"Also, about the media keeping America informed. I believe that as we speak, most news stations are backed up and running at half staff, or will be by the end of the week. Newspapers, radio, periodicals and broadcast media on television were just as affected by this pandemic as any other business that had to rely on people to run its operation. Most of these businesses became hot zones very quickly due to the large volume of people that pass through them. So, many crucial positions were affected. Most companies suffered a sixty percent drop in their work force. Certain specialty services and functions were irreplaceable. Again, I apologize on behalf of these institutions. Next question, please." Jules pointed to a tall African American man.

"From my understanding, many of the country's foreign suppliers have been paralyzed. What is being done to fill this void, and will this have a long-term impact on the nation's economy?" stated the gentleman.

"Yes, of course many foreign suppliers as well as domestic manufacturers have been affected by the recent turn of events. I believe that once treatment is made widely available, as it soon will be, the goods and services that require transport will be up and running. As far as long-term economic fallout is concerned, right now my concern is on care for those that need treatment. Economics, I believe, can wait; next question?"

"What is the situation with power, water, and sanitation services?" an angry gentleman asked.

"Services are being brought back to working order as we speak," stated Jules, pointing to another person.

The conference went on for two hours with Faith's present, and it had begun an hour before she arrived. But, Jules didn't get winded or stumble on one question. He did, however, bring out experts in the various fields of social services to address different community needs. Every expert's contribution to the information pool was always followed by Jules, bringing it back to the fact that the proper treatment was now available. That was the only answer that seemed to calm the masses.

Every major network that was up and running carried the conference. The Internet was also abuzz, as well as blogs and many social networking sites that had been operating as media sources from the very beginning.

"My husband is missing!" shouted a woman. "He was sick and they took him away!"

Her voice rang out over everyone else's, forcing Jules to comment.

"Ma'am, I don't understand," he told the woman. "Could you explain, please? Who took him away?"

"May I?" asked Buddy, stepping up to the microphone and relieving the director.

"He got sick at the airport coming back from a business trip." The woman had tears in her eyes.

"Ma'am, my name is Buddy Defoe and I'm with the Centers for Disease Control and Prevention. I've been fielding similar questions all week from concerned loved ones about the nation's quarantine procedures. If your husband was ill at the airport, coming in on a flight from overseas, he was most likely detained and placed in involuntary quarantine. You can call the airport that he flew back in on - they'll give you the number of their quarantine facility.

There are over seventeen airports inside United States borders that have quarantine programs. If your husband was detained at one of these airports, they'll have a record of this. Now, I understand that for many of you out here a lot of our answers have been very uncomfortable ones. But believe me, your questions and the last several weeks have been equally uncomfortable for us. We are here to help and assist you however and wherever we can. So, please take that into account.

Buddy did a good job; quelling the crowd, thought Faith, as she watched the director take a phone call, then quietly slip away. The government was forcibly isolating the sick, but Buddy didn't make it sound that bad.

Someone asked about the Pandemic Severity Index and how it classified the number of fatalities. John stepped up at that point, to articulate a response that would be both sensitive to the delicate issue and informative.

He began by saying, "A flu pandemic today is rated in very much the same way that we rate a hurricane…"

*   *   *   *   *

When the first contingent of federal officers swept into the headquarters of Meyer-Burke, the security officers in the lobby thought, *Whoa!* When the next wave entered the building, it felt like a tropical cyclone.

"What's happening?" asked one of the pharmaceuticals officers.

"We have a federal warrant," stated Hunt, leading the pack. "For all records, data and patents owned by Meyer-Burke. Please comply and don't obstruct these men."

Hunt took five officers up stairs with him to Norton Burke's office.

He didn't need that many officers, but he did this for effect. He had brought one hundred and fifty officers for the raid.

Hunt was convinced that there was something nefarious going on within the upper echelon of Meyer-Burke. He just didn't know what it was.

For the second time in one day, he burst into Norton Burke's office.

"Gentlemen!" stated Hunt. "Let me see some identification." He is looking at the angry African man sitting across from Norton Burke.

"What now, officer?" asked Norton Burke.

"I need all of your company's records, patents and ledgers," Hunt told him. "Along with your employee records and phone records."

"What is this about? asked Burke. "Did one of our drugs harm someone?" He asked Hunt sarcastically. "If so, there are other channels, you know. Besides, the FDA cleared all of our drugs. We went through their gold standard on each one of them."

"That's good to know," Hunt shrugged. "You shouldn't have anything to worry about in the records department. But, then there is the matter of the dead mercenary two blocks up."

*　　*　　*　　*　　*

Hunt didn't have anything substantial on Meyer-Burke as a company. Or on Norton Burke, the pharmaceutical giant's Chief Execute Officer, personally; nothing more than a hunch. He could have charged Burke with obstructing justice and lying to a federal agent, but, that charge was too small in his opinion. Burke had lied about knowing Pete Carpenter, but Hunt felt like there was something much bigger going on. The math was simple.

The extortion letters from Cimmerian had suddenly stopped. And, the plague that had been Cimmerian's bargaining tool had been released around the globe.

Then, within a month, Meyer-Burke had developed a successful treatment plan and vaccine. Shares in Meyer-Burke had skyrocketed one hundred percent. The company made several billion dollars in one day. No one was that lucky, thought Hunt. No one!

"Sergio Moshe." Hunt reading the African man's identification once more before handing it back. "May I ask you in what capacity do you operate here?"

"I am a consultant," stated Moshe.

"On what?" Hunt was ready to bet dollars to donuts that it wasn't medicine. Even just sitting there, the man had a distinctly military aura and an aggressive disposition.

"Security," answered Moshe.

"That's what I thought," replied Hunt, looking up in the corner at a small camera. Where are the tapes for that video monitor?" he asked Burke, who suddenly seemed dumbstruck.

"We destroy the tapes daily if they're not needed," he informed Hunt.

"I'll take today's, then," stated Hunt and smiled.

CHAPTER 27

Faith, wanting to address the crowd, decided to go up after Edna.

"Isn't it true that the major drug companies have a cure for the common cold?" asked a short, heavy-set man. "But they won't release it because then they couldn't make billions of dollars every year?"

"A cure?" questioned Edna, not knowing how to answer that inquiry.

"A vaccine!" shouted the man. "Don't play stupid! That can prevent a person from ever catching cold!"

Several security officers looked at Edna to see if she wanted them to remove the man, but she wasn't ruffled by his comments. She didn't take his anger personally.

"Sir, not that I know of; obviously you are more informed than me," she advised him, just as Faith's cell phone rang.

"Hello?"

"Faith," stated her mother. "Listen, we had to call an ambulance because he just would not stop coughing."

"Mom, what are you talking about?" asked Faith. Her heart was slamming against her chest. "Who wouldn't stop coughing?"

"Mel," answered Fanny, clearly distraught and crying.

Faith stood up so abruptly that she knocked her pocketbook from her lap sending the contents tumbling across the floor.

"What happened to Mel, Mommy!" she yelled over the phone. "Tell me again, slowly?"

Edna stopped speaking and the entire front row of the crowd followed Faith's voice. Edna's glanced over at Faith as Buzz began to gather the contents of her purse.

"He went outside, but only for a half an hour. He didn't play with anybody; he just wanted to sit in front of the house."

"And, you let him mommy!" screamed Faith. As tears began to roll down her face, she tried to control her voice. "Where...what hospital did they take him to?"

"Grady Memorial Hospital; Yvonne and Jeff went with them."

Faith hangs up on her mother and took her pocketbook from Buzz. Edna looked over at her about to ask her if she still wanted to address the crowd, but Faith was already running, headed the other way, away from the podium and toward the parking lot.

*　*　*　*　*

Faith cried all the way to the hospital. On the way there, Sterling called her and she couldn't even speak.

"What's the matter?" he asked her; and waited almost a full minute for her to compose herself enough to tell him.

"They had to take Mel to Grady Memorial. I think he's caught the flu."

At the hospital, Faith brushed past her sister and Jeff. She was in no mood to hear their explanations for letting her son go outside.

"Faith, he's in room three-eleven," stated Yvonne. We..."

Faith kept walking. She caught the elevator and went up to his room. There was a doctor in Mel's room and a nurse. Both wore protective masks like her baby had the plague, Faith thought. They even had a mask over Mel's mouth and nose.

"What's happening?" asked Faith.

"Who are you, ma'am?" asked the doctor.

"I'm his mother, my name's Faith Millicent; I work for the Centers for Disease Control. What is happening with my son?"

"We have to run some tests. We don't know as of yet what your son's condition is. All we know is that he was having a coughing attack and trouble breathing. Has he been vaccinated for the flu?"

"Yes," replied Faith, wiping several tears away from her cheek as she looked at Mel. "He received an inoculation several weeks ago."

"It may be nothing, ma'am." The doctor got a good look at Faith's face. She didn't want a placebo; she wanted the truth. "We'll run the tests and let you know as soon as possible. My name is Dr. Klein. I will be right here with your son, but you cannot wait in this room." Faith looked as if she was about to refuse to leave.

"If you don't leave, Ms. Millicent, they may try and quarantine your son. We don't want that, so please just wait outside in the waiting area. He's been sedated to suppress his cough and relax his respiratory tract. There's nothing you can do for him in here that can't be done out in the waiting area."

Faith was no fool; she knew what he was saying. He was telling her to pray. Faith went back downstairs to the waiting area and found a quiet corner.

Yvonne saw her come back down, but didn't approach her. She had never seen such hurt on her sister's face and was very afraid. Faith, Yvonne and Jeff all sat down in the waiting area, with a dozen or so other people, none of whom were talking.

Faith didn't waste any time, following Dr. Klein's subtle suggestion, as she silently requested counsel with her Dear Friend.

*   *   *   *   *

John saw the urgent way in which Faith left the news conference and wondered where she was off to. Buzz Shaw had followed her and come back with some information.

"It seems that her kid is sick." Buzz said matter-of-factly as he spoke to Edna and Buddy. "She's over at Grady."

John left the podium, but not before rolling his eyes at Buzz Shaw. He headed back to the Center and took the elevator upstairs.

He needed to ask the director if it would be all right if he went over to the hospital to check on Faith.

Jules was in the office with his back to the closed door. He was on the phone.

"Did he mention my name?" asked Jules.

"Why would he mention your name?" Norton Burke replied. "He doesn't know anything, not yet. He stumbled across Pete and got curious. So, he came here to investigate. Pete panicked and got himself killed. End of that part of the story. Pete's death doesn't bring Mr. Rhinehart any closer to the truth. He's still at square one and my company's records are impeccable. If anything, they will question how we remain on the cutting-edge of everything."

"Yes, from me. That's the part I am worried about, Burke. I've given you classified information, not for monetary gain, but for the greater good of humanity."

"Oh, please," interjected Burke. "If that's what you believe, why didn't you ever return my funds?"

"That was just extra compensation. A man must have money in order to live, to do the other things that must be done. It is an enabler, but not the basis or motive for my actions."

John listened to the conversation from just outside the office. He could hear both parties because the director had the call on speakerphone; as if it was an ordinary conference call.

"At this point Jules, it really doesn't matter. I've called you out of professional courtesy; you and I have been co-partners for a long time."

"Yes, too long. You are a greedy man, Burke, with no sense of morality. You don't care who you hurt in order to get your way. I didn't realize that when I formed this union."

"Whose fault is that?" asked Burke, looking at Moshe, who sat there listening with a smirk on his face.

"The devil is in the details," stated Burke, as if that statement said it all. "You have to do your homework. Maybe step out of that Never-Never Land that you live in and smell the compounds that are all around you. Now, I've given you this information and not so you can become a nervous Nellie, you pompous idiot!"

Jules was speechless, but only for a moment. "Listen to me you pond scum!" He said. "I told you to keep me *au courant* about everything, not just the back end. If I find out that you had any part, a hand or finger, in spreading this plague, or the blackmail, extortion, of this government, whatever you wish to call this Cimmerian mess, you won't reap one nickel of your rewards for your miracle drug. I'll go to the authorities on you, Burke! Do you hear me!"

"Yes, I hear you, old friend," replied Burke. "Regretfully, I do. I don't know why you think of me as a monster of mega-disaster proportions. I'm just a businessman whose business isn't death. I have merchants for that," warned Burke, leaving the word death off of the word merchant. He understood that Jules Marceau knew exactly what he meant. "I told you that I had nothing to do with the spread of any plague, that's the truth. And, the other thing, the extortion attempt? That's news to me. I never attempt anything, let alone extortion, it's too petty. Why extort, when you can extirpate? Are you listening to me, you fool? That's what I will do to you, destroy you and rip your life apart at the roots if you cross me!"

"You're dirt," replied Jules. "And, you don't scare me! I won't be a part of your dirty politics anymore! Now do you hear me?"

"I heard you before you even said it," replied Burke and hung up.

Jules picked up a drink that sat at the edge of his desk with a shaking hand and took a sip. Then he heard his office door open and he turned around. Standing there was John Lovejoy, with the most peculiar look on his face.

"What have you done," asked John?"

*   *   *   *   *

"I believe that the little Frenchman has become undone." Norton Burke was shaking his head. "I fear that, now he must be taken out of the equation."

"That's not a problem," replied Moshe. "Who else?" he asked, ready and willing to commit multiple murders, if need be.

Pete "The Pistol" Carpenter was no longer among the living. As Moshe saw it, his share of the money was now his since Norton Burke had no one else to put in his grunt work. His ace in the hole couldn't play the front line, not at this point in the game. Moshe was his only go-to man.

"What do you mean, who else?" Burke asked.

"Just what I said," replied Moshe. "I am not going to prison in this country, it stinks!"

"No one is going to prison," snapped Burke.

"That's not what the Federal Agent that was here thinks," countered Moshe. "I say we kill him also, and everyone else who poses a threat."

"Are you mad? We can't kill that federal officer!" Burke exclaimed. "It's too hot for that now. We're just going to tie up loose ends and that's it! Someone was trying to extort the Federal government. A terrorist, that's who the Federal government is chasing, that has nothing to do with us. We spread the virus, we created it. But someone jumped on the bandwagon and tried to squeeze some money out of the government. I don't know how and I don't know who. God damn capitalism! It has nothing to do with us!"

"If you say so," replied Moshe, staring straight ahead, calm, cool and reserved.

* * * * *

"I heard you," stated John.

"What?" Jules repeated for the third time, looking at John bewildered.

"Don't deny it. I heard you. What is exactly going on?"

The director set his glass down. He'd been trying to calm his nerves, but at this point, it wouldn't do him any good.

"It isn't how it may seem," he told John.

"So, how is it?" John asked. He was waiting for an explanation.

"I was trying to help humanity," stated the director. "But, things went awry."

"Don't give me that best-laid plans crap!" John raised his voice sarcastically, mocking the director's diction. He was shaking. "Even the best-laid plans can go askew? Who do you think you are; some kind of modern-day Aesculapius?!"

Although Jules was French, he knew of Roman mythology and he recognized the name of their God who provided medicine and healing.

"No, he replied in a low voice. I don't. I am a Poilu, a front line soldier and I always have been."

"This isn't a war, Jules. People didn't have to die."

"Oh, but it is a war," countered Jules. "It has always been. Since the beginning of time, both organisms; human life and pathogens, have always battled. And, both have always died."

"You're crazy," stated John. "This is your justification?"

"Would you have rather I left it up to the survival of the fittest?" Jules asked. "I remain stalwart in my convictions. Charles Darwin was wrong. Natural selection would have allowed pestilence to wipe us out. They adapt to all conditions better than us."

"Jules," John was gritting his teeth. "What are you babbling about? We're at a category four on the severity index; close to one and a half million people worldwide have died. Are you insane? If we go up one more category, we'll be at the highest!"

"I had no hand in that, none whatsoever! So, don't attempt to captiously trap me. I admit that I bear some fault because I may have known how the pathogen spread from susceptible host to susceptible host. But, that doesn't make me culpable - this is how medicine has always been practiced in your country. Have you forgotten the Tuskegee syphilis experiment? I hope not, you being a black man!"

"Don't even try it!" snapped John. "Don't play the race card on this one. You're not qualified to go that route. And, don't try to distance yourself from guilt. You're caught in the crosshairs on this one, Jules. You knew the viruses' port of entry when Faith and I were first investigating it, and that was before tens of thousands died. You knew its transportation system and its reservoir!"

"I also assisted in identifying its port of exit," defended Jules. "Don't leave that part out!"

"Oh no," replied John. "You get no accolades for that. You were a part of its chain of infection! All this time that I have been working here, I thought you were laudable, but you're not. You're far from it!"

"Don't make a knee-jerk decision on this one," offered Jules. He wasn't pleading with John, nor was he demanding his cooperation.

"Don't you try and manipulate the facts," yelled John. "Faith's son has taken ill! Do you have any extra Trivium 1 around for him?" John asked sarcastically.

Jules couldn't say anything because he knew that no words would suffice. All he could manage was a low whisper, barely audible. It sounded like the Irish swear word "begorra."

"Yeah, by God," repeated John. "You need to say more than that; how much of that one billion in extortion money was coming to you?"

"I had no part in that! I didn't give Meyer-Burke any information for monetary compensation." Jules stated.

"Yeah, I heard you tell your co-conspirator that, but I don't believe it."

"That's because you believe the truth, you are misrepresenting the facts."

"Which are...?"

"A billion people were at risk." Jules was pacing now. "A billion people, but not in this country because it is one of the richest, and not in my homeland because we have resources as well. But, in the developing world: Asia, where the Avian Flu and SARS originated, had the potential for catastrophic devastation and what about Africa? Look at what is going on over there, from plague to famine...." He paused for a moment. "...to genocide," added Jules. "Some kind of measure needed to be taken. Doctors, scientists and learned minds claim to be trying it all. But, are they, I ask you? I don't think so. The only time you see a government intervene in a nation's troubles is after there has been a considerable loss of life, or where this is some benefit for the intervening government. No one aids another altruistically."

"But, you do?" questioned John.

"I tried", answered Jules. "That is all a man can do, is try. What about you? Have you tried? Did you speak out about Darfur or Rwanda? Will you speak out tomorrow when people of that continent begin to die by the millions because they can't afford the lifesaving medications that we have? I will. I always have. Or, will you wait until others make it politically correct to speak about? By then it will be too late. Right now the powers that be have a devil-may-care attitude. I don't wish to be cavalier, or even laudable, but I cannot stand by and do nothing in the face of such suffering while others sit back eating caviar and getting fat."

"Jules..."

"Governments turn a blind eye, I won't!" Jules ignored him. "What do you suppose they do at their leisure? Pray for the less fortunate? Give pennies when dollars are needed? Hope that viruses will fall into agenesis? Can you truly not see why I had to take action?" He had recognized a glimpse of understanding in John's eyes and spoke urgently.

"Everyone in government right now is talking bureaucrat-ese, nonsense and drivel. They do things in dribs and drabs. That won't work for the needy, it won't save a life. Not one! I haven't done the unthinkable, as you might believe, and neither has Meyer-Burke. The chief executive officer and me, we have a relationship, an understanding. He has assured me that he knows nothing of this Cimmerian mess and his company didn't spread the plague. All we did was share information, so that we could quickly attack any pathogen that developed. You have my word on that, Lovejoy!"

He had John. He knew it the moment he stopped speaking. John had stopped attacking his assertions immediately; John was looking for a peccavi, a confession of sin. That, he would not get, Jules told himself. Jules had always had the gift of persuasion and he used it. He believed in his heart, that most people were the same; they reacted best to what they heard. If you got into someone head, Jules told himself, you could control their mind.

"There was no other way anyone would have been able to come up with a drug," continued Jules. "A medicine, which was both a vaccine and a treatment, for those who had already taken ill. Not in time to save the lives that we'll save. Ours is the best! It has a cross-immunity, whereas it can recognize and kill hundreds of different strains of influenza. Never before could that have been accomplished. We needed to work together, don't you see?"

He stopped, looking at John with a sinking feeling. The look of interest on John's face had become disgust. John rolled his eyes at Jules, and turned his back to him, not wanting to look at his face anymore. He considered his next move. What should he do? A split second later something came crashing down on his head.

CHAPTER 28

Someone sitting by Faith had a small portable radio, tuned in to a twenty-four hour news station that was reporting incidents of widespread rioting throughout the United States and the world. People were in a frenzy over the availability of the miracle drug Trivium1. Everyone wanted it right away. Even those still healthy wanted it as a preventative, so that they would not fall ill. Everyone in the little hospital waiting area listened to the disheartening report.

"Today is a sad day in the annals of American history." stated the newscaster. "Never before have I seen such selfishness on such a wide scale. It is understandable to a certain degree, because people have an innate will to live and be healthy. But, when do we, as conscious, God-fearing human beings,   give our fellow man just a little bit of the love and compassion that we want for ourselves? That's what I am asking."

Faith thought about the question asked and looked over at her sister and Jeff. She always felt as if she gave everyone, family, friends and acquaintances, the same care and concern that she wanted for herself. That was why she'd chosen the career she had; to help her fellow man and woman live long and healthy lives. She understood the newscaster's question. This was how she lived her life.

"In Paris, France, there has been mass rioting in the Seine-Saint Denis region, north of Paris; which is eerie and very similar to the three weeks of rioting that region suffered in late 2005," she heard the newscaster continued.

Faith remembered the incident, mainly because the rioters had been youths. The interior minister at the time had become infamous by referring to the youths as scum.

Listening to the news report was becoming stressful. Faith tuned in one more time and heard: "Shop windows were smashed along the Place de la Bastille in Paris and hundreds of people were arrested in Nantes, western France. The crowds had to be dispersed with tear gas."

Faith got up from her seat and tuned the report out. She was on her way outside to get a breath of fresh air when she saw Dr. Klein approaching out of the corner of her eye.

Abruptly, she turned and began to walk towards him. Before, she got there; Yvonne and Jeff appeared at her side.

"What is the diagnosis?" Faith asked, expecting a straight answer.

Dr. Klein didn't pussyfoot around. He was painfully blunt, a little too blunt for Yvonne's taste.

"Your son has influenza, Ms. Millicent. It isn't the avian flu or SARS, but another difficult strain that has a forty percent mortality rate. From what we have seen in the past few weeks, I am not saying that your son will die, mind you, but I'm saying it's a real possibility."

The tears exploded on Faith and Yvonne's faces immediately. Jeff pushed the doctor's shoulder.

"You couldn't tell us that any kinder?" asked Jeff, not knowing what else to say or do.

"I don't wish to upset you," stated the doctor. "I just thought Ms. Millicent would appreciate hearing what I told the hospital staff about her son's condition. Sugarcoating the truth doesn't help. We need to take action. I've been here for five days straight and I've had maybe six hours of sleep at the most. I don't want that child to die, but we don't have any medication to give him that I think can successfully treat his condition. We are all out of the Trivium1 that was ordered. So, I must lay the facts on the line."

Many things went through John's mind as he lay on the cool floor, semiconscious; he thought about the director's comment about the English naturalist Charles Robert Darwin and the director's ill-gotten notion that he was advancing the human survival in the battle between natural selection.

He also thought of Africa, particularly, the Darfur region. He'd spent months in the chief city of El Fasher providing the local residents there with medical assistance. So, the director was wrong on that assertion, too.

The last fleeting thought that passed through John's mind amid an aching headache that was developing, was the Tuskegee syphilis experiment and how the director had made a partial point.

The United States Public Health Service and the Tuskegee Institute had conspired to deny treatment for syphilis, so that they could document its degenerative effects on close to four hundred African American males, in the name of progressive medicine.

Much like what the director and Meyer-Burke were doing today, thought John, some seventy-six years later.

Yes, it was similar, conceded John and it was just as wrong. The government had conceded that in 1997, when the president of the United States had apologized for the experiment, calling it "profoundly and morally wrong."

John could hear radios, all of a sudden and voices in his head speaking. They were talking about murder and what might make a person snap.

"Alright," someone said, not from the inside of his head, but standing directly over him. Get up!" they shouted.

Water fell on his face and inside of his nose, suffocating him. He opened his eyes and attempted to sit up. He was very wobbly, so two strong hands helped him up, or rather hoisted him up, thought John, as he was slammed down hard in a wooden chair.

"What the hell did you do that for?" John heard Buzz Shaw's voice say. Buzz had taken the words he was about to ask the men who'd slammed him down in the chair out of his mouth.

"What?" John asked. He tried focusing in on Buzz and felt blood running down the back of his head.

"That!" stated Buzz. He was pointing past two uniformed police officers to where Jules Marceau lay on the floor dead, with a letter opener protruding from his chest.

* * * * *

"Faith, Faith!" Edna said, trying to get her attention.

Faith was hysterical, trying to call Sterling. She needed him to get her some of Meyer-Burke's treatment drug as soon as possible.

"Faith," said Buddy, trying to get her attention.

"Not now!" Faith screamed, walking off to a corner of the waiting room that was unoccupied. Buddy and Edna had come over to the hospital to check up on Faith, hoping the situation wasn't dire.

Faith tried to reach Sterling for about five minutes without success. She kept at it until Yvonne approached her, grabbing hold of her arm.

"I can't get him." Faith was sobbing. She dropped her phone to the floor.

"Faith listen!" Yvonne shook her sister out of her trance. "Edna and Buddy brought some medication with them!"

Faith looked over at the little blue bottle in Buddy's hand and saw the miracle drug for the first time. There was a tiny blue ribbon on the bottle's front, over the name Trivium1 which Faith figured was supposed to be a symbol for the drug's excellence, much like the award given for the first prize in a competition. Or, that was at least what Faith hoped. She snatched the bottle from Buddy's hand and went looking for her son's doctor.

No one said anything about Faith's new temperament. They all understood, had they been in her shoes they might have behaved the same way.

Yvonne was the only one that had the advantage of recognizing every act that was so unlike her sister. This made her look at the people who rioted over access to the treatment very differently and much more humanely.

* * * * *

"Start from the beginning," stated Buzz.

"I came upstairs to ask the director if it would be okay for me to go by the hospital and check on Faith. And, I heard him on the telephone arguing with the chief executive officer over at Meyer-Burke about a pact that they had."

"Tell me about the struggle you had?" stated Buzz, cutting John off, before he could say anything about the collusion he felt the director was involved in.

"There was no struggle between us!" stated John.

"No?" Buzz questioned while looking at the two uniformed police officers that he had brought upstairs with him.

"So, why are you bleeding from a gash to the back of your head?" Buzz asked. "And, why is there a dead man over here?"

"I don't know what happened to him," stated John. "He hit me in the head when I turned my back to him."

"Why would he do that?" Buzz asked, looking at the director's desktop.

"Because we were arguing," replied John. "And he was…"

"You were also drinking." Buzz cut him off again, picking up the glass Jules had been drinking from. "What's this, a little aperitif before dinner?"

"I wasn't drinking," said John. "That was the director, he was drinking by himself. I'm telling you, he hit me with something over the head."

"And, you hit him back," countered Buzz.

"No!" John said. "I was knocked completely out. I don't know what happened after that."

"That's your story and you're sticking to it?"

"I didn't do that!" John said, looking at a dead Jules Marceau. "I didn't have any reason to want him dead."

"That may be true, Mr. Lovejoy," said Buzz. "But, consider our position. Someone heard noise that sounded like an altercation was taking place. They called the police, who in turn showed up and I accompanied them upstairs."

John looked like he wanted to interrupt Buzz, but, he didn't.

"We find you unconscious and bleeding from the head, with a dead body several feet away. "Tell me," said Buzz. "What are we supposed to believe?"

"That there's a killer out there somewhere who you should be outside looking for," replied John.

"Well, maybe later," said Buzz. "After we process and fingerprint you."

"Why do you have to arrest me?" John asked. "I didn't kill him!"

"If that's the case, you don't have anything to worry about," countered Buzz. "Call for some medical attention for him," Buzz told one of the officers. "And read him his rights."

* * * * *

"Excuse me, doc," stated Yvonne, getting up to speak with Dr. Klein as he walked by. Faith had never come back, after taking the medication from Buddy and Yvonne was curious about just what was going on. "What's happening with my nephew, Melvin Millicent? And, have you seen my sister?"

"We're all waiting. We had to give him the medication intravenously. His mother is with him, I arranged it so that she would be able to stay beside him for the night. Everyone's got their fingers crossed. We're hoping his body responds - it's always difficult with the little ones. It's up to the big guy upstairs now," concluded the doctor. "Excuse me, I have to go check on some other patients, but, I will keep you informed, okay?"

"Yes, thank you," replied Yvonne, returning to her seat.

"So, what's going on?" Jeff asked.

"They gave Mel the medication. Faith's in the room with him. She's waiting bedside," added Yvonne. She was about to use the word *vigil* to explain what Faith was doing, but abruptly changed her mind. The others nodded; silently acknowledging what was said and left unsaid. Everybody remained quiet for a long time, just sitting around lost in their own thoughts as the night progressed and the sun set.

"You two are a nice match," said Yvonne, breaking the silence finally, looking at the Defoe's and noticing their harmony. "You both just seem to be in such accord."

"Thank you," replied Edna and Buddy in unison which made all four of them laugh for the first time.

"Can I ask you something personal?" Edna asked Yvonne.

"How personal?"

"Just a tad," replied Edna.

"I guess so," answered Yvonne, hoping that it wasn't an 'oh no she didn't ask me that' kind of question.

"How did you two meet?" Edna asked.

"He pursued me every day," Yvonne laughed. "Actually, I met Jeff while I was out at a dance club. He sent me flowers, candy and books. I had gotten the first two from men before, but never any literature. That was different. The fact that he'd actually read the books himself was a nice touch as well."

"Have you read Jamaica Kincaid?" Edna asked curious. "That's your last name, right?"

"Oh my God!" said Yvonne. "Yes, I've read her books. I like, *At the Bottom of the River*. Have you read it?"

"Yes, I have," said Edna.

That surprised Jeff and Yvonne both. Edna had a little flavor, thought Yvonne. No wonder she and Buddy were so cool and down to earth.

"You know, continued Edna." My supervisor Jules Marceau actually recommended that book to me."

"The French guy, Faith's boss?" Yvonne asked.

"Yeah," confirmed Edna. "I think he likes her writing, because he can identify with her plight in this country. It mirrors his mother, somewhat. Jamaica Kincaid once worked in New York City as an Au Pair and so did the director's mother."

CHAPTER 29

Most of the area precincts were full so John was taken directly to the Fulton County Courthouse where he was promptly arraigned on murder charges. A public defender stood in as his attorney being that he didn't have one. John wanted to explain his case, but the attorney didn't want to hear it.

"Look," stated the attorney, "I just handle arraignments. You can retain a private attorney later to defend your case and clear your good name. But, right now, I could care less if you are innocent or guilty."

John was shocked, having never been in trouble with the law before. He was afraid of going to lock-up where he would encounter real murderers.   The prosecutor took John's community service into account and his lack of a criminal record and asked the court to set bail for John at a quarter of a million dollars. John made good money working for the CDC, but he didn't have that much money saved up.

"Can you make bail?" asked his court-appointed attorney.

"Not at that amount," replied John, feeling like a novice. "So, what happens now?"

"Have you ever played monopoly, Mr. Lovejoy?" asked the attorney.

"Yes why?" John asked. "What does that game have to do with anything?"

"Actually, nothing," answered the attorney. "I just like to bring it up whenever I have to explain to a client that they're about to go straight to jail."

* * * * *

At around three in the morning, Edna and Buddy left the hospital. Jeff wanted to go home, take a shower, change clothes and come back. Yvonne let him go, but she couldn't leave without first speaking to her sister. Once the coast was clear, and the hospital security retired someplace out of sight, Yvonne slipped upstairs to her nephew's room. Faith was there, sitting bedside, staring at her son. Yvonne entered the room slowly, but didn't speak until Faith acknowledged her by turning her head.

"Hey," said Yvonne, walking a little closer, "how is he doing?"

"I don't know."

"I'm sorry, Faith. I shouldn't have let him go outside. I wasn't thinking." Yvonne had tears in her eyes. Faith didn't speak, but she did hold her arms out so her sister could come in for an embrace. The hug lasted for nearly a minute. Then Yvonne pulled up a chair and sat next to Faith and the bed.

"I thought those flu shots would be enough," mumbled Faith. She was staring off into the distance. "But it takes a few weeks for the shot to kick in, Dr. Klein told me. I was afraid at first that I may have done it wrong, by having Mel and Kimberly vaccinated. Maybe their little bodies couldn't fight even a weakened strain of influenza. Because that's what the vaccine is, it's the flu bug. But, Dr. Klein said no, that wasn't the case. The infection from the vaccine was wiped out by Mel's immune system very quickly; he just came in contact with a very strong strain. The Trivium1 that they gave him combats hundreds of different strains. So…" stated Faith, letting her voice trail off. The last part was unknown, the part whether the medication would help Mel's little body. Yvonne didn't say a word. She just sat there and gave Faith her ear.

"We thought about the flu virus that we were chasing." Faith was speaking about the CDC's work now. "We knew it had the potential of becoming widespread. We knew it could go global in pandemic form. But we thought we could catch it and the person spreading it while it was still just an epidemic spreading in one or two geographic areas. Now, look what's happened."

She turned to her sister. "If this Trivium1 treatment doesn't halt the virus, then what do we do?" she asked. Staring at the blank look on her sister's face, Faith sighed. "I know you don't know. No one does." The sisters were quiet for a minute.

"I found myself thinking in terms of mega-death earlier," confessed Faith. "Maybe even the end of the world, or human life forms. That battle between man and germ will finally be over, with pathogen emerging victorious." Faith paused for a moment, as if she needed a minute to really ponder that thought. When she came back, she was in a different place mentally.

"Do you remember the day when mommy brought us both Schwinn bicycles?" Faith asked.

"I do!" Yvonne was smiling at the memory.

"I had the flu that day," confessed Faith. "But I didn't want to cry about it because I wanted my bike. Mommy was our Dr. Mom back then. She was the in-residence medical expert. I wanted to be smart and a good mother just like her."

"You are," said Yvonne.

"Am I?" asked Faith in a low voice. "I'm always running off some place and leaving the kids with you or mommy."

"You're not going on vacation, Faith. You're a mother, but you're also a professional that has a very demanding job. No one can fault you on anything."

Faith shook her head slowly, as if she were debating the issue with herself, inside her own head.

"There was a report I read in *Nature* when Mel was just an infant. It spoke about motherhood altering the brain's learning centers making mothers more adept at caring for their children. Maybe I don't have those necessary instincts?" questioned Faith. "I didn't go through the hormonal changes associated with pregnancy. I didn't experience the powerful sensory events many women speak about."

"Neither did I," reasoned Yvonne. "But as women, we still have innate maternal instincts. So, don't lean toward that theory. I've seen you in action for years. You even guide me like a mother from time to time. So I know your cognitive abilities regarding motherhood are intact. Don't beat yourself up over this, sis'. Everything is going to be alright. God has got us on this one, trust me. To me, mommy, Jeff and the kids, you're our unsung hero."

CHAPTER 30

Several days after Jules Marceau was murdered, Sergio Moshe arrived in Atlanta. He was very disappointed that someone had beaten him to the punch on that murder. The press was all over the killing, vilifying the research expert charged in the incident.

The CDC was in shambles, or at least the department working in coordination with the agents investigating the Cimmerian plot was anyway, thought Moshe. That was a good thing, he told himself. It was clean-up time and for the cleaner, disorganization was a plus.

Moshe was tracking Sterling Rayford because the plan to quell him had changed: Pacifism was out and brute force in.

Sterling was somewhere in Atlanta. Moshe just didn't know where, exactly. He did have his own idea about it, so he went by the CDC looking for Sterling's lady friend, hoping to bump into him or even both of them.

"Why didn't you contact me, before you went over there?" asked Buzz.

"I was just following up on a lead," Hunt told him. "I didn't think the guy would respond like that. I was all prepared to just speak with him. Not arrest, but I guess he was afraid of something."

"His name was Pete Carpenter?" asked Buzz.

"Yeah, he was a mercenary. Burke has another ex-mercenary employed over there, a guy name Sergio Moshe, a serious-looking South African. I'm asking myself, why Meyer-Burke feels as if it needs to employ ex-mercenaries?"

Buzz didn't comment; he wasn't even sure if Hunt was asking him a question. They were traveling in Buzz Shaw's Avalanche truck.

Hunt glanced over at the truck's cubbies and saw that Buzz had jumper cables and tow hooks placed there.

"Nice truck." Hunt was pacing himself, before he approached a subject that he really wanted to elaborate on. "What happened with that Jules Marceau thing?"

"The guy flipped out, I think," replied Buzz. "They were under a lot of pressure during the first wave of this thing. I guess he just couldn't take it."

"Yeah," uttered Hunt. "It just seems odd. What about the Russian woman I asked you to follow up on?"

"There were no leads out here," offered Buzz.

"No?" replied Hunt. "Did you know that Pete Carpenter was in town, around the time that the woman was shot in the back?"

"You think he had something to do with that?"

"I don't know, you tell me. We're talking about an experienced killer, who they call the Pistol, in a city where a chief suspect, agent and turncoat is killed. Whatever, you want to call her."

"Scientist," offered Buzz.

"Okay scientist," shrugged Hunt. "This guy Carpenter didn't have any identifiable business in the Atlanta area. Also, I checked several flight manifests. He was also in many of the cities where the virus first started popping up."

"Was he in North Carolina?" asked Buzz. They found that reporter Allen Taylor's body down there; dumped in a ravine - no forensic evidence. He wasn't shot, though."

"I know," said Hunt. "Carpenter was down there, but he didn't kill Taylor. I did."

"What?" asked Buzz, turning to face Hunt momentarily as he drove. "Why'd you do that?"

"It was an accident. I found him prying around and I was trying to cut off his oxygen so I could knock him unconscious and I broke his neck. Not what I intended, so I dumped his body in the ravine."

"You talk like his death doesn't bother you," said Buzz.

"It does, maybe not as much as it should, but, I'm somewhat desensitized now. Sometimes the innocent die in these wars we fight. It's all a part of the rules of engagement. I notified Washington of my mishap," said Hunt.

He sounded like a programmed soldier, thought Buzz. They were on their way to the home of Jules Marceau and Buzz wanted to know why.

"Why are we executing a search warrant at the home of Marceau again?" he asked Hunt.

"In Lovejoy's statement, he alleges that Marceau had some type of conspiracy going on with Meyer-Burke. I don't know how much of that accusation is valid, but I'd like to know. I think Meyer-Burke is involved in much more than vaccine production. There are too many indicators pointing to them." He had his eyes back on the road. "Besides, Carpenter, this other ex-mercenary was in several cities as well where the virus first surfaced. There was a Meyer-Burke detail man there too, a guy named Sterling Rayford. I don't believe in that many coincidences happening in such a short period of time. I just don't. I think that Meyer-Burke may have had a hand in this pathogenic swan song we're hearing played around the globe."

CHAPTER 31

It took three days for Melvin's health to improve. By the fourth day he was back to almost eighty percent of his old self and Faith took him home. They stayed at their home overnight and then went to her mother's home in Stone Mountain.

Fanny had been worried that Faith would hold the incident against her. But, because her son was well, Faith held no malice in her heart and she brought Mel back to his grandmother's home so she could participate in nursing him back to health.

The CDC put Faith in charge of her division and gave her the title of acting director. She hadn't spoken to John yet, but was deeply concerned about him.

Edna and Buddy went to go visit him and reported back. John looked frail and haggard. It was disheartening, thought Faith.

"Here mommy," Kimberly came into the spare room that Faith had equipped as a command center. "This is for you." She handed her mother a cup of coffee and took a seat.

There was a large map fastened to the wall that Kimberly stared at. Since her brother had gotten sick, Kimberly had a million questions about influenza. She wanted to know where it came from, who it was mad at and how much it weighed. They were all very serious questions for her and stress releasers for Faith.

"What are you writing down, mommy?" Kimberly asked.

"Some proposed guidelines; guidelines for states to follow throughout this crisis and hopefully, a roadmap for the future."

Faith was troubled by some confusion during the initial days that the drug Trivium1 was being distributed. The Federal guidelines regarding distribution of the treatment and vaccine had been ignored in several states, resulting in a large number of deaths. Atlanta had followed the letter of the law, for which Faith was eternally grateful.

Since the treatment was in low supply, Meyer-Burke was having a difficult time keeping up with the demand. The hospitals and other health organizations had distributed Trivium1 to health care workers, children like Melvin and the very sick and elderly. The rationale was that this segment of the population was most at risk and therefore should have priority. Faith thought that this was logical. Being a health care worker, she told herself, didn't have anything to do with her stance, or with the recommendation. Not every state felt this way; many elderly patients in five key states were denied treatment. This ethical mishap, in Faith's opinion, had resulted in the patient's deaths. These five states, wrote down Faith, through their infinite wisdom, saw fit to provide the limited supply of treatments and vaccine to otherwise healthy twenty-something's. Most of them had been police officers and health care workers. Politicians somehow also got in the first wave of inoculations. Then healthy teenagers were inoculated. When the vaccine ran out, the sickly seniors were placed in quarantine. Faith considered the word 'quarantine' in this case to be another word for 'death camp.' It was inexcusable, thought Faith.

The door to the room opened and her mother and Yvonne entered.

"Where's Mel?" Faith asked.

"Jeff is in the room with him, they're looking over comic books. Jeff used to be a collector," stated Yvonne. "So he brought some over to go through with Mel."

"Okay," replied Faith. She stood and stretched.

"What's the story with the states you have the blue tacks in?" Fanny asked. She was staring at the map.

"Those were the states that were hit the hardest," answered Faith. "I had to send decontamination systems down to them to help clear some of their hospitals, office buildings and residential complexes of any and all germs."

"What about the states with the red tacks?" Yvonne asked, pointing to Minnesota and a few others in the West?

"Those are the ones that I'm pissed off at," answered Faith.

Faith had just recently cut her cell phone back on now that her mind was a little clearer. It had been ringing non-stop; it rang as soon as she turned it on, right when she was about to go get something to eat.

"Hello?" She said, answering it as Yvonne and her mother exited the room.

"Faith!" It was Edna. "Did you see the news tonight?"

"No Edna," replied Faith. "I don't have time to watch it, why what happened?"

"The justice department is launching an investigation of Meyer-Burke," stated Edna.

"Who...What... Why?"

"They're not saying explicitly, but it involves some kind of impropriety."

"There's nothing wrong with the treatment, right?" Faith asked, afraid that the miracle drug might somehow be flawed. That would be catastrophic; it was their last and only line of defense.

"No, no wait! There's nothing catchpenny about the drug. I hear that it involves the CEO and our late director. The FBI even raided their New York headquarters. It must be very serious."

"Hold on, Edna," said Faith. Her phone was beeping, letting her know she had another call coming in.

"Hello?"

"Faith?" Sterling Rayford sounded calm.

"Sterling," replied Faith. "Are you alright?"

"Yes," he replied. "But I was worried about you. I've been trying to reach you for several days. I went by the CDC, but that place is a madhouse. I..." Sterling was about to speak about the director's murder, but changed his mind. "How's your son?"

"He's recovering," answered Faith. "And I had my phone off for a couple of days. I'm sorry about that. I should have called you, but my mind was elsewhere."

"I understand," replied Sterling. "Can I see you?"

"Are you in Atlanta?"

"Yes," Sterling told her. "I've been here for a few days."

"Okay," said Faith, glancing at her watch. She needed to go by the CDC to pick up some data from her office. "Can we meet at that southern eatery two blocks from the CDC? I can't remember the name, but you know which place I'm talking about, right?"

"Yes, I know the place," replied Sterling. "How much time do you need?"

"About an hour," stated Faith.

"Okay, I'll see you then."

Faith was about to hang up when she remembered that she had Edna on hold, so she clicked back over. "Edna?"

"Yeah, I'm here."

"I'm sorry about that," stated Faith. "Now, you were saying?"

"Meyer-Burke is up a creek and there are feces everywhere."

"Edna! That's a little extra with the information."

"I'm sorry," said Edna. "Anyway, they just said on the news that there's going to be a summit conference held in New York City concerning the global response to the pandemic."

"When?"

"Two weeks from today, at the United Nations. Oh yeah, John is coming out on bail tonight."

"Where did he find the funds?" Faith asked. She had planned to round up his supporters and create a fund, but never got around to it.

"He got a bail bondsman and only needed to put up ten percent," answered Edna.

"Great!" said Faith, checking her watch again. "I have to go Edna, I'll call you tomorrow."

*   *   *   *   *

Hunt Rhinehart's phone kept ringing, so he finally stopped reading the paperwork before he decided to answer it.

"Yeah," he said.

"Are you still going over Marceau's paperwork?" Buzz asked.

"Yeah, I can't shake this feeling I have that there's something here," stated Hunt.

"You're better at that tedious work than I am, I need the action. Let me know if you find anything. I'll be out here in the field."

Hunt clicked his phone off and glanced over at one of the scientists sent over by the Department of Homeland Security. There were four of them in total. The search warrant had taken longer than anticipated. Jules Marceau had left mountains of paperwork lying around, as well as a laboratory hidden within the closet. Inside this lab was the mountain of paperwork, along with strips of DNA, lying on a table, waiting for two proteins from a virus Jules was researching to lock onto it.

One of the scientists advised Hunt that the proteins matched that of the Ebola virus, but the strips here didn't contain the entire virus; it had snippets of it, rather than every piece the virus needed to infect and kill. This entire mess was a puzzle, Hunt thought. But, the answer had to be here. He just had to keep looking.

*   *   *   *   *

Sterling got to the restaurant a good twenty minutes before Faith arrived. He reserved them a table in the rear, making sure he'd have a good view of the entrance. Then he ordered himself one strong drink. He needed it to lower his inhibitions, and loosen up his tongue.

The place wasn't crowded at all, barely five people dining. Things weren't back to normal quite yet, thought Sterling. But, just the fact that restaurants were open for business let him know they were on their way.

Faith rushed in the door as he was looking at his watch, momentarily catching him off guard and sending his heart aflutter. She looked alive, in a powder blue pants suit and low comfortable shoes.

She saw him right away and made her way over.

"Hey," she said, appearing winded. She set her pocketbook down on the seat and kissed him briefly on the lips.

"Sorry - I had to stop by the Center real quick," she informed him. "It's been crazy! What's up with you?"

Sterling didn't smile or even respond right away. He needed a minute, he told himself.

"Melvin?" he said, trying to form a question.

"He's making remarkable progress," said Faith, smiling for the first time in a good while. "It was touch and go for awhile, but we came through. That treatment your company developed is a God-send! Really it is."

Sterling was in pain, not physically, but mentally and emotionally. Faith thought that the treatment was heaven? Yes, he thought bitterly, because it had saved her son. She wasn't going to feel the same way after he told her the truth: Trivium1 had been crafted and created through devilry.

"You know, several countries are attempting to seize your patent," Faith informed him.

"They are?"

"Yes," said Faith. "I hadn't thought about it before, but World Trade Organization rules allow for countries to seize patents in times of national emergency for non-public, commercial use. We had a debate about this once - my department at the CDC, I mean. John and Buddy felt that Africa should use these rules to seize patents from any and all pharmaceutical companies that make drugs that the poorer countries need, but can't afford. That's what's currently taking place with Trivium1 in low-economic countries. I'm sorry."

"That's quite alright," replied Sterling. "They're doing the right thing. Meyer-Burke doesn't deserve to profit one dime from the sale of Trivium1. That's why I've given my stock and profits from it to over a dozen health organizations. Many of those service low economic areas."

"Wow!" replied Faith, befuddled. "That's a strange position for you to take, isn't it?" She noticed the long look on his face for the first time. "Sterling, what's up? Is there a problem with you? I heard that they were launching an investigation into Meyer-Burke."

"Yeah, the giant is feeling heartburn," stated Sterling, answering her question with a metaphor. He took a deep breath.

"Faith, listen. I did some things that I fear will come out. I want to tell you first myself."

Sterling paused, wondering where to begin. Faith reached over and clasped her hand in his. He squeezed her hand, and then released it.

"I feel as though I should start from the very beginning," he told her and took another breath. "Scientists at Meyer-Burke began getting curious about three or four years ago when a number of squirrels began to pop up in Denver with the plague."

"Black Death?" questioned Faith, referring to the clinical name that the plague was given when it first hit America in the 19th century traveling in rats on large ships.

"Yes. They found over a dozen dead in City Park, two miles from the state capitol. As you know, Black Death killed millions of people in Europe during the 14th century, but its curable today. Meyer-Burke is always on the watch trying to anticipate when and where the next significant health crisis will be and how can it be prevented."

"Like most pharmaceutical companies, I would imagine," interjected Faith.

"Yeah, but Meyer-Burke unfortunately allowed their zeal to take over, in the wrong way. Our scientists read about the CDC discovering the Spanish Flu and piecing it back together. They began to wonder about what would happen if that strain got out of the laboratory, the way SARS did several times during the epidemic. This is when the idea for Trivium1 was born: A treatment that could defeat many different strains of influenza. Norton Burke loved the idea, as did everyone. Me included. Our drug was going to be lightning in a bottle."

"And it is, right?"

"Yes, it is," agreed Sterling. He looked very grim. "At a very high cost: our morals, my spirituality and countless lives."

"I don't understand," said Faith, bewildered.

"I know," replied Sterling. "Bear with me, I'm getting to it. There's a public database called Haplotype Mapping Project, or HapMap. It breaks down the genetic variation of the human species. It gave our scientists a roadmap that identified why certain populations before us survived environmental changes through genetic mutation. As you know, a single strand of DNA comprises about three billion chemical units."

"Of course, the double helix, joined by the hydrogen bonds, between complementary bases; Adenine, Thymine, or Cytosine and Guanine."

"Yes, well, our scientists looked at the genetic disparities listed between western Europeans, the Yoruba of Africa, the Japanese and descendants of the Han Chinese."

"Looking for what, exactly?"

"Susceptibility to disease," answered Sterling. "With this template, our scientists were able to distinguish classes of people who had certain genetic factors that made them prone to disease. They were also able to exclude environmental factors. The research led us to Jakarta, Indonesia. Do you remember a few years ago, Indonesia's health minister asked the world, 'What does her poor country get out of sharing bird flu samples with scientists and vaccine makers?'

"Yes," replied Faith. It was a very delicate issue being that Indonesia, like many poor countries, was at great risk of being hit by the deadly virus first, but lacked the same resources to develop life-saving vaccines as the countries they were sharing their samples with."

"No one could really answer that question. Meyer-Burke did pledge to assist any poor country that would supply us with samples of any virus discovered in their borders. That stopped the one-way exchange of information. But sometime after that initial agreement was formed, things got a little gray."

"What do you mean by gray?"

"Norton Burke began to get bright ideas about facilitating a pandemic." Sterling looked straight into Faith's face and said, "being the only pharmaceutical company with a vaccine for it."

Things began to become clearer to Faith now as Sterling watched her expression change.

"Norton Burke uses ex-mercenaries for company and personal security. He's always feared a kidnapping attempt just as much as he fears infectious disease. There was a rare find in one of the poor nations, I don't know which one, but a sample was sent to the infectious disease lab on Plum Island. Norton Burke hijacked this sample and some important data."

"How did he do that? The Plum Island lab has a BSL-4 security rating. You don't get any higher than that."

"Norton Burke is personally worth over thirty billion dollars, Faith. That kind of money can buy you information, professional killers and people in high places. He has connections in Washington and some foot soldiers that he calls his aces in the hole. The Department of Homeland Security began investigating the theft, but that didn't slow Norton Burke down. He had someone find four top scientific experts. The Russian woman killed in Atlanta a few weeks ago was one of those experts." Sterling stopped for a moment, letting the information sink in. "The others are all dead also, I believe."

Faith was aghast, but she didn't say anything. She needed to hear it all.

"I didn't argue. I honestly believed a pandemic was unavoidable and nascent in the near future. I believed all of the hoopla that Burke was feeding me. Then something amazing happened, a scientific phenomenon; a baby rhinoceros was discovered to be immune to all disease and viruses. Scientists stumbled upon this discovery while treating several other different animal species that had suddenly taken ill with Newcastle Disease, East Coast Fever and the Rift Valley Fever."

"That's why the influenza virus has these animal disease properties," Faith mind was jumping ahead, making connections. "You doctored the virus and gave it all of its properties?"

"The four experts that Norton Burke found; yes, they did that, along with putting several dozen different influenza strains together as well. They tested it on the baby rhinoceros, but couldn't infect the animal with anything. That's when Burke became obsessed with his Rhinovirus project - he had them alter one specific common cold virus, the adenovirus, AD-14."

"But, why couldn't the animal be infected?" asked Faith, while her medical mind started kicking in.

"The mammal had a natural protein in its blood that was very similar to properdin, the natural protein in human blood serum that helps provide immunity from many infectious diseases."

"So, this is how you were able to develop the vaccine?"

"Yes, the scientist in Indonesia gave us access to the rhinoceros. And, we killed it."

"With a virus?"

"No, it died from exhaustion. Meyer-Burke worked the animal to death. Because we needed to know that we could cure the virus before we unleashed it on the world. The rhinoceros died before we were satisfied."

"So you took a chance?" asked Faith with a very tight voice. "You gambled?"

"No, we didn't do that," replied Sterling. "The animal was an import from Tanzania. Its relatives carried the same genes and the same mutation. So we went there and commissioned its entire family. We were hoping for a ceteris paribus." Faith had a strange look on her face, so he asked her, "Are you familiar with the term?"

"Yes," she told him. "It's new Latin and means with all other factors, or things being the same."

"Exactly," agreed Sterling. "We got five of them from the Serengeti National Park. We stayed in Dar es Salaam for months, testing the animals and the locals. The locals speak English, by the way. We used the Hap Map template and their theory of natural selection. We found several descendants of the Yoruba living in the mountains of

Tanzania. It seems that they didn't all progress into the government of Nigeria. They live on the lower slopes of Mount Kilimanjaro. These people call themselves the Chagga. They're the third largest ethnic group in Tanzania and outstanding farmers. What made them interesting to us was how they could resist infection and influenza. The research we did on them, coupled with that of the rhinoceros, enabled us to create the first compounds used in the formation of Trivium1."

Faith couldn't help but think about how great minds always ran contrary to social norms. With all this great ingenuity, they created a killer bug. Then they set out to find a cure for their own creation. Faith felt deeply pained because she really liked Sterling. She thought they had something special together. She had entertained thoughts of him being the silver lining in her life; but, not anymore.

"What do the locals call that mountain?" asked Faith, remembering but wanting Sterling to say it.

"Kilema Kyaro."

"Which means?" asked Faith, looking very sad.

"That which makes the journey impossible." He understood perfectly how she felt and what she was thinking.

"How could you be a part of something like that?" She recalled when they first met; he had been reading *Natural Cures for the Common Cold*. She also remembered his comments about the terrorist attacking New York City. Sterling hadn't answered her question, so she asked another. "You extorted, or tried to extort, the United States Government?"

"No! Not me. That was Pete Carpenter and Sergio Moshe, I believe. I don't even think that Norton Burke knew they were doing that. He only wanted to have the virus mutate, so he could sell his treatment. Norton-Burke is a businessman, not a killer. He just underestimated the greed of the killers he had around him. They had help, but that wouldn't be too difficult for them to find. We were all promised fifty million dollars and given down-payments of five million."

"You were in all the cities that I was in," said Faith. Her face was stony. "Were you there to spread the virus?"

"Not maliciously," answered Sterling. "I was just there for observation purposes. Moshe and Pete basically let the pathogen out. But, since I was also in many of the cities myself, they have a traveler's guide book on me, an attempt to place all of the blame at my feet."

"They aren't doing anything to you!" snapped Faith. "By your own admission, you participated in the plot, you knew all of the particulars, and you helped them facilitate the plan. You observed everything and, you almost killed my son!" She was shouting now. A couple of people glanced up from their food in their direction.

"Faith, please," said Sterling, with a pitiful look on his face. "I'm sorry, I didn't…"

"What?" snapped Faith. There were tears on her face. "You didn't think my son would get sick? What about all of the other sons? Do you know how many sons died in that poverty-stricken neighborhood in Washington, D.C., next to the Anacostia River? You're just as guilty as the two men that tried to extort our country. That's right, it's mine too; I help protect it! And, I make contributions. You are just as bad as Norton Burke! I don't care if he wasn't a part of the extortion plot. I don't care if the only thing on his mind was business. What did you have on your mind? Good intentions? A lot of good that sentiment did! Those kids have a one in twenty percent chance of making it out of Washington, D.C. alive before they reach the age of twenty-one. And, here you come, another black man, and cut their chances down to less than half of that!"

Sterling couldn't get a word in; Faith verbally abused him as she read him the Riot Act. He didn't shy away because he knew that he deserved to hear everything she had to say and then some. Prison, Sterling felt, was even too good for him.

"You're nothing more than a well paid slave!" Faith said, almost spitting the words out. "Did you even notice that they were unleashing it, all of the lower economic areas? Why do you think they did that?"

"Because they thought that the government would ask fewer questions," answered Sterling. "Poor people get the worst care anyway, they figured. They unleashed it at Four Points, close to the New

Mexico side - they had three deaths out of eight cases of the Black Death plague over there in 2006. New Mexico, Colorado, Arizona and California are the main states where it exists. So Four Points seemed like a good place for Meyer-Burke's virus to materialize - of course, substituting California for Utah."

"Of course," repeated Faith sarcastically.

"Faith, I'm being candid and, this is unscripted," stated Sterling. "I'm trying..."

"To what?" Faith stated cutting him off again. "What are you trying to do? Make amends, maybe? I hope not. It's entirely too late for that! I want evidence, Sterling. That will be your reparation." She dropped her voice. "I want Burke," she told him. "Give me what links him to this atrocity."

Sterling thought for a moment. "The first attack was on April 24th, Africa Malaria Day."

Faith frowned, not following him. "What were you celebrating; the one million deaths annually from the disease?"

"No," answered Sterling. "They were celebrating Norton Burke's birthday."

Sterling spent twenty minutes giving Faith account numbers, access codes to the safety deposit boxes where he'd been keeping detailed information about all Meyer-Burkes' dealings for all the years he has been with the company.

Faith felt that she could remember it all, as mad as she was, but just to make sure, she wrote most of the information down.

"You want me to go to the police with you?" he asked her.

"No, that won't be necessary. What about Jules Marceau? Was he privy to the extortion part, or just the spreading of the virus?"

"Neither, the way Burke roped him in had very little to do with money. Jules Marceau, from what I determined, was looking for a *raison d'etre;* as Burke always joked."

"Which is?"

"A reason or justification for existing," he informed her.

"The stuff you told me about your mother?"

"I didn't lie to you about that, Faith. Every moment that we shared was real; I told you the truth, when we spoke about us."

"Yeah, you just conveniently left out the part about how you had helped create a Frankenstein monster." Faith felt like she needed to leave. She was getting very upset and couldn't stop clenching her fists.

"You want me to go to prison?" Sterling asked.

Faith stood, shaking with rage and threw a glass of water in his face. "No." She grabbed her pocketbook from the next seat. "I want you to drive to the Golden Gate Bridge, and jump the hell off!"

CHAPTER 32

As Faith stormed out of the restaurant she had her cell phone in her hand, already trying to call Buzz Shaw. Sergio Moshe watched her and wondered what the trouble in paradise was all about. He had picked up Faith's trail earlier when she'd dropped by the CDC. Faith got in her truck and drove off. Moshe let her go; was no longer concerned with her. She had done her part by leading him right to Sterling Rayford.

*　*　*　*　*

As Faith tried Buzz Shaw's number, her cell phone began to ring.

"Hello?"

"Faith, where are you?" John asked.

"I'm on my way home. I just found out some information I need to get to Buzz Shaw, it's about the Cimmerian mess and Meyer-Burke. It's all crazy, John! I'm so confused, that I don't know what to do."

"Faith, calm down; could you tell me briefly a little bit about what you've learned?"

"Okay," *I might as well*, she thought; telling John would be good practice. She knew she was probably going to have to tell her story several times over for Buzz Shaw and Hunt Rhinehart and whatever authorities they brought to her to talk.

Faith gave John the story. She began with her first meeting with Sterling on her way to Washington, D.C. and expanded, telling him how, after Jules had requested everyone to use their contacts in the pharmaceutical business to see what their companies had in the pipeline, and she'd thought of Sterling and called him. At that point, their chance meeting blossomed into a friendship.

"Do you think Jules might have known?" asked John abruptly. "I mean, known that you had met a detail man from Meyer-Burke?"

"I don't know," answered Faith. She realized now how convenient it had been for Jules that she had advocated for Meyer-Burke's miracle drug first, rather than him doing it. He, of course, had signed on later, but only after several of his subordinates had requested he do so. That suppressed any appearance of impropriety or collusion.

Faith continued, telling John about Vegas, about how Sterling had told her all about his company's clinical trials. John took very detailed notes: times, locations, and subjects. The most intriguing part of all was Faith's account of how the drug's properties were discovered. Africa, he thought, the birthplace of everything.

*   *   *   *   *

Sterling was taking an unusually long time in exiting the restaurant. Moshe got out of his car and went to have a look. He didn't need his prey slipping out the back door. Sterling was still there, still sitting in the back of the place at the same table. Maybe someone else was on their way to meet him, thought Moshe, until he saw Sterling signal for the waiter. The waiter handed him a small white slip of paper that Moshe figured to be his bill.

Moshe quickly looked up and down the block, thinking fast. Sterling probably hadn't come to the restaurant on foot. There were only four cars on the block besides his, but none of them looked like a rental. Maybe he came by cab, thought Moshe.

As he watched, Sterling left the restaurant and walked swiftly up the block. Darkness had fallen. Moshe was confident that Sterling hadn't seen him hidden in the doorway of another eatery. Sterling walked the length of the street and then he turned the corner.

He had a rental car, but had parked it a block away, having misjudged the distance to the restaurant. Both hands were jammed inside his jacket pocket. Although it wasn't cold out, Sterling walked briskly, as if he were chilly. He stopped in the middle of the block. His rental was parked directly behind a large truck that blocked a streetlight.

As he placed his key in the door, he sensed, rather than felt, the cold gust of air. Something was rushing towards him. With anticipation on his mind, Sterling moved to his left and jabbed outward with his right hand. It connected solidly with Moshe's mid-section. Moshe gave a loud grunt, but that was it. The knife that Moshe held flew swiftly through the air, touching the top of Sterling's chest and nicking his chin.

Moshe kicked him hard in the groin and ran at him. Their bodies crashed into one another and Sterling's back smashed the passenger side window of his car. Moshe head butted him, hard on the nose once, twice in his right eye. Sterling felt intense pressure on his stomach and back before he managed to push Moshe away.

"What did you say to that majestic young lady of yours?" asked Moshe, with a cold smile on his face and all his teeth showing. "She looked so very upset."

Sterling moved away from the car, but stayed facing Moshe. The man looked like a wounded animal, Sterling thought. His face had a feverish look, his black eyes filled with agitation. His teeth looking like shears to Sterling.

Moshe touched the gaping wound in his abdomen. Then he looked at the bloody butter knife that Sterling held in his right hand. Not figuring Sterling to be armed, he had attacked him. He'd figured wrong. Moshe knew he didn't have long; that was why he had continued to fight, so intensely. Sterling looked at the critically injured man as his blood dripped from the tip of the knife.

"I saw you peeking in the restaurant window," Sterling told him. "And I remembered what you told me at my apartment."

Moshe smiled, because death was funny to him, he thought, even if it was about to be his own...

"Who was Cimmerian; you or Pete?"

"It sure hell wasn't Burke." Moshe was having trouble breathing. "He didn't have the guts for it. But, I'd give him the credit. The mastermind was his inadvertent creation. He created the monster."

Sterling shook his head, silently agreeing. "That's the second time that I've heard that description tonight," he told Moshe. "They say if people keep telling you the same thing, maybe you should listen. I'm listening. Is there anything else that you would like to tell me?"

The life seemed to run right out of the man and pool up at Sterling's feet. Moshe held on to the pit of his stomach, wishing their confrontation hadn't ended so quickly. How he loved a good long snickers née, he thought.

"You'll never be privy to everything," stated Moshe, and fell down to one knee. "No one was, only Burke knew all of the players. He just didn't understand the game." Moshe grunted and fell over on his face.

Sterling looked up and down the block. There wasn't a soul out. He quickly went through Moshe's pockets, removing all of his identification. That way, it would take a while for the authorities to identify him.

"I don't need that long, only a half day," Sterling thought.

CHAPTER 33

"Okay, Okay!" Faith was whispering, out of breath, as John hugged her tightly. "You're suffocating me." When he released her, Faith quickly pulled him into the apartment and shut the door.

"You're hugging me like I was the one inside prison, are you alright?"

"Yeah" stated John. "I told you that. I was just concerned about you and after everything you've just told me. I can see that my concerns are valid."

"Sterling wasn't going to hurt me," said Faith. "I know that, because if he felt that way about things, he didn't have to tell me anything."

Faith walked into her living room and plopped down on the couch. She looked at one of her metallic-looking throw pillows and rolled her eyes. Anything resembling sterling silver now upsets her.

"I thought about what happened with me and Jules, non-stop." John took a seat beside her on the couch. "I couldn't figure out who killed him. It damn sure wasn't me – he'd hit me first. As embarrassing as it sounds, I was knocked right out."

"That's so odd," replied Faith. "Do you think he could have stabbed himself? You know, maybe thinking that the gig was up, his personal and professional life was over?"

"I know that desperation can make people do a lot of different things, conceded John. "But I never pegged him as someone who would take his own life."

"Well, I never pegged him to be foolish enough to get mixed up in a plot like this. So, hey... right about now, the possibilities are endless."

John had to agree with that assessment. He'd been trying to categorize everything he knew about the entire investigation. Some things fell into their proper place and perspective, while others didn't fit and made no sense.

"Do you want some green tea?" Faith asked, getting up.

"Yes, please, I couldn't eat or drink anything while I was in that prison. Everything looked and smelled like it was weeks old."

"You do look a little thin," observed Faith. "But, your okay right," she added, happy he was there keeping her company and providing her with a sounding board to vent her frustration.

As Faith prepared the tea she asked John about his experience being incarcerated.

"Was it really as bad as I envision it to be?"

"I would have to say yes," replied John very thoughtfully. "You know how people sometimes joke that they would rather die than go to prison? I see why now."

Faith brought him the tea and sat back down. "I'm glad Melvin's alright," John told her.

Faith nodded as she took a sip of tea. "Did they have any cases of influenza in prison?" she asked. "I can't help wondering about how the penal institutions handled the pandemic."

"I heard they were quarantining prisoners left and right," John shuddered. "But I guess I didn't come in contact with anyone affected, or infected, thank God."

"You know, Meyer-Burke has to make about ten billion annually, probably much more. But, still they're greedy! So greedy, that they would allow millions of people to die just to stuff their coffers with a few dollars more. How much money is enough?"

"No one has ever been able to figure that amount, Faith. But Meyer-Burke isn't the only pharmaceutical company that's dealing in death. Many would rather let their medications expire than give it to the needy. The money goes in their coffers, like you said, but the sick, poor and needy go in a coffin."

John's analogy sounded shocking, but it was true. Faith had never looked at it that way until now; not until she really needed some medication for her son. That was when most people thought about it, she theorized: When a loved one of theirs was on their death bed. When that happened, there was very little time for debate, barter or bargain.

A life, thought Faith, should never be negotiable. Not under any circumstance.

"I need to call Buzz Shaw," said Faith getting up from the couch.

"And I think I need a shower," said John, sniffing at his own underarms. "Do you mind if I take one here?"

"No," picking up her cell phone. She looked up and gave him a sudden smile. "Just don't walk around my house naked."

John smiled back and held onto the provocative comment he had for her. Faith pointed toward the hallway. Then she dropped her arms, figuring that he would find his way. She had a small card with both Buzz and Hunt's number on it. She opted to call Buzz. Hunt seemed to have an attitude a lot of the time and Faith wasn't in the mood for any more drama.

*   *   *   *   *

Sterling hustled out of Atlanta catching a flight back to New York. His business in Atlanta being finished, he was able to kill two birds with one stone.

On the flight, he went into the bathroom and cleaned himself up while tending to his wounds. There wasn't much in the bathroom, so he didn't have much to work with. Several passengers stared down seeing the blood on his shirt. His face looked battered and bruised from where he had been cut and head butted.

"I had a bit of a skirmish with my girlfriend," he joked, to one passenger who actually asked him about it. "She did all of the hitting." Although skeptical, most people either shrugged or laughed his comment and explanation off.

He had a car waiting for him at the airport; that had been good planning on his part, he congratulated himself. Driving along, Sterling wondered if anyone had found Moshe's body yet, or whether it was still lying out there on the cold pavement, soiled, like his life on the earth.

*   *   *   *   *

"John!" Faith called from outside of the bathroom. "Can I come in?"

"Yeah."

Faith entered the bathroom and sat down on the toilet seat. John was inside the shower with the partition closed. Faith couldn't see him clearly and he could barely see her.

"I spoke with Buzz Shaw; he's on his way over here. He sounded stressed. He wanted to know about Mel. I told him Mel was okay, that he was over at my mother's recuperating."

"I'm surprised he asked," said John. "He's quite a callous man."

"Yeah, but we don't know all that he has seen. When I was sitting in the hospital praying that Mel would be alright, I heard two women talking about how they hated hospitals." Faith sounded a little introspective. John opened the partition just a crack and peeked at her. "One of the women said that visiting a hospital was like going to an automotive place; because they seem to always fix what you come in for, but break something else so that you have to come back. How horrible is that, when a person should feel that way?" John just shook his head. He had no answer to that question.

"By the way," stated Faith, "I picked up your mail while I was over at the CDC. It's in that pile with mine on the kitchen table."

Faith heard John turn the water off and got up. "Hand me a towel, please?" asked John.

Faith grabbed a big yellow towel that hung on a rack behind the door and handed it to him, not looking in his direction.

"Thank you," he told her, fighting the urge to grab her and pull her close to him.

"Let me go call my mother," said Faith, heading out of the bathroom and leaving John standing there with a look of longing on his face.

*   *   *   *   *

Burke walked slowly through his living room wishing that he didn't ever have to travel back into the city. What for? He asked himself. His company was in disarray.

The Feds didn't have one shred of evidence on him. They were just fishing. But their fishing expedition had managed to tarnish his good name with the consumers; and that, Burke didn't like.

Hunt Rhinehart had been so cocky, he thought. After Killing Pistol Pete, or was it 'Pete the Pistol,' he thought, "Ah, who really cares?"

Hunt had killed a foot soldier, no one really important; and he had saved Burke fifty million dollars. Burke wasn't mad at him for that. He'd have his ace in the hole kill Hunt later, of course, once everything blew over, as a matter of professional courtesy to Pete Carpenter.

All this killing, thought Burke. Things had been so much easier when he was only a millionaire.

The only sounds Burke was used to hearing at his glass house were those of the male crickets in the area. The females were the quiet ones in the Gryllidae family. The males produced a loud shrill sound, that Burke called chirping, by rubbing their front wings together.

That was the sound that he had been hearing all night, but it wasn't the sound that he heard now jarring him out of his relaxed state.

The loud crash was the sound of his security gate crashing down. Burke knew this instantly as he looked out at the vehicle barreling towards his home.

Had he not been frozen with shock and fear, Burke might have run, or at least attempted to move. Instead, he stood there, looking Sterling directly in the face as Sterling crashed through the glass wall that protected Burke's living room area from the outside elements.

As luck would have it, Sterling knew nothing of the huge black steel support beam that sat a few inches away from where he broke through the glass. Had he hit it, the beam would have stopped him, his vehicle and the assault. But he missed it; he was lucky.

Norton Burke wasn't. The vehicle smashed into Burke with no resistance beyond glass shards scattering in all directions. The impact knocked Burke back into a concrete pillar that sat in the middle of the living room, breaking his backbone on contact.

"Augh!" yelled Burke, as blood oozed from his mouth. Sterling exited the vehicle slowly, making his way over to where Burke sat a shattered husk of a man.

"How does it feel?" asked Sterling, sitting down across from Burke, "to have the life knocked right out of you?"

The lights in the living room had gone out with the vehicle's impact. It was very hard for Burke to see Sterling's face now. Some dark adaptation had to take place first.

Then Sterling's gaunt-looking face came into view.

"You stupid dolt," stated Burke, coughing up even more blood.

"I knew you thought of me as an imbecile," replied Sterling. "But I never cared about what you thought. Not even now."

"We could have worked this out." Burke couldn't feel his lower extremities; he was desperately trying to. Sterling had damaged his spine, he thought, staring at him.

"How do you figure we could have worked his out?" asked Sterling, conversationally. There was blood dripping down on his pants. "The F.B.I. is all over this. It was only a matter of time before they put the puzzle together."

"You think this was my first difficult conundrum?" asked Burke, finding it very had to breathe. "I had a contingency plan for this. I had an inside connect who would have fixed this."

Cimmerian, thought Sterling, as he realized that Moshe had done him in, too. Moshe had stabbed him in the side and in his back. Not deep, but just enough so that he would be severely injured. I could have been all right, thought Sterling, if I'd gone to the hospital, instead of exacting revenge on the man who everyone said had created the monster. That was Meyer-Burke.

Using his great skills in motivational research, Sterling came to realize that the monster manipulative and grotesque was Meyer-Burke. So it was up to him to ferret out the evil. Money was the unfilterable virus that had infected Norton Burke. No fan or filtering device would work on it; anything attempted or tried would fall short of Norton Burke's desire to always win and make money.

Just like he said, thought Sterling. He would have fixed this. Burke didn't have much strength left. He looked around. His house was in ruins and he could hear sirens off in the distance.

"You are just like me," he told Sterling. "Hoggish. We are both filthy men. Had you been in my place, you would have done the same thing."

Dying immediately after making this declaration and thinking to himself: *'never negotiate'*.

Sterling didn't kid himself. He knew that Norton Burke was most likely right. For Burke, the power had always been in the dollar. It was only right that he should die chasing what he lived by. He only hoped that had he been Norton Burke, whoever would have been him would have done the same thing that he was doing now.

* * * * *

"Hello?" Faith answered the phone.

"Yes, it's me Buzz. Come downstairs?"

"All right." John, I'm going downstairs - Buzz Shaw is down there. He says they just found a body a few blocks from where I had my meeting with Sterling."

"Was it Sterling?" John asked coming into the kitchen and picking up the mail.

"No. It was some guy named Sergio Moshe. But he worked for Meyer-Burke also."

John knew the name, so he nodded his head. "You want me to go down with you?"

"No, I'll be right back," said Faith. "Wait here and try to find out everything you can on Norton Burke."

John had already had plenty of information. He was confident that anything Faith needed to know, he could tell her. John picked up the mail and went through it. He found several letters there addressed to him. But one jumped out at him. It was signed 'R. Klebb' and postmarked a day before the Russian woman was killed.

John tore the letter open and read through it very quickly. Then he picked up the photo that had been downloaded from the internet and looked at it closely. His heart sank and his mind raced as he ran out of the door, dropping the letter on the floor as he went.

*   *   *   *   *

Faith walked out of the building and saw Buzz standing by his truck talking on the phone. He was cussing up a storm. Obviously, she thought, there had been more developments. She walked over and stood in front of him, not eavesdropping on his conversation, but waiting for him to finish. Buzz looked at her and nodded. Then he looked down the street as he held the phone to his ear.

"Was that everything that Sterling Rayford told you?" he asked her, cuffing the phone.

"Yes," replied Faith, shrugging her shoulders.

"Are you sure?" Buzz asked, sounding agitated.

"That's what I said," becoming agitated herself.

Buzz nodded again and then he reached out and grabbed Faith by her throat.

"I'm asking you a simple question; did Sterling Rayford tell you anything else?"

He was choking Faith as tears sprang from both of her eyes. She grabbed at his t-shirt he wore ripping down the top half of it revealing a tattoo of two bones placed crosswise under a bloody skull. The tattoo meant death and danger.

"I know you can't speak," said Buzz looking down the street, "but you can nod your head. If you don't tell me what I want to know, I will kill you. Do you understand?" He decided to loosen up his grip somewhat so she could breathe a little.

Faith controlled herself suddenly realizing the gravity of the situation. She nodded an acknowledgement a second later.

"Very good." Buzz put his telephone away without saying goodbye. Faith understood: it was a front. He hadn't been speaking to anyone.

"Did Sterling Rayford say anything about me?"

Hunt pulled up alongside of them and John ran out of the building.

"What are you doing, Buzz?" Hunt asked, jumping out of the car. "She doesn't have anything to do with this!"

Buzz pulled Faith in front of him while reaching for a small gun from his back.

"It's him!" John yelled. "He's part of it!"

Hunt waved John off. John wasn't telling him anything he didn't already know.

"Shut up!" Buzz turned and fired. The shot missed John and shattered a glass window behind him.

"Buzz!" Hunt had his own gun in one hand. He held it loosely, not raising it, or pointing it. "It's over. Norton Burke and Sterling Rayford are both dead - they found them about twenty minutes ago. I just got the call."

"You're lying!" Buzz stated. "I spoke to Burke an hour ago!"

"He's dead," Hunt informed him again. " And so is Sergio Moshe. You are the last one. You don't have to die here."

"Die?" Repeated Buzz, laughing. He was remembering the incident with Pete Carpenter. "I don't intend to die, not unless you're gonna shoot through this pretty lady to get me."

"I'm not going to do that," stated Hunt "because you're going to let her go."

"I am?" Buzz asked. "Now, why would I want to do that?"

"Because she can't help you." Hunt sounded completely calm. "I'm going to let you drive out of here, but not with her. It's your choice."

Buzz looked around quickly. He wanted to kill all three of them; he knew that if he left them alive he would be on the run forever.

"You promise that you won't chase me?" Buzz asked, turning quickly and shooting John in the shoulder.

"Buzz!" Hunt yelled pointing his gun at him. "It doesn't have to be like this!"

"Sure it does," replied Buzz, holding his gun to Faith's head. "Now you lower your gun," he told Hunt. "Mine has a hairpin trigger. So even if you shoot me between the eyes, she still dies." Years ago, a much younger Hunt would have fired and taken his chances. Not today. He didn't want death to be Faith's karma for today. She deserved better than that.

"I know what you're thinking." Hunt glanced at John, who was laid out on the ground. "You want to kill us all, but you can't. Look around, Buzz - there's already a crowd forming. You fired shots, so the police will be here shortly. Leave now, Buzz. I knew you were Cimmerian and I wrote my suspicions in the reports I sent to Washington."

"Why would you suspect me?"

"The chemical weapons used in the first attack; they were all specialties of yours. Then when the virus developed, the first agents used didn't make any sense, unless whoever Cimmerian was started their extortion campaign before Meyer-Burke released the virus."

Buzz stared around. There were sirens in the distance.

"Those extortion notes were mailed to the right departments; and went through the correct channels." Hunt kept the urgency out of his voice. "The sender knew the inside workings of our government. You did everything correctly, Buzz; a little too correct. And then I found your phone number in Pete Carpenter's pocket."

"That convinced you?" Buzz asked.

"No, but it made me wonder. That's why I gave you less and less information when Jules Marceau popped up dead and I heard you'd found the body. It was way too convenient. How did you make it look like Lovejoy did it?"

"That was easy." Buzz was grinning, showing his teeth. "Lovejoy was unconscious when I got there and Marceau didn't put up any struggle as I stabbed him in the chest."

The sirens were closer now. Buzz heard them and estimated they were only blocks away.

"You still didn't tell me what sealed the deal?" He told Hunt, trying to get him to come out from behind his car, so he could get a clean shot at him.

"I found at note in Jules Marceau's paperwork. It said that Burke addressed one of his contacts as 'Crossbones.' Then I remembered your tattoo, the one on your chest that symbolizes death, much like Cimmerian symbolizes a land of perpetual darkness."

The first police car screamed around the corner. As Hunt looked towards it, his attention distracted for a crucial moment, Buzz took two shots. The first missed. The second shot hit Hunt in the chest, dropping him.

Buzz threw Faith on the ground. "Your turn," he told her. The gun was aimed square at the back of her head. John, half-conscious, closed his eyes and waited for the sound of gunfire. Two shots cut through the night. John opened his eyes and saw Hunt, upright and firing, with Buzz in his sights.

The first shot tore through Buzz's cheek and the second one followed the first. The impact spun Buzz around, so that he was facing Hunt again. Hunt's aim was steady, but the shots required no precision. He emptied his gun, five shots into Buzz Shaw's torso.

*   *   *   *   *

By the time Edna and Buddy got to Faith's address, Buzz Shaw's body had already been removed. John had been taken to Grady Memorial with a gunshot wound to his shoulder. He was expected to live.

Hunt Rhinehart and Faith were treated at the scene. Hunt had been wearing a bulletproof vest which deflected the shot he took to his chest.

"Are you alright?" Edna asked, running over to where Faith stood.

"Yes, I'm okay. Thank you."

Edna was looking at Hunt Rhinehart; Buzz's truck was being towed away.

"What happened with John?" Buddy wanted to know.

"He got shot in the shoulder," stated Faith. "They took him to the hospital. Hold on, that's my phone."

She answered it and found her mother on the line. "We saw you on the news!" Fanny sounded frantic. "What happened? The kids are worried sick!"

"I'll need that, ma'am." A man in a dark suit reached out and took the phone from Faith's hand before she could answer her mother's question.

"Wait a minute, that's my phone!"

"It will be returned," he told her, "once it is determined that there is no evidentiary value."

Faith stared at him and at Hunt Rhinehart, who stood off in the distance talking to another man in a dark suit. She noticed, for the first time, how efficiently these men cleaned up. All traces of Buzz Shaw had been erased; he could easily have never even existed. His name wasn't listed anywhere, either. She knew this.

"Faith," stated Edna, "Why did that man take your phone like that?"

"I don't know," stated Faith. She was watching several men with dark suits enter her building, along with the police.

"That's the United States Government for you," commented Buddy. "They only dole out information that has been censored and everything is clandestine."

"Come on," said Faith, passing the bloody spot where John fell and entering the building. She took the elevator upstairs and found the police already in her apartment. The mail John had been reading was still on the floor. Faith picked it up as she and Edna and Buddy entered the apartment.

"We're just gonna have a look around," said the police.

Faith nodded. Then she walked off into the living room and began to read Rosa Klebb's letter. The letter was telling John how she saw the man who had flown her and the other three scientists into the country. He had been on the news. This was the only man they had seen; he put them up in apartments and took them to the laboratory where they did their dirty work. She'd copied a photo of him and enclosed it. Buzz Shaw.

"What is it?" asked Edna.

"Let me have that," Faith heard Hunt Rhinehart's voice and turned.

"I know you don't understand," he told her, taking the letter and photo from her hand. "But some things are best left unexplained. Buzz Shaw worked for the United States Government, a fact that I'm not very proud of at the moment. But the facts can't be changed. I need to ask all three of you not to speak about him, or our investigation at all, to anyone as a matter of national security. Do you understand?"

Even though none of them did, they all nodded yes.

"Thank you," said Hunt. "I knew that you would."

CHAPTER 34

Luckily for John Lovejoy, the bullet in his shoulder didn't cause any major damage. Doctors were able to remove it easily. His first visitors were the people that he wanted to see the most: Frank Smith and Doug Edwards, his handlers at the Central Intelligence Agency.

"Why the hell did you guys leave me in prison for so long!" yelled John from his hospital bed. "And this only-here-for-observation crap! It's over! I almost got myself observationally killed!"

"Lovejoy, how long have you been an undercover field operative with the agency?" replied Frank, the Senior Special Agent with the C.I.A.

"Five years." He was furious and not bothering to mask it.

"Then you should know how these things work. We couldn't compromise your cover by pulling you out too quickly, or our friends over at the State Department would have known that we had our own operation up and running."

"So you let me sit in prison where I could have gotten shanked up by some disgruntled convict that we put in prison years ago?"

"That would not have happened," joined in Doug, the only other African American Special Agent in John's division. "We had eyes on you. But like Frank said, you're more valuable to us as long as you can stay under the radar. If the entire intelligence community learns of your identity, you'll no longer be useful."

"And if I get killed one day while working out in the field, undercover and unarmed, then what? How useful will I be to the agency then?"

Doug looked over at Frank and gave him a he's-got-a-point look.

"We'll see if we can find a way to issue you a firearm," stated Frank. "But until then, you're just going to have to shoulder the responsibility!"

"The hell with you, Frank!" shouted John, recognizing the pun that his senior officer put in his comment.

Frank laughed and walked towards the room door. "Just making sure you still have your good spirit, he said. "Get better. We need you to get back out there."

Frank turned to Doug. "Debrief him," he told Doug, "and I'll be down by the car."

Frank left and John stared at Doug.

"You know this assignment was bull!" John snapped. "The State Department puts a rogue agent on an assignment this sensitive? Then they don't have the decency to let us know that his loyalty was in question? I almost got killed. A friend of mine almost got killed. And who knows how many other people could have gotten killed!"

"They didn't know," stated Doug. "I spoke with them before coming over here. Their other man suspected something, but wasn't sure. So, he stuck it out. They didn't want to spook him; but they got him and they cleaned up their mess. We had no idea when we sent you in, to watch Jules Marceau. You were the only one at the agency qualified to work at the CDC. You knew chemical and biological elements, and you talked all that infectious disease jargon. So what could we do? Plus, you volunteered for the assignment."

"Yeah, I volunteered three years ago before rogue agents from other agencies got involved; and before deadly pathogens were used as biological and corporate weapons. Shall I go on?"

When Doug didn't respond, John continued. "Ex-mercenaries, murder charges, before being shot!" John yelled.

"Okay, okay, I get the picture," stated Doug. "If you're mad, I can understand. But we didn't think the assignment would turn out this way either. Come on, John. When we picked up the correspondence sent from Jules Marceau all those years ago, it looked like impropriety, but on a small scale."

"If it was such a small scale, why'd you have to send me in? And why did the C.I.A. care?"

"Because we didn't know who he'd sent the correspondence to. He was a foreign national working in a very sensitive position. That made it a matter of National Security, and he was French, need I say more" replied Doug.

"No, please don't," answered John. "Let's just get this debriefing over with. I don't know why we are letting the State Department take all the credit for this case either."

"It's because they broke it up, and it was their agent that went rogue; professional courtesy."

John nodded, exhausted and unwilling to argue anymore. He just wanted to give his oral report on the Russian woman's last letter and the exchange of gunfire at Faith's apartment, so he could get some rest.

"I guess the Agency will be re-assigning me after this. Do you think I could get a desk job?"

"I don't think so. Actually, they want you to stay on at the CDC. They believe that it is good cover for you and a strategic position."

"And if I refuse?"

Doug smiled and shook his head at his old friend. Then he replied in his best Marlon Brando impersonation, "This is an offer that you can't refuse."

CHAPTER 35

Several months later while at Faith's mother's house for Thanksgiving dinner; a special program came on the television that brought many memories back.

"Mommy!" Kimberly called out from the living room. "Come here, hurry!"

"I'm coming." Faith was in the kitchen, having an adult conversation with John, her mother, Yvonne and Jeff, Edna and Buddy and a gentleman friend of her mother's. "Please, excuse me, what is it dear?"

"It's ours, right mommy?" Kimberly asked.

"No, it's not!" Mel stated, shaking his head. "Tell her, Mom!"

Faith looked at the television screen. It was a report about a rare rhinoceros that was about to leave the Los Angeles Zoo on its way home to Jakarta, Indonesia.

"No baby," said Faith turning the television's volume up a little.

"This is the first Sumatran Rhino not born in the wild in 112 years," stated the reporter. *"Andalas will be heading to the Sumatran Rhino Sanctuary in theKambas National Park."*

"What's this?" John asked, coming into the room and embracing Faith from behind. They were a couple now, dating seriously and committed.

"A Rhino that was leaving the Los Angeles Zoo," answered Faith, "as part of some international breeding program."

"Oh," replied John, kissing her on the neck. "Why do you sound so somber?"

"Nothing particular," said Faith. "I'm just not a big fan of Rhinos anymore."

———————————————————————

THE END